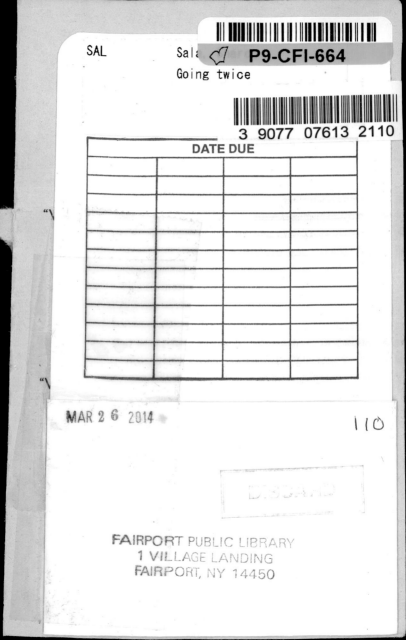

SHARON SALA

GOING TWICE

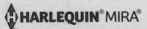

Recycling programs
for this product may
not exist in your area.

ISBN-13: 978-0-7783-1592-6

GOING TWICE

For questions and comments about the quality of this book, please contact us at
CustomerService@Harlequin.com.

Printed in U.S.A.

This book is about strength of character and strength of heart, something of which we are rarely aware. It's not until life throws us a curve, testing our mettle as to how much it takes before we might break, that we even know it is there. But when the need arises and we tap into that strength, it is then that heroes and heroines are born. They are the survivors, but not in just the physical sense. They endure, then they persevere, until finally they prevail.

I dedicate this book to the quiet heroes and heroines who go about their lives without medals or awards, who take care of business and walk away knowing they did what they had to do to take care of the people they love. Their legacy is their reward.

GOING
TWICE

One

It was the bird chirping outside the bedroom window that woke up Jolene Luckett, but her mood did not match the peppy sound. Even though it was her day off, it was going to take everything she had to get through it.

After a quick shower, she dug out her favorite pair of jeans and an old Washington Redskins T-shirt. It was a relief to wear tennis shoes rather than the leather half boots she often wore to work, but the soles made little squeaking noises on the hardwood floors as she headed for the kitchen. Yet another cheery sound that felt like an irritation.

A preprogrammed coffeepot had hot coffee waiting. She filled a to-go cup with the hazelnut-flavored brew, grabbed her purse and car keys, and headed out the door.

Next stop was the flower shop. The owner was just opening up, and her stomach rolled as she followed him inside. The smell reminded her of funerals.

"Give me a couple of minutes to get my register up and running," the salesclerk said.

"I want to look around, so take your time," Jo said.

She knew what she needed, but it was going to take her a few minutes to work up the nerve to pick it out and pay without breaking into tears.

Music began to play somewhere in the back as she moved toward a display of potted mums. Her grandmother had an entire flower bed of chrysanthemums on the east side of her house when Jolene was a girl. Seeing them made her remember a time when she still believed in happy-ever-afters. Now she knew different, and she also knew she couldn't stare at plants all day. Not when she had another appointment to keep. As she moved down the length of the room, she caught sight of a table piled high with stuffed toys and immediately looked away. She wasn't ready for that. Not yet.

The clerk was at the register now, whistling beneath his breath as he worked. She curled her fingers into fists and lifted her chin as if she was readying for battle.

Focus, Jo. Focus.

She walked to the other side of the room, toward the cooler holding large buckets of cut flowers waiting to be made into arrangements. She saw blue flowers, but they were not the kind she wanted, and she moved on to another display with smaller potted plants. There were colorful pansies with their happy faces, and delicate violets with their green velvet leaves. Then she saw the small pots with the tiny blue flowers, and her eyes filled with tears. Forget-me-nots. Perfect. She sorted through them for a bit and then chose the one with the most blooms.

To get to the register she had to pass by the display of stuffed animals again, but this time she stopped. It hurt her heart to look at them, but it hurt even more to choose one, knowing where it was going to wind up.

"Anything I can help you with?" the clerk asked.

Jo flinched. Some FBI agent she was. He'd walked up beside her and she hadn't even heard him coming.

"No, thank you. I'm just about done."

As he walked away, her gaze fell on a small fuzzy giraffe. The first time she'd chosen a toy she'd picked a little teddy bear. Last year she'd chosen a small green turtle. This time it would be the giraffe. She picked it up and headed for the register.

The man was talking to her as he rang up the purchases, but for the life of her she couldn't remember a thing he'd said. She handed him her credit card and signed the slip he gave her.

"Would you like to attach a card to the flowers?" he asked.

"No, thank you," she said again, then picked up her purchases and walked out the door.

Traffic was heavy as she drove toward North Capitol Street, but it was good to have something to concentrate on.

Her cell phone rang, but she wouldn't look. Didn't care—couldn't care—when she was on a mission this important. By the time she neared her destination, she began moving into the proper lane so she could exit on a service road to get to the entrance.

Her heart was hammering so hard when she drove through the entrance to Prospect Hill Cemetery she felt faint. The first time she'd come here she hadn't come alone. Wade had still been with her. But no more. She blinked back tears, refusing to admit most of that was her fault. It had been a subconscious reaction to the guilt she felt, pushing him away instead of letting him in to grieve with her.

She drove through the cemetery with a heavy heart, found a place to park at the foot of the hill, and got out with her flowers and the toy.

The sun was warm, but the breeze blowing on the back of her neck kept it from being uncomfortable. As sad as it was to have to come here, it was also a strangely beautiful, peaceful place. She saw an older couple a short distance away, and a woman sitting on a bench farther up the hill—reminders that grieving for the dead was a part of living.

When she finally reached her destination, the weight in her chest was so heavy it hurt to breathe. Wade had insisted on this plot. He'd said it was because little boys needed trees to climb. She knelt in front of the grave marker to brush away freshly cut grass and a couple of leaves. The stone was cold and hard, the opposite of what you would associate with a baby, but she finally reached out and traced the letters carved into the granite: *Samuel Joe Luckett.*

The Samuel was for his daddy, Samuel Wade.

The Joe was for her, his mother, Jolene.

They had planned to call him Sammy.

Jo's hands were shaking as she put the flowers against the marker.

"Happy birthday, little guy. I brought some pretty flowers and a new toy. The flowers are called forget-me-nots. I never forget you, because you're always in my heart, and the toy is called a giraffe. He has a long funny neck, doesn't he? They have some real ones here in the zoo, but this one is about your size."

Everything began to blur as her voice broke and the tears welled. "If I could take back what happened, I would do it in a heartbeat. I didn't know going to work that day would hurt you or I wouldn't have gone. I know it's my fault you're not here, and I'm sorry. I'm so, so sorry."

Her cell phone rang again, and again she ignored it. She knew who it would be. Even though Wade surely hated her guts, he still called her every year on this day. She couldn't talk to him now. She didn't want him to hear her cry.

For the past three years Wade Luckett's plan had been to fill up his days with so much work that he wouldn't have to think about what he'd lost. But every year, when this day came around he stepped out of denial, and made himself face what had been the worst day of his life.

He hadn't slept worth a damn last night and had dressed for work early. The thought of food made him sick, which was a sure sign something was horribly wrong. He drank a cup of coffee while watching the early morning news, and fielded a couple of texts from the office, answered a half-dozen emails, all the while watching the time.

They opened the gates to the cemetery at sunup, but he wouldn't be the first one there for fear of running into his ex-wife. He still didn't understand how losing their baby had turned her against him. He wasn't the one who shot her, and he damn sure wasn't the one who walked away after it was over. Still, what was past was past. If he could have, he would have gladly died in Sammy's place, but nobody had given him the option.

For whatever reason, life had kicked them both in the teeth, and today was just the reminder. As soon as he thought enough time had passed, he began gathering up his things. His car keys were in a bowl on the table, and the little yellow Hot Wheels truck he'd picked out at the store last night was right beside them. His hands were shaking when he picked up the truck and dropped it in his pocket. Moments later he was out the door.

He drove to the cemetery with a painful knot in his chest, and the closer he got, the greater the pain became. He took a deep breath as he drove through the entrance, then kept driving. When he saw a car in the distance and the tall, dark-haired woman kneeling at the grave, his eyes filled with tears.

Ah, damn it, Jolene. You still break my heart.

Unwilling to intrude on her moment, he parked, took the little yellow truck out of his pocket and held it like a talisman against welling pain, but the longer he sat there, the worse the pain became.

Without thinking, he reached for his phone and called her, just as he did on this day every year. He saw her react as the phone began to ring and knew before she turned around that she wasn't going to answer. He watched as she left the grave and began walking back to her car.

Her shoulders were too damn straight.

Her steps were uneven.

He knew she was crying.

After she was gone, he drove up and parked beneath the tree near the grave and walked over. When he saw the yellow giraffe, the pain in his chest bloomed. He looked down at the yellow truck he was carrying and shook his head. They'd always been on the same page with everything.

Then he focused on the name and smiled.

"Hey, Sammy, it's me, Daddy. I see Mama's already been here. That's a great giraffe you have there. I brought you a birthday present, too. You're three years old today, and I brought you your first Hot Wheels. This one is a little yellow truck like the ones I used to play with when I was three."

He dropped to his knees, set the truck on the marker next to the giraffe, and then laid the palm of his hand on the engraved name.

"This is the closest I can get to you here, baby boy, but I carry you in my heart."

Then he got up and walked away, his shoulders a little too straight, his steps staggering. He couldn't see for the tears in his eyes.

Houston, Texas

Hershel Inman hardly remembered the man he'd been before his wife, Louise, died in the aftermath of Hurricane Katrina, and could barely cope with what he'd become, since Louise wouldn't let him forget it.

She alternated days of crying and begging him to stop killing with preaching at him for his sins. If he didn't love her so much, and if she wasn't already dead, he would gladly have strangled her just to make her shut up.

His mission had begun as payback to the authorities who'd come too late to save her, and to

God for picking and choosing who lived and who died. Then the FBI showed up, and his power grew as he continued to kill and escape detection. He had been invincible—until he'd made that first mistake and missed a survivor who'd witnessed what he'd done. After that, everything began to unwind. He'd tried to silence her, but the FBI kept interfering, and then, to make matters worse, she married the agent who'd saved her.

Their lives got better and his got worse, ending with the explosion in his getaway boat that nearly killed him. He'd dropped off the radar to let his burns heal and thought about disappearing altogether. But when he closed his eyes at night, all he saw was Louise's face and the fear in her eyes as the water rose higher and higher around them, so he stayed in the wind, waiting for a chance to strike back.

Spring arrived, bringing with it the chance of tornadoes on a weekly basis through the heartland of America. He knew people would die, but even more would survive, and he thought about starting over with the killings, and wondered if he would be able to contact the FBI team like before. He wondered if they had deactivated the stolen phone he had used to communicate. He told himself if the phone still worked when he recharged it, it meant he was to continue. If it didn't, then he would disappear.

When it activated, he took it as a sign. He packed his pickup with new camping equipment and headed north out of Houston. Storms were predicted within the next two days. If he got out there ahead of time and set up near where the outbreaks were expected to occur, and if the storms were bad enough, he would be close at hand when the survivors started crawling out of the debris.

Hershel drove north all the way to Wichita Falls, which was near the Texas-Oklahoma border, found an out-of-the-way place to camp and set up his tent.

When the storms started building, his anxiety built along with them. As they finally formed into wall clouds and began moving through the countryside, Hershel moved into action.

"This is it. It's time to party."

He checked his shoulder pack for Tasers, ropes and leather gloves, tossing them in the front seat of his truck beside the flashlight. He wore dark clothing with a black hooded sweatshirt to hide the side of his face burned in the explosion, and heavy boots for walking through the debris.

The wind was rising, and the sky was getting dark. It would be sunset within the hour, and the storm would move through the area soon afterward. He got in the truck and started driving north, pacing himself so that he would be coming in behind the weather, and the bigger the storm clouds grew, the more hyped he became.

According to his radio, the tornado watch had just been upgraded to a tornado warning for Wichita Falls, even as he was nearing the city. A side draft from the powerful storm cell made it difficult to drive, and he finally pulled off the road and parked, unwilling to get any closer until it had moved on. He had the radio tuned to a local weather station with a minute-by-minute update on what was happening. When he heard the frantic announcement that tornadoes were touching down in city neighborhoods, he began planning how he could get into the area before police and rescue sealed it off.

As soon as the storms began moving away, he drove straight into the chaos they'd left behind and, as he'd hoped, became just another person on the streets trying to help. He'd thought long and hard about how this would play out, leaving bodies with his mark on them. He'd been dreaming about the condition of Louise's body when they finally found her—naked and coming apart at the seams. She would have hated the humiliation, but she was dead, so he hated it for her.

Rain was still coming down hard as he jumped out of his truck. He shouldered his backpack, grabbed his flashlight and began moving down the street, quickly getting lost among those who were already afoot.

Some were searching for survivors, while others appeared to have rescued themselves. They were wet, blood-stained and disoriented. Soaked by the downpour and on the lookout for live electrical wires, he kept moving through the area with an eye on his surroundings. At any moment the police or emergency services could show up, and then he would have to move on.

He saw a trio of men already working to free a couple from under what was left of their home. He wanted no part of that and kept running, dodging downed power lines and using the light from the intermittent lightning flashes to see a broader area than what his flashlight beam showed. Finally he heard what he'd been waiting for: a faint cry for help. He stopped, waiting for the cry again, and when he had a location, he headed into the debris.

At first he was just moving broken lumber and huge chunks of insulation, then he realized there was a standing wall with a partially attached staircase behind it. He removed a broken commode, cushions from a piece of furniture, broken table lamps and the water-soaked contents of a closet before he finally got to a door. As he dug his way closer, the shouting got louder.

"I hear you, man. Stay calm," Hershel said, and the man quit shouting. Nothing like having the victim cooperate in his own demise.

Finally he cleared away enough to see that the man who lived here had taken refuge under the stairs. Hershel got out the Taser, grabbed a piece of rope from his backpack and reached for the doorknob.

An old man stumbled out into the rain.

"Thank you, thank you, you saved my life," he cried, reaching for Hershel's shoulder to steady himself.

"I didn't save it. You don't deserve to live," Hershel said, and pulled the trigger on the Taser.

The man dropped to his knees, paralyzed by the electrical current pulsing through his body. Hershel glanced over his shoulder and dragged the man behind the wall, making sure there was no one around. Then he wrapped a short length of rope around the old man's neck, yanked it tight and held on.

The old man's body was seizing. Lightning

flashed long enough for Hershel to see the shock and horror on his victim's face, but he felt no guilt. When the man finally went limp, the release of endorphins that flowed through Hershel's body was nothing short of elation.

Working quickly, he removed the electrodes from the man's chest and then proceeded to strip him naked. Once the dead man was completely nude, he tossed the clothes and pulled a piece of Sheetrock over the body. There was nothing sexual about the act. It was all about humiliation and how the family would feel when their loved one was discovered in such a condition.

Satisfied with what he'd done, he stepped out from behind the wall and walked back down to the street just as a pair of young men came running toward him.

"Anyone in there?" they yelled.

"All clear," he said, ducking his head, and kept moving in the opposite direction.

He added two more victims before the police and rescue workers closed off the hardest hit area, then returned to where he'd parked, jumped in the truck and began trying to find his way out of town. The power was out almost everywhere, and the place felt like a ghost town as he drove carefully through the streets. After a lot of stopping and backtracking, he found the highway he'd been looking for and pulled off the road. He took out the cell phone and sent FBI agent Tate Benton a text. Sending texts now and then had been part of his ritual since the agents began hunting him, and he needed to feed off their frustration to make this work again.

I am not dead, so do not weep. It was not my time. I have vows to keep.

Then he turned off the cell phone so it couldn't be traced, and plugged it into the cigarette lighter to recharge as he pulled back out onto the highway.

As he drove, he could tell how far the power was out by the lack of house or security lights along the way. About five miles from his campsite, he began seeing the occasional light off in the distance, where people still had power.

When he finally found his turnoff and drove off the highway onto the old dirt road, he pulled around behind the abandoned ranch house where he'd set up his tent and parked so the truck couldn't be seen. He checked to make sure nothing had been disturbed, and once he was satisfied all was well, he zipped himself inside the tent, took off his filthy, rain-soaked clothes and crawled naked into his sleeping bag. He was asleep in minutes.

Washington, D.C.

Tate Benton was in the den eating salted cashews and nursing a bottle of beer. The television was on CNN, and his wife, Nola, was in her art studio, working on a commissioned painting. He was coming off of a long, drawn-out kidnapping case that had ended badly, so when his cell phone indicated an incoming text, he almost didn't answer.

Then he glanced at Caller ID and the skin crawled on the back of his neck. The last thing he expected was a message from the Stormchaser.

I am not dead, so do not weep. It was not my time. I have vows to keep.

"Son of a bitch," he muttered, and immediately forwarded the text to his partners, Cameron Winger and Wade Luckett.

Within moments his cell phone rang. It was Wade, and he had Cameron conferenced in.

"We're absolutely sure it's him?" Wade asked.

"It came from the same phone he used to use," Tate said.

"I didn't know the agency kept that old phone activated," Cameron said.

"That's on me. I told them to," Tate said.

"I turned on The Weather Channel," Wade said. "There's a tornado outbreak along the Texas-Oklahoma border."

"Do we wait for the bodies to begin showing up or go now?" Cameron asked.

"He's already killed or he wouldn't have sent the message. But we won't know for sure that's where he is until the medical examiner makes that determination," Tate said.

"I'm packing tonight anyway," Wade said. "I'll be ready when you call."

"I'm going to talk to the Director and then I'll let you know what he thinks," Tate added.

"I'm with Wade," Cameron said. "I'll pack and wait for you to tell us when and where to meet up. And just for the record, this sucks big-time, even though it means I'll probably see Laura again."

There was a click in Tate's ear, and then the line went dead. It appeared Cameron's attraction to the pretty Red Cross worker they'd met last year was ongoing. He knew the rest of his news wasn't going to set well with Nola, but he had to tell her what had happened. After the hell the Stormchaser had put her through last year, he hated to let her know the bastard was starting up again.

He smiled when he walked into her studio. The painting she'd been working on for several weeks was almost finished, and the child's face, which was the subject of the work, looked alive.

"Hey, pretty lady, do you have time to be bothered?"

Nola looked up and smiled. There was a smudge of paint on her cheek and more on her fingers.

"I always have time for you. What's up?"

"Not-so-good news."

She frowned. "Oh, no. Please tell me you're not going to be leaving again so soon."

He showed her the text and watched the blood drain from her face. Then, without speaking, she put the brush in cleaning solution and began wiping her hands. When she looked up at him, she was trembling.

"I thought for sure he was dead. I wanted him to be dead."

"So did I, honey, so did I," Tate said, and slid a hand beneath her hair to rub the back of her neck.

"Do you have a location?" she asked.

"Not yet. There's a tornado outbreak on the Texas-Oklahoma border, which might be where he is, but we'll have to wait for the autopsies to know for sure."

"Dear Lord. Those poor people," Nola said, and wrapped her arms around him.

They held each other without speaking, lost in the memories of what they'd gone through before.

"You have to stay safe," Nola whispered.

"I will, honey. He's not after us. We're part of the package that feeds his ego. If we're dead, he doesn't have anyone to needle, you know?"

"Okay…I get it, but still, he's not normal. I was with him, remember. He talks to his dead wife like she's right there beside him."

"I remember. I remember everything—including thinking I was going to lose you."

"Am I in danger again?" she asked.

"I don't think so, but I'll know more once we find out what he's done."

Nola hid her face against Tate's chest. "I hate this. I just hate this."

"So do I, honey, but we won't quit until we get him." He hugged her close, then leaned down and gave her a quick kiss. "I need to call the Director."

"And I need to make sure you have enough clean clothes," she said, and began cleaning her brushes and covering up the painting.

He frowned. "I didn't mean to mess up your work."

She shook her head. "I couldn't work now if I had to. I'm going to do laundry. I have this over-whelming need to do something for you to make it all better, and that's all I've got."

He watched her leave the room with her head up and that familiar take-charge stride, and knew she would be okay. It was the Stormchaser's latest victims he was worried about.

After a quick phone call to the Director to let him know what had happened, he was given the go-ahead to proceed as the team saw fit and told to stay in touch daily.

He went back into the den and changed channels until he found one giving early reports of the storm front that had just gone through Wichita Falls. It had produced three funnels, one of which had cut through part of the city. Victims were being taken to the local hospitals, and so far two bodies had been taken to the morgue. Tate knew all they could do now was wait and see if the Stormchaser was truly back.

It took exactly sixteen hours for the news to break that storm victims had been murdered, and by that time five bodies had been pulled from the rubble, three of which had been identified as having survived the storm and killed afterward. And they were all nude, which was a new twist to his M.O.

Tate called his partners, then made a call to the local police in Wichita Falls to tell them what they were dealing with, and that the team was on the way.

Keystone Lake, Oklahoma

Hershel was no longer in the state of Texas. He drove all of the next day, following the storm front as it moved into Oklahoma. According to the National Weather Service, the chances of storms firing up in the northeastern part of the state were high, so he'd set up his campsite at Keystone Lake, near Tulsa. The camping area appeared to be a popular one. He'd chosen a site on the far side of the campgrounds in the hopes that the sound of his portable generator would not disturb nearby campers. He had a waterproof, two-room tent with zip-up windows and a heavy-duty floor, a fan for hot, muggy nights, and a laptop computer with a satellite connection for streaming live TV and keeping an eye on weather systems, as well as the FBI's investigation of the Stormchaser murders. He liked knowing the media had given him a special name, and he liked hearing that the agents were catching fire for not stopping him last year in Louisiana.

The sun began to set as he was cooking his supper. He ate a solitary meal in the growing dusk, listening to a pack of coyotes announcing their arrival for an evening hunt, yipping in a high-pitched tone that morphed into brief howls.

The mournful sound made Hershel shiver. He wasn't by nature a man who enjoyed sleeping out under the stars, and the thin walls of his tent weren't much more reassuring. As it grew darker, he put out his fire, started up his generator and went into the tent to settle in for the night.

He kicked off his shoes at the front and padded across the floor to the sleeping bag beside his laptop. His choices were limited, but he finally found reception from a local station. When he saw footage of the agents in Wichita Falls standing at his first kill site, he upped the volume. He knew them well enough by now to read the frustration on their faces and actually laughed out loud.

Shame on you, Hershel Inman, laughing about people dying. You're sick and mean, and I'm ashamed I was ever married to you.

Hershel frowned. Everything had been going just fine and now Louise had to put her two cents into his business again.

"Well, you can just be pissed all you want, Louise, because you went off and left me. I didn't leave you."

I didn't leave you on purpose, and you know it. I died. I didn't want to die, but I died anyway.

Guilt hit Hershel like a kick in the belly.

"You blame me for not getting your insulin. It's my fault you died. My fault. Why don't you go ahead and say it!"

I never said it was your fault. But I died, and that's not my fault, so don't you dare say it was.

Hershel shut down the laptop, but the night air was still. Without any breeze coming through the screen windows, he knew sleeping would be uncomfortable. He set up his fan so that it would blow on him during the night, trying to ignore the constant sound of Louise's rants.

"I'm going to bed now, so you need to go away. How do you expect me to sleep when you're talking in my head all the time?"

I don't talk to you, Hershel. I'm dead, remember?

"Then who am I hearing if it's not you?" he yelled.

Don't ask me. You're the one who's crazy. Remember? You're the one who turned into a killer. I just died. Now you go away and let me rest. I'm tired, too. I'm tired of watching you break my heart all over again.

Hershel zipped and locked up the flap to his tent, and then threw himself onto his sleeping bag. He wanted the knot in his gut to go away. His euphoria from his kills was gone. He needed the storms to come back. Rain washed him clean, and killing made the pain go away. He fell asleep to the rattle of the generator, and when it ran out of gas toward early morning, he never knew it.

Two

Jo Luckett was at her desk, tying up the loose ends of her last case when her phone rang. She answered absently, still locked into what she was doing.

"This is Jo Luckett."

"Agent Luckett, this is Julie. Hold for Director Thomas."

Jo's focus immediately shifted as her boss came on line.

"Good afternoon, Agent Luckett. Good job on closing that case."

"Thank you, sir. Good teamwork, as usual."

"Speaking of teamwork, what do you know about the Stormchaser murders?"

She tensed. Her ex-husband was on the team, but she was certain that wasn't what he meant.

"Probably not much more than what anyone would hear on the news, why?"

"He's killing again. We've activated the original team, but I'm adding you to it. Julie emailed you the file. Familiarize yourself with all the details and await further orders. At the moment the team is on the move. Once they get settled, I want you to join them."

Even though her stomach was in knots, she answered firmly. "Yes, sir."

There was a pause, and she thought he would hang up, but he didn't.

"Will you have a problem working with your ex-husband on this?"

"No, sir, of course not," she said shortly.

"Good. Agent Benton is lead investigator. You will take your orders from him."

"Yes, sir."

"I want this man stopped. Find his money trail. Find the aliases he's been using. Do what you do best and make that happen, understand?"

She got the message. Her skill at tracking perps via the latest technology was needed once again.

"Yes, sir, of course, sir."

She hung up and immediately checked her computer, found the new message from his office and pulled up the attachment. The file was massive, far more than she had time to go through at her desk. She forwarded it to her laptop at home, then finished the report she'd been working on and filed it.

She wouldn't let herself think of what the days to come would be like. She hadn't had more than a half-dozen brief encounters with Wade in the past three years, and the thought of working with him made her sick to her stomach. She'd loved him so deeply—then, in one reckless afternoon, destroyed their world and their unborn child. She couldn't imagine how this was going to turn out, but all she had left was her job, and she wasn't going to fuck that up, too.

Tulsa, Oklahoma

On day three, Hershel pulled a hit-and-run during the storms that hit Tulsa, taking out three more people who had initially survived. He was back at the campgrounds at Keystone Lake long before daylight, sleeping peacefully while the city waited for sunrise, fearing the scope of the disaster.

The air at the scene of the debris field left from the tornado was hot and heavy, mingling with the scents of decaying food and diesel from the big machines the cleanup crews were using farther down the next block.

The yellow crime scene tape around the area

where the two agents were walking marked the spot where the first body had been found. As soon as the body was identified as a murder victim, cleanup efforts in the immediate vicinity had been shut down, although the site had been so badly compromised, there was no way to tell what was storm-related and what might have been left by the killer.

Over the next sixteen hours the medical examiner had found two more murder victims among the bodies that had been recovered, and all three shared the same cause of death. They'd been rendered helpless with a Taser, and then they'd been strangled.

Once the media caught wind of the news, they quickly linked these victims to the earlier killings in Wichita Falls, Texas, and that was when the FBI had shown up, still following in the Stormchaser's path of destruction.

Two hours later police cruisers from the Tulsa Police Department blocked off access to both ends of the street as the FBI agents moved through the third crime scene. A couple of news crews had stationed themselves at the far end of the next block with their cameras trained in the agents' direction. They weren't interfering with the investigation, but the long-range lenses could make it appear as if they were filming on-site.

Wade Luckett was standing less than a yard away from the bathtub where the third body had been found. He checked the picture on his iPad against the scene before him, then turned to look for Tate, who was standing a few yards away. "Hey, Tate, here it is," he said.

Tate moved across the debris field for a closer look. "You're right. And check that out. There's a wall between that tub and the street, another impromptu barrier between the body and immediate discovery."

"Just like in Wichita Falls," Wade said, and then added, "Have you heard from Cameron today?"

"Yes," Tate said. "They located the guy who thought he witnessed the killer leaving the James Atwood crime scene. He's interviewing him sometime today. He also said that Laura Doyle showed up yesterday with the Red Cross."

"He's still sweet on her," Wade said.

Tate grinned. "Sure looks like it. They stayed in touch after we came back from Louisiana last year. I know this because my lovely wife keeps me apprised of the important things in life."

Wade heard the pride in Tate's voice and remembered how close they'd come to losing Nola Landry to the Stormchaser last year.

"Okay, so she's a great wife and phenomenal artist, but I'm all about her cooking."

Tate laughed. Wade Luckett was never full.

Talking about cooking made Wade hungry, which prompted him to dig some gum out of his pocket and pop it in his mouth as he got back to business. He pulled up the pictures on his iPad, eyeing the similarities between the first scenes in Wichita Falls and the ones here in Tulsa.

"What I don't get is how the hell he gets on site so fast. How does he manage to commit these murders while rescue crews are still at work?" Wade asked. "He hid among the Red Cross volunteers before, but there's no sign of him with them now."

"Obviously he can't repeat that scenario because we know what he looks like. Although I would guess he has some burn scars now, after surviving that boat explosion," Tate said. He was the profiler in the team and they depended on his instincts and knowledge.

"We've furnished both the Red Cross and local authorities with a photo of Hershel Inman, but it doesn't mean much, not when we know how skilled he is at disguises."

Wade stepped around the broken headboard of

a bed, saw what was left of a child's stuffed teddy bear and had a moment of déjà vu, remembering finding the giraffe at his son's grave.

He was sad for the end of his marriage and the loss of his son, but he was still damn mad at Jolene for shutting him out. He'd been just as devastated as she was by the baby's death, and yet she'd taken all the burden of grieving as her right only, and acted as if he'd lost nothing but the time he'd invested in the marriage.

He looked away from the toy and then glanced up as a police car sped past three blocks up, running hot with lights and sirens. He wanted this killer caught and put away so bad he could taste it. Then he shook off the anger and got back to the work at hand.

"So, taking it as a given that Hershel Inman's appearance has changed, he's apparently changed his method of killing to go with it."

"If you think about the kill sites, it makes sense, though," Tate said. "The first victims were stranded in rural areas by high water, so the sounds of gunshots would not be a concern. Now that he's moved into a city, that kind of noise would be noticed. His method now needs to be swift and silent. The Taser would render the victims both mute and immobile. Strangling them afterward would be simple if they couldn't fight back, and leaving the bodies naked further feeds his need for domination."

"That's damn cold," Wade said.

Tate thought about how close Hershel had come to killing Nola. "Yes, and so is Hershel Inman's heart."

Hershel would have been pleased if he'd known they were talking about him. He hadn't seen them in months. Now here they were going through the rubble while he was sitting less than two hundred yards away, watching. They weren't so damn smart after all.

There were only two of them this time, which made him wonder where Winger was, but then he let it go. As long as he had their attention, he didn't care how many people they sent to cover his handiwork.

He rolled down the window, aimed his camera, and took several pictures of the agents as they poked through the debris. Every time the camera clicked, he imagined he was looking through the sight on his rifle, pulling the trigger and taking them out one by one. When Luckett stopped digging around and started to turn around, he rolled up the window and drove away.

* * *

It was nearly four o'clock in the afternoon and Cameron Winger was in the police station in Wichita Falls, Texas, waiting for his witness Coyle Hardison to show. Clouds were building back in the southwest part of the state again, and some forecasters were predicting another round of storms. He knew Hardison had left the city after the storm, but when contacted by the FBI he had willingly agreed to come all the way back from his grandfather's ranch over two hours away to give his statement again.

They had given Cameron use of an interrogation room, and he'd already set up his camera to record the witness's statement when there was a knock on the door. He turned around just as an officer escorted a young man inside. The man was dressed in blue jeans, work boots and a T-shirt. When he saw the agent, he promptly took off a wide-brimmed cowboy hat and ran a hand through his hair to smooth it down. There was a healing cut on his forehead, a bruise under one eye, and both the backs and palms of his hands had bruises and shallow cuts, as well. It appeared he, too, had suffered some from the storm.

"Agent Winger," the cop said, "this is Coyle

Hardison. Do you have everything you need to proceed?"

"Yes, I do, and thanks," he told the officer. He started to shake the young man's hand and then stopped. "Uh, sorry, it looks like you need to skip handshakes for a while, but thank you for coming back. Have a seat and we'll get started."

"Yes, sir, happy to help," Hardison said.

The officer shut the door as the young man sat down. He looked a little nervous, but also curious.

"Are you going to film me?" he asked.

Cameron nodded. "Yes, but it's only protocol. Just relax and answer the questions as best you can."

"Okay," Coyle said, then locked his fingers across his belly and leaned back.

"State your name, age and occupation."

"Coyle Hardison, twenty-two years old, and I work in construction."

"How did you come to be in the neighborhood right after the tornado hit?"

"I live there. At least I used to before my house blew away."

"How did you know James Atwood?"

"We lived in the same neighborhood. I've known him and his wife, who died last year, just about all my life."

Cameron moved to stand beside the camera, making sure the man was facing it as he answered.

"You stated earlier to the police that you believed you saw the Stormchaser. Would you please explain what you saw, in detail, and what led you to this conclusion?"

Hardison nodded, and then began to relate his story again.

"It was right after the tornado had gone through my neighborhood. Me and my friend Charlie Reeves were out checking on neighbors and helping in any way we could. It was still raining, and we were making our way down the street, dodging debris and downed power lines when a guy came out of the dark from behind a big pile of rubble, walking straight toward us."

"Did you know where you were at the time?"

"No, not at first. You couldn't tell anything in the dark, but I remembered just after we saw him, we also saw the street sign bent over at a ninety-degree angle, and that's when I realized we'd just passed Mr. Atwood's house."

"What time was this?" Cameron asked.

"It was less than thirty minutes after the tornado went past, but I can't be more specific than that."

"Okay. Describe the man you saw."

"It was very dark. The power was out all over that part of town, so it was hard to see where we were going. Some people were out and about. You could hear some people calling for help and others yelling. It was weird, hearing all that without being able to see who it was, and the rain was hard enough that it buffered the sound. We had a flashlight, but we were shining it down on the ground to make sure we weren't stepping on any hot power lines. There was a flash of lightning just as I looked up. That's when I saw him, and then only for a moment. But I can say for sure he was middle-aged, wearing all dark clothes, and with the hood of his sweatshirt pulled up over his head. It was hard to tell, but I think there were scars on one side of his face."

Cameron's heart skipped a beat. That fit with what they believed Hershel Inman must look like now.

"Could you tell how tall he was, or his general build?"

Hardison closed his eyes momentarily, and Cameron guessed he was pulling up that memory. Then the young man blinked and stared straight into the camera.

"He was average height, maybe five-ten, but for sure not six feet. His clothes were plastered to his body from the rain, so you could see his build. He had what you call a barrel chest. Oh, and he was bowlegged, and he had a small black pack slung over one shoulder."

Cameron was certain now that the guy had seen Hershel Inman, and that ended the slim possibility of a copycat killer.

"Did you happen to see him get into a vehicle or notice him leaving in any specific direction?" he asked.

"No. We just passed him and kept going. I never looked back. I'm sorry."

"No, don't be sorry. Your information has been very helpful. Is there anything else you can think of?"

Coyle Hardison frowned. "No, but I hope you catch the bastard and fry his ass. Mr. Atwood was a really nice old guy. I used to mow his yard when I was a kid, and his wife would give me cookies and lemonade after I was done. He was really sad after she died, and I'd say Mr. Atwood is probably the only one who doesn't regret dying, because now he's with his wife."

Cameron got up and turned off the camera.

"Thank you for coming in. You've been very helpful."

Hardison nodded and left the room.

Cameron packed up his stuff, thanked the police for their assistance and then headed for the parking lot. The heat and humidity hit him like a slap in the face, adding to the chaos in the city as he walked out of the building. He saw the line of thunderheads building back to the south and hoped they weren't in for another round of storms. By the time he loaded his things in the back of his rental car and got inside, he was sweating. He turned on the air conditioner and then called Tate.

The local newspaper, the *Tulsa World,* had run a picture of Hershel Inman alongside a brief back-story of the Stormchaser's murder spree last year in Louisiana, and then connected it to the ongoing investigation. The FBI had also given them an artist's rendering of what Hershel Inman might look like now with burn scars on his face. They'd known it would set off a firestorm of sightings that would most likely lead nowhere, but there was always the chance that one of them would pan out.

The Tulsa Police Department had their own detectives running down the leads, and funneling the more promising ones to the FBI agents, who interviewed the witnesses further. So far nothing had clicked.

It was late in the afternoon, and Wade and Tate had stopped at a Quik Stop. Tate was pumping gas, and Wade had gone inside to get cold drinks and snacks, when Tate's phone began to ring. When he saw it was Cameron, he walked away from the pump to answer.

"This is Tate. What did you find out?"

"The witness definitely saw Inman. He described a middle-aged man, average height, barrel chest and bow legs. And the guy was dressed in dark clothing with a hoodie pulled up over his head. He only got a brief look as lightning flashed, but he thinks the guy had some kind of scars on one side of his face."

Tate sighed. "Well, it's confirmation we're dealing with Inman again, although after we got that text, we pretty much knew it. I don't suppose we hit the jackpot and got a vehicle description or anything specific to go on?"

"No. The guy was with a friend and didn't even put two and two together until he found out James Atwood was one of the victims. They had lived in the same neighborhood, and that's the area where the witness ran into Inman. So what do you want me to do?" Cameron asked.

"Head to Tulsa in the morning. I'll text you the info on where we're staying."

"Okay."

"Drive safe," Tate added, then hung up and finished refueling the car.

Wade came back carrying cold bottles of Pepsi and a couple of candy bars, handed a pop to Tate, then offered the candy bars and waited for him to choose. Tate chose the Snickers.

Wade frowned. "I was gonna eat that one," he said.

Tate shrugged, handed it back and took the other one.

"I was gonna eat that one, too," Wade said, and then grinned at the confused look on his partner's face. "Just kidding. Take both of them if you want. I have three more."

Tate grinned, took the candy bars and got back into the car. He opened the cold bottle of Pepsi and took a big drink, grateful for the cool liquid as it went down. As soon as Wade was inside, they drove away.

All of the tornado damage had been on the far northwest side of the city, and the people displaced by the storm had booked up a large number of available hotel rooms. They finally found a suite at the Hyatt Regency on 2nd Street, which provided amenities they didn't have the time or inclination to check out.

Tate pulled into the underground parking garage beneath a security light and in plain view of multiple cameras. They headed into the hotel, each man lost in his own set of thoughts. Out of habit, Tate paused at the front desk to check for messages.

"Anything for Tate Benton or Wade Luckett?"

One of the clerks spoke up.

"Yes, sir. Something arrived for Mr. Benton about an hour ago. One moment, please."

She went into a back room and came out carrying a manila envelope.

Tate frowned as he took it from her. There was no return address or postage mark and nothing to indicate it had come from a courier service. All it had was his name on the front. He looked inside as he was walking away, and then made an abrupt U-turn and went back to the front desk.

"Excuse me. Who received this?"

"I don't know, sir, but I can check."

"Thank you," Tate said.

Wade followed him back. "What's wrong? What's in it?" he asked, and opened the flap as Tate handed over the envelope.

When he saw the photos of him and Tate taken earlier that day at one of the crime scenes, the hair rose on the back of his neck.

"Son of a bitch! He's *here!*"

Wade pivoted toward the open lobby, eyeing everyone within sight. Behind him, he could hear the desk clerk telling Tate that a bellhop brought the envelope in from outside.

"Is he still here?" Tate asked.

The clerk pointed to the bell stand and a tall, slim man with red hair and glasses. "His name is Rob."

"Thank you," Tate said, and headed across the lobby.

"I'm going outside," Wade said, and bolted toward the front entrance and then straight to the valet stand. He flashed his badge, then pulled Inman's picture up on his phone and started showing it around to the hotel employees who were coming and going parking cars.

"Look close," he said. "It's important. Did any of you see this man? He won't look exactly like this now, because we believe one or both sides of his face will have burn scars. He gave an envelope to a bellhop named Rob. Did you see him? He might have been wearing a sweatshirt with the hood pulled up."

"I just came on duty," one valet said.

"I was parking cars all afternoon. All I saw were car keys coming at me," another said.

"Who was manning this stand?" Wade asked. "Who was in charge?"

"Mario."

"Where is he? I need to talk to him," Wade said.

"He went home. He's off duty now,"

A valet came running up from the parking garage, and turned in the ticket and keys of the car he'd just parked.

"What's going on?" he asked.

Wade flashed the picture and explained himself all over again.

"Did you see him? It would have been around an hour or so ago, talking to Rob."

"Yeah, I saw someone talking to Rob. He gave him a twenty just to carry an envelope inside. That dude is lucky. He's always getting the big tips."

"Did you see where the man went? Did you see what he was driving?"

The kid shrugged and pointed. "He wasn't driving. He walked that direction and then went behind the hotel."

Wade looked up. "Do you have exterior security cameras back here?"

"Yes, but you'll have to talk to Mr. Comfort. He's the manager."

Wade wasted no time returning to the front desk, where he hailed the first available clerk.

"I need to speak to your manager."

The desk clerk looked nervous. He could already tell something big was going on that had to do with that envelope.

"I don't think he's in his office."

"Can you page him?"

"Yes, sir. Just give me a few minutes."

Wade glanced over his shoulder. Tate was on his way back.

"The kid identified Inman," he said.

"So did one of the valets," Wade said. "He said when Inman left, he walked around behind the hotel. I'm waiting on the manager to show up so we can check the security cameras. We might get lucky and see what he's driving."

"Good call," Tate said.

"Either he's getting careless or he's getting cockier," Wade muttered.

"He's challenging us. These pictures are an in-your-face statement. I'd say his failure to kill Nola and then getting injured made him feel helpless. He's angry. That's why he's gotten so personal with his victims. Before, he killed from a distance. Now it's up close and personal, and leaving them naked is a reflection of his own humiliation. He doesn't want to be the only one who was shamed," Tate said.

"That makes sense," Wade agreed. "But it also makes him more dangerous."

The desk clerk returned.

"The manager will meet you in his office. If you'll follow me?"

They followed the clerk through a maze of hallways, then into an office.

"Mr. Comfort, these are the FBI agents staying in our hotel."

"Thank you, Walter. Gentlemen, how can I help you?"

"This is Agent Luckett, and I'm Agent Benton. We need to see footage from the security cameras around the perimeter of your hotel," Tate said.

The expression on the manager's face became one of instant concern.

"What's wrong? Has something happened that's going to endanger our guests?"

"At this point we don't think so," Tate said.

"How far back do you need to look? We don't keep them beyond—"

"Just the last couple of hours," Wade said.

The manager picked up a phone and made a call, then escorted them to yet another location.

"This is Rick Chavez. He's in charge of hotel security. He'll help you from here."

"Thank you, Mr. Comfort. We appreciate your cooperation," Tate said.

Chavez looked to be in his mid-forties and was built like a linebacker: broad shoulders, stocky body, with the biceps of a bodybuilder.

He eyed both men curiously, and then waved at some chairs against the wall.

"Mr. Comfort gave me the timeline you wanted to see. Pull up a chair. I don't have popcorn, but the movie is ready to roll."

"I'll stand, if it's all the same to you," Tate said.

Wade nodded in agreement.

Chavez shrugged, checked the discs and started the playback.

Moments later four different screens were playing footage of the hotel exterior. They leaned in, watching eagerly for signs of Hershel Inman's arrival.

Three

A few minutes into watching the footage, they saw Hershel walk into camera range, carrying the envelope, but there was no sign of a vehicle on any of the screens. They saw him approach the bellhop, hand over the envelope and the money, and then the bellhop walked out of camera range into the hotel. But it was what Hershel did next that startled them. He paused, looked straight up into the camera, then turned and walked away.

"Look at that!" Wade said. "He wanted us to know it was him!"

Chavez frowned. "Who are we looking at?" he asked.

"The man who's been killing survivors of your recent tornado," Tate muttered.

Chavez jumped. "The Stormchaser? That's the Stormchaser?"

Wade nodded. "That's him."

"Son of a bitch," Chavez whispered. "Are we in danger here? Should I put on extra security?"

"That's not been his pattern," Tate said. "He targets people who have survived a natural disaster and kills them at the disaster site."

"Good Lord. He's a piece of work," Chavez said.

"Can you make us copies of that footage?" Tate asked.

"Yes. It'll take me a few minutes to burn them for you."

"We're in room 444. Would you have them sent up when you've finished?"

"Yes, sir," Chavez said.

They left the room with mixed emotions. Hershel Inman continued to move among them like a ghost, taunting their inability to take him down. He was there, and then he wasn't. They knew what he looked like—now they even knew exactly what he looked like with the burn scars—and they still couldn't find him. Frustration was high, and by the time they reached their room they were ready for a change of pace.

"I'm going to take a shower before I start writing reports," Wade said.

"How about some dinner? Do you want to go down to the restaurant or order in?" Tate asked.

"It's your call," Wade said.

"Room service," Tate said.

"I haven't eaten since breakfast," Wade said.

"Except for three candy bars and a Pepsi," Tate countered.

"That's not eating. That's just passing time," Wade said. "I want a medium-well rib eye, steak fries and a salad. You pick dessert. I'm heading to the shower."

"A man who knows the important things in life," Tate mumbled as he reached for the menu to check his own options.

The doorbell rang as Jo Luckett was in the kitchen making coffee. She grabbed the cash she'd set out and ran barefoot through the apartment. She could smell the pizza even before she opened the door.

A few minutes later she carried the food into the kitchen, transferred a couple of slices to her plate, made a glass of iced tea and set the cinnamon sticks aside to have with coffee later. She carried her plate to the living room, plopped down on the sofa with her food and took her first bite before turning on the TV.

She'd been reading Stormchaser files all afternoon. Both the killer's brutality and random choice

of victims made it all the more important to take
him down as soon as possible. Now she was ready
to take a break.

But no sooner had she turned on the evening
news than she realized they were airing coverage
of the murders in Tulsa, Oklahoma. She upped the
volume and took another bite, paying more attention to the tornado damage than she did to what
the news anchor was saying. She'd grown up in
California and gone from UCLA straight to FBI
training. She'd only seen footage of tornadoes, had
never been near one, and hoped she never had to
be. They were horrifying enough on their own,
without the added insult of living through such a
storm only to be murdered in the aftermath.

The program continued with interviews of the
Tulsa police chief and then members of one murder victim's family. She finished her first piece
of pizza and had started on her second when they
segued to another piece of footage. When they
mentioned the FBI investigation, she set the food
aside and upped the volume. Within moments she
saw a long shot of one man standing in the midst
of a massive debris field. Tate Benton. She could
see the yellow crime scene tape around the area,
and police cars parked out on the street, obviously
to deter sightseers or locals who might interfere

with the agents as they viewed the site. But when another man walked out from behind a broken wall, she froze.

It was Wade.

Sound faded as pain shot through her head hard and fast.

The scent of pizza was suddenly sickening.

She hadn't seen him in over a year. He looked good. He looked fit. She wondered if he was happy, if he was seeing someone. What on earth had made her think she would be able to work in close quarters with him? What was that she'd told the Director? Oh, right. *No problem,* she'd said. Lord.

She was watching his every move to the point of obsession when she noticed movement in the shot behind him. Someone in an older-model black pickup was rolling down the window. The driver had something in his hands. There was a moment when she'd thought it was a gun, and then she realized it was just a camera and breathed easier. Just another lookie-loo taking pictures.

She carried what was left of her pizza into the kitchen and dumped it in the trash, then put the rest of the food in the refrigerator, and the whole time she was giving herself a pep talk. She could do this. She'd never wanted to do anything with her life except be in the Bureau. All she had to do was focus on the job.

She sat back down with her laptop, pulled up the files she'd been reading and went back to work. One hour passed and she got up for a cup of coffee, then kept reading, making notes as she went. Another hour passed and she got up to go to the bathroom. When she returned her steps were dragging. Seeing Wade had resurrected every ugly memory of her last months with him.

She sat back down again and within moments realized she was reading the report detailing Nola Landry's kidnapping. When she got to the part about Agent Cameron Winger being attacked and ending up in the hospital, she sat staring at the words. What if it had been Wade? Who would they have notified? Then she pinched the bridge of her nose to stop the tears and took a deep breath. What was the matter with her? She was no longer his family.

After a few moments she closed the laptop and went straight to her bedroom, changed into a different T-shirt and put on her running shoes.

It was after 7:00 p.m., but there was still plenty of light. She pocketed her cell phone and door key and headed for the park across from her apartment building. Staying fit was a big part of the FBI protocol, but this wasn't about physical fitness. She needed to break a sweat, to wear herself out until she was too tired to think about Wade and death and babies that didn't survive.

After a half hour at a steady pace she lost focus on everything but the run: feeling the blood surge through her veins, the expansion of her lungs as she breathed in and out, the burn of muscles as time continued to pass, testing her endurance.

She was bathed in sweat and still running when the sun went down, and then she ran all the way out of the park and back to her building before she finally stopped. In an effort to cool down she took the stairs up to her third-floor apartment rather than take the elevator, but even as she went inside she felt as much panic now as when she'd first left.

Her FBI training kicked in as she measured the pros and cons of what she was going to face, and came to one simple conclusion. There was no way to outrun the past.

Cameron arrived at the hotel in Tulsa before noon the next day and left his rental car's keys with valet parking.

He shouldered his luggage and headed for the elevator, bypassing the front desk as he went. When he knocked on the door, Wade let him in.

He could tell by the look on Wade's face something more had happened.

"Don't look so glad to see me," Cameron said.

"Sorry," Wade said. "We've been looking at security tapes all morning. I'm glad you're here. Did you have any trouble on the road?"

"Not a bit," Cameron said. "Where's Tate?"

"There's a small conference room attached to the suite. He's in there. That door leads to a bedroom with two beds. You're with me."

Cameron dumped his things in the bedroom and then followed the sound of voices into the conference room. It had a long table, a half-dozen chairs and a small sink and counter at one end of the room. He saw a bucket of ice, some soft drinks and a couple of uneaten doughnuts under a plastic cover. He made himself a cold drink, grabbed a doughnut and then moved toward the computer screens set up at one end of the table.

"Glad to have you back," Tate said as Cameron walked up behind him.

"Good to be here. What's going on?"

Wade pointed to the photos spread out across the table as Tate hit Pause and stopped the security footage.

"We had a visit from Inman," Wade said.

Cameron jerked, almost spilling his drink.

"Here? He came here?"

"Long enough to drop those off," Tate said. "Those were taken of us at one of the kill sites yesterday morning. We got him on the hotel security cameras paying a bellhop to bring them to the front desk that afternoon. The cameras caught him coming to the front door and leaving around back, but we didn't get a look at what he was driving. So we confiscated video from as many businesses in the immediate area as we could get in the hopes of spotting him in one of the vehicles passing by. No luck so far."

"Wow," Cameron said. "He's right under our noses again, and we still can't get our hands on him."

"Yes, and once again the media is having a field day with that," Wade grumbled.

Cameron knew how he felt. They'd been making excuses for a year as to how he got away.

Tate's phone signaled an incoming text.

"The Director sent us an email," he said, and went to get his laptop. He pulled up the message, then read it aloud.

"I'm adding Agent Jolene Luckett to your team. She's been studying all the files for the past two days. Use her as you see fit. If you're planning to move locations, wait for her before you leave. She arrives tomorrow at 10:30 a.m. at Tulsa International Airport."

Tate had gone numb right after the first sentence, and was trying to figure out what possessed the Director to do something like this. Granted Jo was a whiz at tracking down people through the internet, but Wade didn't deserve this.

Tate wouldn't look at Wade, and he could see Cameron doing the same as he went to refill his soft drink.

Wade took a deep breath, walked to the windows and shoved his hands in his pockets. He had an overwhelming urge to hit something.

"I never knew the Director had such a sense of humor," he drawled. "I can handle working with my ex-wife. Either one of you have a problem with it?"

"Not me," Tate muttered.

"I'm good," Cameron added.

"Fine. Then that settles that," Wade said. "I hope the Director knows he's just upped the team's traveling costs. She doesn't snore, but I'm damn sure not sharing a room with her."

Tate laughed and Cameron grinned.

Wade grinned, but inside he was screaming. There was no way in hell this was going to work.

And at the same time he thought that, he wondered what her reaction had been when she got her orders. He would lay odds she wasn't any happier about this than he was. Still, if she didn't make waves, he wouldn't, either.

"So what are we doing for dinner?" Cameron asked.

Wade turned around. "I don't know about you, but I think after that piece of news, the Director just bought us some fine dining."

Tate was inclined to agree. "I say we check out the hotel restaurant."

"Do we need a reservation?" Cameron asked.

"I'll find out," Tate said.

Wade heard them talking, but the words were all running together. Except for seeing her a few weeks ago at the cemetery, he hadn't come face-to-face with her in over a year and a half. She was so angry, but for the life of him, he couldn't figure out why she was angry with him. He hadn't shot her, nor was he responsible for the death of the baby she'd been carrying. He'd never been so scared, never prayed as hard as he had that day. Losing the baby had been terrible. But losing her would have been unthinkable. Or so he thought, until she turned into someone he didn't know and walked away. He had yet to wrap his head around why. Hell, maybe working with her would be good after all. Maybe he would finally get some long-overdue answers.

Jo had already packed except for the small stuff. Now all she had to do was run a few errands and catch a very early flight tomorrow. According to her info, one of the team would pick her up at the airport. She hoped to God they didn't send Wade. She didn't want one-on-one time with him right off the bat.

The more she thought about what she was going to be doing, the more anxious she got. She'd been gone for almost a week on another case and home only two days when she'd gotten this call. There were bills due, a prescription to get refilled, some toilet articles to replace, before she headed out again. Unfortunately there was nothing she could buy to protect her from the inevitable gut reaction to seeing Wade. It was such a bitch still being in love with the man she'd divorced. This wasn't the first time she'd second-guessed her reason for doing it, but she had been slightly insane from her guilt and grief at the time, and it was too late to explain all that now.

She sighed. Whatever would be, would be. Either they would get through it or they would wind up killing each other. One way or another, this day had been a long time coming.

It had been five days, maybe six, since this killing spree began. Hershel had actually lost count, but it didn't matter. He felt safe and sheltered at the campground at Keystone Lake.

The first thing he did after he woke up that morning was turn on the laptop to see what was happening, and the first thing he saw was his own picture. It wasn't the first time he'd seen it on-air, because it was being aired daily in conjunction with the murders, and he feared it was only a matter of time before someone took a closer look at him camping out here.

He'd spent over an hour last night watching the Weather Channel, trying to second-guess where the next serious storm threat might hit. There were a couple of places he could go and wait for it, but he couldn't go home—not ever again. Once he would have just grown a beard, changed cars and locations, and disappeared under another name like he'd done after the Louisiana floods. But he had healed with severe facial scars, and the ability to grow a full, healthy beard was gone. He could always go to Mexico and disappear, but that felt too much like running away. If he did that, it would mean they'd won, and that didn't set well.

He rolled out of his sleeping bag, reached for his jeans and began to get dressed. A few minutes later he was out of the tent and heading for the public bathrooms. Although it was still early, the day was already showing signs of heat. The air was still and muggy. Even the little ground lizards seemed uninterested in his passing, lying motionless beneath the underbrush.

Very few of the other campers were up, and the ones who were seemed occupied with making their breakfast. He saw one camper heading off toward the lake with a rod and reel, possibly to go catch his meal. It seemed like an iffy proposition to Hershel. In a pinch, he would rather rely on bread and peanut butter.

He made quick work of the toilet and washing facilities and was on his way out when he heard voices just outside the doorway. The last thing he wanted was to come face-to-face with someone and have to acknowledge their presence, so he stopped.

A few moments later the voices faded, and he took a quick look to make sure they were gone before heading out, walking with his head down.

The next time he looked up he saw a little girl sitting on the picnic table near his tent.

"Hi!" she said. "I'm having breakfast."

He frowned and kept walking, hoping his silence would deter her. It didn't.

"My name is Louise. What's yours?"

He stumbled. What the hell? Was this the universe making fun of him, or was this his Louise trying to communicate?

He turned around and gave her a closer look. She couldn't have been more than six or seven years old and didn't look a thing like his Louise. The moment he thought it, he told himself he was a fool. Of course she didn't look like Louise, because she *wasn't* Louise.

The little girl took another bite of the sweet roll she was eating, then licked her fingers as she waited for him to talk. When he didn't, she offered up another question.

"What happened to your face?" she asked.

"Go away," he said shortly, and moved toward his truck.

She got down off the picnic table and followed him, still eating and licking her fingers between bites.

"Does your face hurt? I fell off my bike and skinned my knee. It hurt a lot. Did your mama kiss your face and make it better? My mama kissed my knee and put three Cinderella Band-Aids on it."

"Get lost, kid," Hershel muttered, and began unhooking his generator. He needed to get the hell out of here.

The little girl frowned. "Getting lost is dangerous. I'm not supposed to get lost," she said, and took another bite, chewing while she talked. "You said a mean thing. You shouldn't be mean to people. It's not nice. Do you go to church? You should go to church. It might make you nicer."

Hershel froze. For just a moment he could hear his Louise nagging him, talking about God and changing his ways. He looked back at the kid again, wondered if Louise had somehow sent her, and then shook off the thought.

"Go back to your own campground," Hershel said, and turned his back on her.

"I'm gonna tell my mama on you! I'm gonna tell her you told me to get lost."

Hershel spun around, but she was already running back across the campground.

"Damn it."

He wasn't into offing kids, but this complicated his situation. This little altercation could bring unwanted attention, which he didn't need. It was time to leave.

He began loading up the heavier pieces of his camping equipment, and then packed up what was inside the tent. As soon as it was empty, he took it down, as well, working with one eye on the campsites behind him, hoping he didn't see some irate parent coming his way. Still, it verified what he'd been thinking all along. No more public campgrounds for him.

It's your own fault.

Hershel groaned. *Now* Louise decided to show up. If she'd spoken up earlier, he wouldn't have been so antsy with the kid.

"Well, hell, Louise, of course it's my fault. You continue to remind me that everything is my fault, including your demise."

Leave now, Hershel. Stop now and go to Mexico. We talked about it once. You can go there now and disappear.

"You don't get to tell me what to do anymore. I'll go when I'm ready and not before."

You are a mean man, Hershel Inman, and you are going straight to Hell.

"Yes, so your little doppelgänger said a few minutes ago…or words to that effect. Now beat it. I need to finish packing."

You're going to be sorry…be sorry…be sorry…

Hershel was livid. Louise's nagging was so off

the wall she was beginning to echo. He threw the rest of his things into the truck and took off from the campground without looking back.

Four

"We are beginning our approach into Tulsa International Airport. Please turn off your electronic devices, return your seat backs to the upright position, stow your tray tables and prepare for landing."

Jo turned off her iPad, handed the flight attendant the rest of her trash and glanced at her watch. She hated to fly and disliked landings most of all, which made the knot already in her belly grow tighter. Between falling out of the sky and coming face-to-face with Wade Luckett, this day was already screwed.

God, help me through this.

She leaned as far back against the headrest as she could go, clutching the iPad against her chest as if it was a protective shield. The man in the seat beside her coughed. Again. He had been sharing that ongoing hack with the other passengers ever since they boarded the plane, and she hoped to God it wasn't something contagious. She'd been sick on location before, and she couldn't afford to be sick now. She was going to need all her resources to get through this assignment.

Her overwhelming fear of showing weakness was a holdover from her days as a rookie with the Bureau. If you were tough, they called you a bitch. If you had a pretty face or showed weakness, then you couldn't possibly do a good job.

A few minutes later she both heard and felt the jarring thumps as the landing gear went down. She tightened her grip on the iPad, not realizing she was also holding her breath until her seatmate coughed again, at which point she exhaled in sheer disgust.

When she began feeling the drag of the wind against the flaps she knew they were on approach. She planted her feet beneath the seat in front of her and leaned back, as if by sheer will alone she would stop the plane and get them on the ground. First there was the screech of tires on the tarmac, then a slight bounce, and then another thump as the tires made final contact and began to roll. Finally they were down. As they began to taxi toward the terminal she opened her eyes.

And here we go.

* * *

Tate Benton was in Baggage Claim, waiting for the newest member of their team to show up. He hadn't seen her in years, probably since right before she and Wade divorced. He and Cameron used to have dinner at Wade and Jo's home at least once a month. Then everything went to hell after she lost the baby. They knew grief split up just as many couples as it brought closer, and assumed that was it. Wade hadn't volunteered any information, and it wasn't something he felt comfortable asking about.

He glanced at his watch, then back up at the people filing into the area, suddenly curious to see her again. She'd been with the agency for twelve years and had a good reputation. He knew her well enough to know that she would be forthright and competent, despite her past with Wade. Then he saw her coming and took a step forward.

At five feet nine inches tall, she had a commanding presence. Her stride was long, her shoulders military-straight. Her dark, shoulder-length hair swayed in opposition with her stride, a subtle hint to the stubbornness of her spirit. But as she came within speaking distance, he saw something else that he hadn't expected. The look on her face was the same look he'd seen on soldiers coming back from combat. He wasn't prepared for the shadows in her eyes or the grim set to her lips. When she saw him, the relief on her face was obvious, which told him she was probably as unhappy about having to work with Wade as he was about working with her.

"Good morning, Tate. It's been a while," Jo said.

He smiled and lightly touched her shoulder in greeting.

"Hello, Jo, and yes, it has been a while, but I'm really glad to have you on board with this case."

She smiled briefly. "Thanks. I only have one suitcase. Give me a few minutes to retrieve it and I'll be ready to go."

"Sure thing," Tate said. "Want to leave your carry-on with me?"

She started to say no and then realized that was silly. He wasn't showing preference to her because she was female. He was just being helpful so she would have both hands free to get her other bag.

"Yes, sure. That would be great." She slipped the bag off her shoulder, handed it to him and then moved toward the carousel.

Tate wasn't a profiler for nothing. He knew it wasn't easy for women in high-profile jobs and guessed she'd been burned enough to be touchy about accepting help of any kind. A few minutes later the carousel began turning. After snagging her bag, she pulled the handle up and rolled it toward him.

"I'm ready," she said.

He led the way out of the terminal and across the drive to the parking garage, with Jo coming along behind him. They loaded her luggage, and then got in the SUV and drove away.

"It's sure hot here in Oklahoma," she said.

Tate nodded. "Part of why the thunderstorms get so severe when a cool front comes in." Then he grimaced. "This case has been a tough one. Chasing down a serial killer whose urge is triggered by natural disasters has been crazy."

Finally, something Jo felt comfortable discussing.

"I read all the reports your team filed, along with everything else I could get my hands on regarding this man. So his wife's death made him crazy and he compensates by killing. I understand the death-and-grief-can-make-you-crazy part, but I don't quite get how murder fixes his problem."

Tate heard a personal note in what she'd just said and wondered if she realized how much she'd admitted, then shook it off.

"His killing is pure retribution against the authorities who didn't come to her aid soon enough to save her. He wants them embarrassed by their inability to catch him, and that's where we come in. It has nothing to do with the victims. They're as random as they could possibly be. The only thing they had in common was surviving the storms."

"But he doesn't kill children," Jo said.

"So far," Tate agreed.

"Do you think he would?" she asked.

"I can't predict what this man will do. As you know, he's changed his mode of killing. No guns this time around."

"Why do you think he did that?"

"I'd say part of it had to do with locations and noise, but it's hard to be positive. Last year, when his killing spree began, he did kill tornado victims with a gun, then he moved on to the flood victims, which made it easier." He tapped the brakes, and then turned off the street and into a parking area. "Home sweet home," he said.

Jo glanced at the hotel and grounds.

"Fancy."

"The storms have destroyed so many homes that a lot of the hotels are full up. We took what we could get."

He found an empty space and parked. They exited the SUV at the same time. Jo grabbed her suitcase, pulled up the handle, dropped the carry-on strap over it and followed Tate inside.

Wade and Cameron were still going through security footage, although Wade kept glancing at the time and losing focus. Jo was afraid of flying, and by the time she got here she would be on edge. It wouldn't make their reunion any easier, but he doubted there was anything that would ease that moment.

In an effort to be cordial he'd ordered a couple bottles of Diet Dr Pepper sent to the room, along with some packages of peanut butter crackers. She wasn't big on sweets, but she loved savory. The suite they were in didn't have another bed, but Tate had managed to get the adjoining room for her. Beyond that, Wade couldn't imagine how this was going to play out.

When he heard a key in the door, he jumped up.

"Easy, partner," Cameron said quietly.

"Shit," Wade muttered, and then the door opened.

She came in pulling a suitcase and talking on the phone. She glanced up just long enough to give everyone a quick nod and then kept talking.

Tate closed the door behind them, glanced at Wade and shrugged.

Wade sighed. The tense moment had just been put on hold, which gave him a few moments to look at her unobserved.

She looked good—damn good. He'd been concentrating on being angry and had forgotten about the sexy part. She shed her jacket as she talked, then tossed it on the back of a chair, revealing even more of her curves.

Wade headed for the wet bar to get something cold to drink. He needed something to cool his thoughts.

"I'm sorry," Jo said as she ended her call. "That was my cleaning lady. She said there's a leak in my bathroom. I told her to call the landlord. This stuff always happens when I'm gone."

"Last time something like that happened at my place I was asleep. I woke up with half the ceiling in bed with me," Cameron said.

"What in the world caused that?" she asked.

"Was that the wild party where the girl got high and wanted to swim, so she locked herself in the bathroom and tried to flood the room?" Tate asked.

Cameron nodded.

"That's horrible," Jo said, then laughed. "I'm sorry, but the image is pretty funny."

Cameron grinned. "It was a mess for sure."

Wade was standing on the other side of the

sofa, determined to wait her out, but he might as well have been invisible. Tate was showing her the door that connected to their suite and giving her the room key. She smiled, grabbed her bags and started toward the door, and Wade's patience ended.

"I lost a couple of pounds last month, but I'm sure that didn't make me invisible. Hello, Jolene. Yes, I'm fine, and it's just great to see you, too. I trust you had a safe flight, since you're here. There's Diet Dr Pepper and peanut butter crackers at the wet bar with your name on them, and you're welcome."

He glared, turned on one heel and strode out of the room without looking back.

Jolene felt like crying, but it was the last damn thing she would do in front of them, so she smiled, instead.

"I think that went well, don't you?" she said, then went into her room and shut the door.

Tate sighed.

Cameron rolled his eyes.

They could hear Wade cursing and banging drawers in the adjoining bedroom, and then a short while later they heard the door slam.

"Did he just leave? Where the heck did he go?" Cameron asked.

"Knowing Wade, he's gone to the gym. He'll come back in about an hour all hot, sweaty and hungry," Tate said.

Moments later they heard the outer door to the adjoining room open and close.

"Did she just leave, too?" Tate asked.

Cameron shrugged. "I seem to remember that habit of working out when they were bothered was true of both of them. What are the odds of them ending up in the gym at the same time?"

Tate sighed. "Hell if I know. I just hope whatever they're doing, they get all the crap out of their systems before they come back."

Wade was at the weight bench when Jolene walked in. She saw him and almost walked out again, then realized he wasn't looking at her and didn't know she'd come in, which was fine. She paused at the desk to pick up a towel and a bottle of water, and then went to the opposite side of the room, chose a treadmill and started walking. As soon as she was warmed up, she increased the speed, then increased it some more until she was running full-out.

More than one man in the gym turned to watch in quiet awe, but Wade wasn't one of them. He was concentrating on his lifts, while one of the employees spotted for him. He worked at the weights until the muscles in his arms were burning and then he stopped and for the first time sat up. That was when he saw her, bathed in sweat with an expression on her face that made him ache. If he didn't know better, he would have thought she was crying.

He got up, grabbed a towel and, without giving himself time to change his mind, walked over to her treadmill and stopped squarely in front of her.

She blinked, almost stumbled, and then hit Stop. The track rolled to a halt. Now they were standing face-to-face, sweat rolling out of their hair and down their faces.

Jolene couldn't move. This was the closest she'd been to him since the day of their divorce, and it still hurt to know she no longer had the right to touch him.

He wanted to hug her but handed her a towel instead, then wiped his face with his own.

"It's good to see you," he said.

"It's good to see you, too."

"That was awkward. Sorry I flew off the handle," he added.

She sighed. "Very awkward. I didn't know what to say, either, and made the mistake of saying nothing, which was rude."

"I'm through here," Wade said.

"So am I."

They dropped their dirty towels in the bin as they passed by the desk and walked out together, still careful not to touch each other. He punched the button for the elevator, then stared at the floor while waiting for it to arrive. Two girls walked up behind them. There was a moment of silence, and then Jo heard them whispering and giggling.

When the elevator opened they all got on together, and the moment the doors went shut, one of the girls cornered Wade.

"Are you Channing Tatum? You are, aren't you? OMG, can I have your autograph?"

Wade frowned, and Jolene grinned.

"No, I'm not Channing Tatum, whoever that is, sorry."

"Oh, please, can we have your autograph? We won't tell anyone you're here."

"Look, ladies, I'm not—"

Jo shrugged. "The jig's up, Channing, you might as well give them the autograph and be done with it."

"Oooh, thank you," they squealed, then eyed Jo, trying to figure out if she was famous, too.

"Don't look at me," Jo said. "I'm just his bodyguard."

The girls' eyes widened as they digested the thought that someone like him would have a female bodyguard.

Now he was frowning at all three of them while the girls were scrambling to get out a pen. One wanted him to sign her arm, while the other wanted him to sign the back of her shirt.

It was all Jo could do not to burst out laughing. Just as the first girl handed him a pen and then held out her arm, the elevator stopped on their floor.

"This is where we get off," he said, and started out.

"I'll hold the door," Jo said, leaving him no choice but to be extremely rude or do it and get it over with.

He glared at her and took the pen.

"How do you spell *Tatum?*" he asked.

The girls frowned, and then giggled, as if he'd just made a joke.

"With a *U,*" Jo whispered.

He sighed, wrote *Channing Tatum* on one girl's arm and then wrote it again on the other girl's shirt.

"Thank you so much!" they squealed in unison.

They were still giggling as the door shut.

Wade turned and gave Jo a hard stare.

"Who the hell is Channing Tatum?"

"An actor. He was named *People* magazine's sexiest man of the year."

His eyes widened. "Really? I'll have to check out one of his movies."

"Try *Magic Mike*," Jo said. "I'll bet they have it on pay-per-view here at the hotel."

"Yeah, okay, but don't do that again, damn it." Then he looked at her again and snorted. "My bodyguard. Really?"

She was still laughing when they got to the room.

The last thing Tate expected to see was them coming in together with Jo laughing and Wade's face flushed with embarrassment.

Cameron glanced up. "What's so funny?" he asked.

Jolene pointed at Wade. "Ask Mr. Hollywood here about the two girls in the elevator who wanted his autograph. I'm going to shower. Are you planning to go out for lunch or are we ordering in?"

Tate grinned. There had to be a good story behind this. "We're ordering room service, since we're still going through security footage."

"Good. Just order me something like a Cobb salad, or a Caesar salad with grilled chicken… something with a little protein, iced tea to drink and some kind of fruit. I'm not picky. I won't be long, and then you can fill me in on where I need to concentrate my search."

She walked out, still smiling, and the moment she was gone, they turned on Wade.

"Mr. Hollywood?" Cameron asked.

Wade shrugged. "Oh, two girls in the elevator thought I was some actor named Channing Tatum. Jo made it worse by telling them she was my bodyguard. I didn't know who he was and she told me to watch a movie called *Magic Mike*."

Tate laughed out loud.

Cameron grinned. "Damn. I never saw the resemblance, but maybe that's because I wasn't looking at your ass."

Wade frowned. "What do you mean?"

"That movie is about male strippers," Cameron said.

Wade glared. "I'm going to shower, too. Order me two of whatever sandwiches you guys are having and a piece of pie. I'm starving."

"Obviously the man hasn't lost his appetite," Tate drawled.

"I can't believe he doesn't know who Channing Tatum is," Cameron said.

"Think about it. Wade likes to watch hunting and fishing shows, and documentaries about Alaska," Tate said.

"Good point," Cameron said, and then frowned.

"What's wrong?" Tate asked.

"Well, the lucky bastard… It wouldn't hurt my feelings to be mistaken for Channing Tatum."

"I thought you had a thing for that little blonde Red Cross worker," Tate said.

Cameron grinned. "I do, but it still wouldn't hurt."

The awkward meeting had passed and they'd survived. By the time Jo and Wade came back from cleaning up, the food had arrived. Everyone stepped away from the TV and the security footage to eat, but they kept on discussing the case.

Jo was both horrified and fascinated by the Stormchaser's reasoning. She knew Tate's wife was the only victim who had survived and wanted to pursue a question she'd had while reading the files, so she quickly swallowed the bite of salad she'd been chewing and turned to Tate.

"Did you know her before the flood, or did your relationship develop during the investigation?" she asked.

"We grew up together," he said. "It was a fluke

that the killer brought me back to my hometown, but seeing Nola again was a plus for me."

"I wasn't asking to be nosy. I was thinking along the lines of Inman targeting people connected to the team."

"It's hard to say what was in his head," Wade said. "I mean, Nola became a target before we ever showed up when she witnessed him murdering some of her neighbors during the flood. We came on the scene in the midst of all that, and it pretty much went downhill from there."

"After the explosion, and after you lost track of him, did all three of you think he was dead?"

"I didn't," Wade said. "I was with Tate when we found where he'd pulled himself out of the flood, then when we found where he'd parked his truck and it was actually gone, I thought if he lived through all that *and* the gators, he could live through anything."

"I wanted to believe he was dead," Tate put in. "For Nola's sake as much as for mine, but I asked the Bureau to keep his phone activated, just in case, and as it turned out, that was a good thing."

"That's another thing," she said. "He actually sends you text messages?"

Tate pulled up the most recent text on his phone

and slid it toward her. "This is the latest. We got it just after the Wichita Falls tornado."

I am not dead, so do not weep. It was not my time. I have vows to keep.

Jo shuddered as she read the words.

"Nothing creepier than a perp on some holy quest. Is this the only contact you've had with him since?"

"No. We got photos here at the hotel yesterday. They were taken of us while we were on-site at one of the crime scenes," Tate said.

Jolene frowned. "And he did this to prove he's right under your noses and you still can't catch him, right?"

"Right," the men echoed.

"Can I see them?"

Wade wiped his hands and got up. "They're over here somewhere."

"They're in that file folder on top of my brief-case," Tate said.

Wade retrieved the folder and gave it to Jo.

The moment she opened it, she had a feeling of déjà vu.

"What the hell?" she muttered, quickly leafing through the stack. When she got to the one where

Wade was walking out from behind the broken wall in the debris field, she gasped.

Wade frowned. "What's wrong, Jo?"

"Oh, shit. Oh, my God," she said, still talking to herself.

Tate grabbed her arm. "What's going on?"

"I need a laptop! Does anyone have one up and running?"

"I do. I was checking email while we waited for lunch," Cameron said, and ducked into their room to get it, and came back running.

"What's happening?" Wade asked.

"I saw this film footage on CNN while I was still at home. There's something in the background that you aren't seeing in the stills."

She ran a search for CNN, then typed in the date and subject she was hunting for. As soon as the results came up, she looked over at the men.

"Look at this. I think I might have seen the Stormchaser in this clip."

They gathered around her chair and then leaned in as she widened the shot and clicked Play. All of a sudden there they were, live and in color.

"Watch for the moment Wade walks out from behind that wall…" Jo said. "There! Now look, wait for the cameraman to take the close-up of him and Tate."

"There we are," Tate said.

Jo clicked Pause. "And there he is," she said, pointing at a pickup on the far side of the scene. "Now watch when I start it back up. When I first saw this, for a second I thought the driver was actually pulling a gun. That's why I even noticed it. And then when I saw it was a camera, I blew it off. So here goes."

She clicked Play again, and the men watched in disbelief.

"That *is* a camera!" Tate said, and shuffled through the pictures they'd been sent until he found the one that matched what they were seeing on the computer. "This is the same scene, but taken from another angle."

Jo nodded. "So is this Hershel Inman?"

"Hell, yes," Wade muttered. "And thanks to your sharp eye, we now know what he's driving. I'm starting over on those tapes. If we can get a license tag, we can put out a BOLO."

Jo allowed herself a moment of pure elation. It was always like that when a clue suddenly fell into place. And having information to put up a be-on-the-lookout bulletin was even better.

Wade grabbed his drink and his pie, and headed back to the security footage they'd been viewing. Cameron followed.

"Good job," Tate said, and gave her shoulder a brief squeeze.

Jo said nothing, but inside she was smiling.

Five

When Hershel finally left Tulsa, he took I-44 East into Missouri. The farther he went, the better he felt. Being on the move made him feel like he had a purpose, that he was going somewhere specific, when in fact his destinations depended on weather, not a job.

He spent the night in the mountains outside of Springfield, Missouri, but didn't bother setting up the big tent and used a pup tent instead. He made a cold camp, eating bread and lunch meat he'd bought a couple of hours earlier, and was listening to the radio in his truck when he caught a weather report that made his heart skip a beat. Storm warnings again for northeastern Oklahoma, with the storms predicted to move into Missouri later on. He got out a map of the state and began looking at highways that would take him into those areas, when Louise appeared.

You have turned into a maniac, chasing storms like a dog chases cars. One of these days you'll get caught up in one of those storms and you will die.

Hershel sighed. "Damn it, Louise, I'm trying to have a peaceful meal here. I should have known you couldn't stay gone long."

I'm just reminding you of what you've become. You have no home. You have no life. You're like some filthy hobo, slipping into one place and out of another. God is mad at you, Hershel.

Hershel flung the rest of his sandwich out the window.

"Well I'm pretty damn mad at him, too. He ruined everything. He could have saved you and He didn't, so don't talk to me about God. As far as I'm concerned, He doesn't exist."

Hershel! That's blasphemy!

"I've killed people, Louise. Between you and me, what's a little blasphemy added to my sins? According to you I'm already going to Hell, so leave me alone!"

Going to Hell...to Hell...to Hell...

Hershel frowned. This echo business was new,

and he didn't know what to make of it. But if Louise had nothing more to say, he wouldn't complain.

Thirty minutes later he glanced at the gas gauge. He needed to stop for fuel. He didn't like facial disguises, but the FBI knew his real identity, so he didn't really have any choice. He was an old hand at wigs and beards, and since he needed to stop, it was time to get one out.

He pulled over to the side of the highway, got a small bag from the floorboard and dug through it, finally deciding on a curly gray wig and a thick gray mustache. For a final touch he pulled out some gold wire-rimmed reading glasses and settled them on his nose. It was a good look. Even the scars on his face were less noticeable because there were other things to focus on. As soon as there was a gap in the traffic, he pulled back onto the highway and continued heading east.

He stopped for gas at the next available Quik Stop and, after he fueled up, went inside to pick up some food. He had cans of tuna and Vienna sausages in one hand, a box of crackers under his arm and was looking to see if they had peanut butter when someone tapped him on the shoulder.

Every fear he had of getting caught went through his mind as he spun around, only to see a young woman smiling at him as she handed him a small shopping basket.

"Looks like your hands are getting full," she said.

Hershel stammered a thank-you as he dropped the items inside and ducked down another aisle, grabbed a couple of cans of soup, a sack of pretzels, a loaf of bread and a big package of doughnuts. His last items were a six-pack of beer and a jar of instant coffee.

As he began to pay, he realized he was also getting low on cash, so he stopped by the ATM on his way out, swiped his card and soon pocketed three hundred dollars in twenty-dollar bills. The transaction was in Lee Parsons' name and would go unnoticed, because no one cared what that man did with his money. He'd set up new identities in several places long before he'd killed his first victim, then taken every penny he and Louise had saved for their retirement and put it in a new bank under the Parsons name. His Social Security check and the retirement money he was drawing from his old job continued to accumulate in a checking account in New Orleans that was still under his real name. There wasn't anything he could do about it at the moment, but he would figure all that out later.

He walked out with his head down, deposited

the sack of groceries in the truck and was back on I-44 within minutes. And, all the while he was driving east, there was a large bank of storm clouds building up in the west behind him.

It was Wade who finally found Hershel's arrival at their hotel on the surveillance video, and even more exciting was the fact that they got a tag number to go with it. Every agent in the room high-fived Jolene, giving her props for catching sight of him—and his truck—in the CNN footage, and quickly put out the BOLO.

"If we get lucky and they pick him up on some highway, this will put an end to a long, deadly investigation," Tate said.

"Well, he's been in our sights before and got away. I'm not popping the champagne yet," Wade muttered. "I can't believe the bastard is still alive. We need to find out what his kryptonite is."

"Maybe it'll be Jo," Cameron said, and gave her a friendly wink.

Wade flinched. *No, she's my kryptonite,* he thought.

Jo glanced up at the clock. "I'm going to check on a search I was running. Yell if you need me," she said, and went back into the conference room.

Wade wouldn't look. He didn't want Tate and

Cameron teasing him later. From beginning to end, there wasn't one thing funny about them. In just shy of five years they'd gone from lovers to married to burying a child and getting divorced. When he thought about it, it still made his head spin.

"We have reports to write," Tate said. "The sooner we get them done, the better. I've been watching the Weather Channel, and it looks like there's a line of severe storms building up in the area. I seriously doubt he stayed around here, especially after that challenging look he gave us in the security camera."

Cameron frowned. "If we're not working tonight, I want to stop by where the Red Cross is set up and see Laura."

"I didn't know she was in town," Wade said.

"Yes. I got a text from her today," Cameron said.

"Lucky you," Wade said.

Cameron grinned. "No. Lucky *you*. Yours will be sleeping next door. Mine is way across the city."

"*Mine,* as you put it, is no longer mine, and sleeping next door is not a plus."

"But, Channing, you guys were laughing and talking earlier," Cameron said.

Wade glared. "Can the Channing crap, thank you, and of course we were talking. What did you think would happen when we had to work together…that one of us would slit our wrists? Give us a little credit for professionalism, please."

"Sorry," Cameron said.

"Forget it," Wade muttered. "I'm going to write up my report."

Unaware she was the subject of conversation, Jo was focused on the search she'd been running, trying to find out how Hershel Inman funded his lifestyle and his killing sprees.

Once they'd learned his identity last year and located the home he'd made after Hurricane Katrina, they'd not only cut off his ability to return but had flagged his personal account in New Orleans. If he drew money from the account or transferred any in, they would know. He had to be living under an assumed name, maybe more than one, so either he was one slick bandit or he had money somewhere else. Either way, she was determined to find it.

She was still at it a couple of hours later when the lights suddenly flickered. She glanced up, surprised to see that it had gotten dark outside. When she saw lightning, she shivered. All of her life she'd been afraid of storms. She went to the windows to look out. The sky was black; there were no stars. She heard thunder rumbling overhead and then jumped when a shaft of lightning struck nearby, rattling the window. More lightning split the darkness, tearing across the heavens like a quicksilver spark, gone as quickly as it had appeared.

"Are you okay?"

She jumped. Wade was right behind her, and she hadn't heard him come in.

"I'm fine. Are storms predicted tonight?"

"That's what they said."

"Crap," Jo muttered.

"You want some dinner? We're going to go down to the restaurant."

She glanced toward her computer. "I should keep working."

"You have to eat sometime," he said. "Take a break and come back with fresh eyes."

She hesitated. It would be amazing to just sit down and share a meal with him again.

"Yes, I guess you're right," she said. "Give me a couple of minutes to wash up and I'll be right there."

"Take your time. We won't leave you behind," he said, and walked out.

Jo stumbled as she moved to save her work and shut down her computer. Her hands were shaking as she typed in the codes. She'd left him behind without a backward glance.

Damn.

Damn it all to hell.

The storm hit just as they finished ordering. The thunder was loud, the lightning louder still, flashing like a disco ball across the sky. When the rain began to hammer against the windows behind her, she flinched.

Wade put a hand on her arm before he thought. "Easy, Jolene, it's just rain."

The lump in her throat was instantaneous. She knew she should say something, but all she could remember was lying in his arms as he whispered those same words in her ear.

She managed a slight laugh. "I can face down the bad guys and outshoot almost anyone on the shooting range, but I'm scared of storms and flying in airplanes. Pathetic, isn't it?"

"I don't like snakes," Tate said.

"To this day I don't like clowns," Cameron offered.

"The only thing that makes me shake in my boots is you, Jolene. I was afraid to make you mad when we were married, and I'm still afraid," Wade said, and then was shocked by what he'd revealed.

She couldn't believe what he'd just said. "You aren't serious."

"Well, at the risk of making myself look like a bigger ass than usual in front of my partners here, I'm serious as a heart attack."

She was stunned. "But why?"

"Remember that Valentine's Day when I snuck into the apartment to surprise you and you knocked me cold?"

She frowned. "You were supposed to be in L.A. I thought you were a burglar."

"You laid me out with a single blow I never saw coming and broke sixty bucks' worth of roses," he said.

Tate grinned. "Wade is—was—our best agent at hand-to-hand combat. Now *I'm* scared of you, too."

Cameron laughed.

She glared.

Without realizing Wade had changed the subject to divert her focus on the storm, she relaxed.

It was almost midnight when Hershel arrived in St. Louis, Missouri. He'd had the radio on throughout the drive and realized that for the first time ever he was in the path of a storm with nowhere to go. He knew the thunderstorm was severe and moving in his direction. Even though he'd stayed on I-44, without daylight to help him find some kind of campsite he'd been forced to keep driving. Now he was in an unfamiliar city with a storm on his ass.

He was going to have to find a place to ride it out, which meant taking a chance on a motel or spending the night in his truck. Worried, he drove up one street and down another while the thunder and lightning came closer.

All he needed was some out-of-the-way no-tell motel and a little luck. Several times he started to pull into one and stop, and each time was deterred by either a cop car patrolling the area, a drug deal going down or prostitutes trolling for johns. He needed a place that was low profile, not something with a waiting line, so he kept driving.

When it began to sprinkle he turned on the windshield wipers. Within a few minutes the rain got heavier and heavier, and the wind began to whine. When the rain suddenly changed to hail, it was so startling that he almost swerved into on-coming traffic.

"That settles it," he muttered, and wheeled into the parking lot of the next motel he came to. The power was flickering on and off as he braked to a sliding halt outside the office.

He was wearing the gray curly wig and mustache again, and when he jumped out on the run he was immediately pelted with golf-ball-sized hail. Wind caught the motel door as he ran inside and slammed it hard against the inner wall before he could push it shut.

"Wow, that shit is sure coming down!" the clerk said.

"I need a room," Hershel said quickly. "How much?"

"Twenty-five dollars for the night," the clerk said.

Hershel slapped the money on the counter. The clerk shoved a key in his hand.

"Last room at the end of this building. Don't call me about the leaky faucet. I already know about it."

When Hershel started to run back out the door, the clerk suddenly called out, "Hey! Stop!"

Hershel cringed.

"I need to see your driver's license, and you didn't sign the register," the clerk said.

"Seriously, man? We're about to blow away here," Hershel said, ducking his head as he signed the register. Then he flew out the door, anxious to get into his room before it got any worse.

"Hey, I need to see your license!" the clerk yelled, but Hershel just kept going.

The clerk looked at the register and rolled his eyes. "Johnny Come Lately. That's a good one," he said, and then jumped and cursed when something blew against his door.

He flipped on the no-occupancy sign, locked the front door and headed for his apartment down the hall.

Hershel's windshield wipers were useless against the onslaught of hail, and he turned them off so they wouldn't get broken. The building was a blur through the wind and hail as he drove down to the room at the end. He was in something of a panic, trying to think of everything he should take inside in case something happened. What did he need that he couldn't live without? He definitely needed his wallet, his disguises and some food. He was hungry and could eat while he rode out the storm. He threw some of the food into his duffel bag, grabbed his big suitcase and jumped out.

The hail hit him on the head, in the face, on the nose, in both eyes. His nose began to bleed before he got inside. By the time he got into the room he was shaking.

He locked the door behind him, slung his things on the bed and turned on the TV to check the weather. Just as the television came on, he began hearing sirens. His heart skipped a beat as he struggled to find a local station. Within seconds of locating a broadcast, he realized they were telling people to take cover.

His heart skipped another beat and then began to pound. This was the real deal, and he had nowhere to hide. He remembered the survivors he'd found and where they'd been hiding: one in a closet, some in bathtubs, under stairs... He threw his suitcase onto the shelf, made sure his wallet and car keys were deep in his pocket, and crawled into the closet and closed the door. He was curled up in the corner with his duffel bag on his lap. When the wail of the wind turned into a roar, he knew this was bad. He'd seen too many aftermath scenes to not be afraid.

"God, oh, God, please don't let me die," Hershel prayed. "Please spare me. Please, God, please."

I thought you were mad at God, and now here you are begging Him for protection? You are a selfish bastard, Hershel Inman. Think about how you feel. Hear that roar? Feel the walls beginning to shake? Hear that ripping sound? It's the roof. This is how scared all those people were that you killed. Think how happy they must have been when they lived through it, and then you came along and

*took their lives. You're going to die, and it's exactly
what you deserve.*

"Not now, Louise! For God's sake, not now!"
Hershel screamed.

Yes, now, Hershel. Now!

The walls were pushing in on him, and then he
heard a loud sucking sound, as if all the oxygen
was caught in an outflow, followed by a whine that
pulled the breath from his body. He heard a rum-
ble so loud it made the floor shake beneath him,
and then the sound of a freight train that seemed
to be coming through his room. His mouth was
open. In his head he was screaming, but in reality
he had no breath left for sound.

All of a sudden the roof was gone and he was
being pelted with both rain and debris. He grabbed
the bag from his lap and put it over his head. Suddenly his face was on fire, like he'd been shot with
a load of bird shot. Then something fell on top of
him and everything went black.

"Mister! Mister! Are you okay?"

Hershel groaned. Someone was tugging on his
arm, and his body was one giant ache. He groaned
again as he tried to move, only to realize something was pinning him down.

"Help me," he whispered.

"He's alive!" someone yelled.

Hershel passed out again, and the next time he came to, rain was falling in his face. He was cold and in pain, so much pain. Then he felt something warm suddenly run between his legs and realized he'd just peed his pants. He heard shouting and turned his head to look, only to realize he was lying on the ground next to two other people, both of whom were dead.

"Shit, oh, shit," he moaned again, and this time he ignored the pain and crawled to his knees.

There was chaos everywhere. People were running and shouting. Power lines were down somewhere close by, because he could hear electricity arcing. He looked around for the motel, but there was nothing but debris as far as he could see. He needed to find his pickup, and then wondered if he still had the keys. He checked his pocket and breathed easier when he felt them, then felt his wallet there, as well.

He tried to get up, then staggered and dropped back to his knees. He needed to find that closet. He needed his duffel bag. Where the fuck was his duffel bag?

It was still raining, but the wind was gone. He didn't know he was crying until he choked on a sob.

I should tell you it's no more than you deserve, but I won't. I still love you, Hershel, and I'm sorry that you're hurt.

"I can't find my things, Louise. I need my bag. Do you see my bag?"

Look at where you were lying. It was underneath your head.

He looked back, saw it on the ground and swung it up into his arms, clutching it to his chest with both hands.

"My stuff. I found my stuff. Thank you, Louise. Thank you," he sobbed. "I need my truck. I need to find my truck."

He made a three-sixty-degree turn, assessing the area and looking for some kind of landmark to tell him where he was. He saw part of the motel sign hanging precariously from a pole and realized they had carried his body to the other side of the street. Part of the motel roof was on top of a vehicle, and when he recognized the taillight, he realized it was on his truck.

"My truck. I see my truck," he mumbled, and staggered into the street.

Three men in hardhats were walking down the street ahead of a city bucket truck. They stopped every few feet to pull debris out of the way so the truck could keep moving.

He stumbled into their path, waving his arms.

"Help me," he said, pointing to his truck. "Help me get the roof off my truck."

One of the men took him by the arm. "Look, man! You've been hurt. You're bleeding all over the place."

"Please!" Hershel begged. "I just need my truck."

"What the hell," the man said, and waved the other workers over. "Come on, guys. Let's get that roof off this man's truck."

"Stand back, mister," a second man said.

Hershel stepped aside and held his breath, praying the truck was still in one piece.

The men grabbed the edges of the roof, lifted it once to get a good grip, then lifted again and began walking backward until it was off.

Hershel ran forward, looked into the truck bed and was stunned that the generator was still there, although it was evident that it had shifted. He had packed things so that his tent and equipment were up against the truck cab, and then he'd shoved the generator against them to keep them from sliding around. Now the generator was on top of the tent and nearly everything else was gone. The top of the cab was banged up, the windshield had been cracked by the hail, and the dents in the body were large and numerous, but if he could open a door, he could get inside.

"There you go, mister," a crew member said. "Hope it starts for you."

"Thank you," Hershel said as they walked away.

He used the remote to unlock the door, but when he reached for the handle and tried to open it, it was stuck. He tried again and again, but without any luck.

"Come on, come on, damn it," he muttered, as he circled the truck to try the other side.

He was in so much pain he was sick to his stomach and his head was spinning. It felt like it had before, when the boat he'd been in had exploded. He probably had another concussion and wondered how many concussions a human brain could sustain before it turned into mush. After two fruitless tries at the passenger door, he rested a moment and then tried again. Suddenly it opened with a pop and a loud creak. He whooped his delight, then winced at the pain stabbing through his jaw and touched his face. It felt ragged. What the hell had happened to him now?

He heard a siren, and when he saw the flashing red-and-blue lights of a cop car, he got out his keys and crawled into the truck. It took two more tries to get the door shut, but the sudden silence and welcome shelter were a huge relief. However, once he *was* inside, he then realized how badly his skin was burning and reached for the rearview mirror. When he saw what had happened to him now, he gasped. Part of his skin looked like it had been peeled off, while other places were black and pockmarked. When he ran his fingers along the surface, he realized debris was imbedded beneath. This wasn't good. He was going to have to take a chance and go to an emergency room or die of infection later.

He took a deep breath, stuck the key in the ignition and gave it a turn. When the engine immediately fired, he began to cry from sheer relief. He put the truck in Reverse, backed up just enough to turn the wheels toward the street, and then drove off into the dark.

Jo woke up needing to go to the bathroom, and then when she went back to bed she couldn't get back to sleep. The storm had long since passed through, but she was still on edge and decided to check the weather. She sat up in bed and reached for the remote to find out what, if anything, they would be facing come daylight.

It didn't take long to find coverage and learn that the thunderstorm that came through Tulsa had not only built in power as it moved into Missouri, but that by the time it hit St. Louis it had dropped a tornado measuring out as an F4 right into the city. She leaped from the bed, ran through the conference room, past the living room and down the hall to the bedrooms, where she began knocking on doors.

"Guys! Guys! Wake up!"

Wade came flying out of his room in a pair of gym shorts. Tate came out in a hotel robe, and Cameron had on a pair of sweats.

Okay, she thought. So they all slept in the nude and had grabbed the first thing they could find.

"What the hell's going on?" Wade asked.

"St. Louis took a direct hit. F4 tornado. It's a mess," she said.

Tate's eyes widened.

Wade ran for the living room television and quickly turned it on.

"What channel?" he asked.

She grabbed the remote, found the channel and then upped the volume as a local St. Louis reporter broadcast live from the scene.

"Dear God," Cameron muttered.

Wade sat down on the arm of the sofa as Tate watched from where he was standing.

Jo knew how long they'd been working this case

and she'd read all the files, but unlike them, she'd never experienced the devastation of weather-related tragedies firsthand. They'd seen the bodies, the families in complete despair, businesses ruined and lives forever changed. And now it was happening all over again—almost certainly with the addition of a madman.

"What do we do next?" Jo asked.

Tate looked up at the clock. It would be daylight in a couple of hours.

"Get packed. I want to be on the road before daylight. It's a long drive across Missouri to get to St. Louis. I just hope to God that Hershel Inman isn't already on the hunt."

Hershel drove until he found a hospital, parked as close to the E.R. entrance as he could and got out, locking his vehicle behind him. He was in so much pain he was shaking as he stumbled inside.

"I need help," he said to the first nurse he saw.

She took him by the arm and quickly led him into an examining room, while a lady from the front desk followed with a clipboard in her hand.

"Lie down here," she said, and when she pulled out a pair of scissors, Hershel balked.

"Don't cut my clothes off. They're all I have left. Just let me take them off."

She gave him a sympathetic glance. "Sorry about that, go ahead and take them off."

He winced, but got up from the bed and stripped down to his undershorts, then lay back down.

"Where were you when this happened?" she asked.

"Inside a motel closet. All of this happened to mc aftcr thc roof camc off."

"How did you get here?" she asked, as she began taking his vitals and looking at his facial wounds.

"I drove myself."

"What's your name?" the clerk asked.

"Lee Parsons. I'm from Chicago and was just passing through."

A man came into the exam room at a lope, took a quick look at Hershel and then glanced at the nurse.

"He drove himself here, and it looks like there's some kind of debris embedded in his face," she said.

When the doctor began issuing orders, Hershel let himself relax. No one knew where he was, and they had no way to identify what he drove or the name he was living under. He felt secure enough for the moment to let nature take its course.

Six

Hershel woke up wearing a hospital gown and lying in a bed in the E.R., and his first thought was, *What the hell?* Then he remembered the tornado and immediately felt his face, discovering a layer of bandages. These newest injuries had solved his immediate problem of being able to move about without detection. Not even Louise would have recognized him like this. When he saw that his shoes and clothing had been folded and put in a plastic bag at the foot of his bed, he breathed a sigh of relief and flagged down a passing orderly.

"Hey, who do I need to see about getting out of here?"

"I'll get someone," the orderly said, and hurried away.

A few minutes later a doctor showed up with a nurse right behind him.

"Good morning, Mr. Parsons. I'm Dr. Levy. I have your discharge papers, as well as a prescription for an antibiotic I want you to take and cream for your face. You'll need to keep your face bandaged for a couple of days or until the stitches are no longer seeping."

"Stitches? What did you have to sew up?"

The doctor smiled ruefully. "Basically, your face, but it's not as bad as it sounds. Some of the debris we removed was so deeply embedded we had to cut it out. There's no more than a stitch or two in any one place, and with time the scars should be nearly impossible to see."

"As you can tell from my other scars, I'm way past caring what I look like, so I guess that's okay," Hershel said.

"Try to keep everything clean. You'll be on antibiotics for eleven days, but if you begin running a fever or suffering increased pain, see your regular doctor."

"Yeah, okay," Hershel said, signed the sheet the nurse handed him, then took the bag with his clothes and scooted off down the hall to a bathroom to get dressed.

He was sore in every muscle in his body, and it sounded like he was hearing voices from the bottom of a barrel, but he was alive, and he wasn't going to complain. He dressed quickly and left the hospital gown on a chair as he headed for the exit.

The sun was shining as he walked out—rather rude, he thought, in light of what had gone on last night. He scanned the parking lot for his truck and for a moment thought it had been stolen, then remembered the damage it had suffered and looked again. He spotted a dark truck with a dent in the roof of the cab and headed toward it. Someone had stolen the generator out of the back, as well as his tent. He sighed. They probably would have hot-wired the truck and stolen it, too, if it hadn't been so damaged.

"Whatever," he muttered, and got in on the passenger side, scooted over under the steering wheel and drove off.

He drove away from the hardest hit area and began looking for a body shop that was open. It took him about fifteen minutes to find one. He pulled up in front, then once more painfully slid himself across the seat to get out.

The owner came out wiping his hands, took one look at all the bandages on Hershel's face and shook his head.

"Wow, mister, I hope you weren't in that truck when you got hurt."

"No, but I need a little help here," he said.

"I'll be happy to fix your dents, but I'm really backed up. Lots of people got hailed on last night."

"I'm not worried about the dents," Hershel said. "I was passing through when this happened. I'd appreciate it if you would take a hammer and pop the roof of the cab back up, then help me so I can open and close the driver's-side door. I'm too damn sore to be crawling across the seat every time I get in and out."

The man eyed Hershel's condition, then shrugged.

"Yeah, sure, I'll see what I can do." He backtracked to the garage and yelled, "Hey, Raymond! Come here for a sec."

A big, burly man in his mid-fifties lumbered out.

"What's up, Boss?"

"Let's help get this fellow on his way. He got caught in the storm last night, and now the driver's-side door won't open. I'm going to pop up the roof. You see what you can do about getting that door to work."

"Yeah, Boss," the man said, and tried the door a couple of times, then got down on his hands and knees and looked beneath the truck. "Right here's your trouble. There's a piece of metal jammed up underneath."

He got up, went into the garage, came back with

a mechanic's creeper and a pry bar, flopped down on his back on the creeper and rolled himself beneath the truck.

Hershel heard the crunch of metal, a loud curse, another crunch, and then a clang as something metal dropped to the pavement. The big guy was up in seconds, tossed the twisted metal into an open barrel near the garage and opened the door without a hitch.

"That'll fix ya' right up," Raymond said, and then looked inside the truck where his boss was working. "Here, Boss. Let me do that."

He took the piece of plywood and a small sledgehammer, got into the driver's seat, pushed the wood up against the dent, then swung the hammer at it as hard as he could. The roof popped back up like a jack-in-the-box. He got out grinning.

"There you go," he said, patted Hershel on the shoulder and walked away.

"Thank you," Hershel said. "What do I owe you?"

The owner just shook his head. "You don't owe me nothin'. Just pass the favor on. Have yourself a safe trip, okay?"

Hershel got in the truck and quickly drove away, but his conscience was bothering him. How could he pass on a good deed when he was in the business of retribution?

See, Hershel? That's how good people treat each other.

He frowned. Should have known Louise would have to put her two cents in, but he refused to comment. His head was beginning to hurt again. He needed to get his prescriptions filled and figure out his next step. He still had the rifle behind the seat, but his Taser had been in the suitcase that blew away. It should be easy enough to replace in a city this large, but he needed a place to hole up and heal a little while he considered his options.

The agents drove into St. Louis just before 11:00 a.m., then went straight to police headquarters to check in and introduce themselves. After a quick conversation with the desk sergeant, they were escorted to the office of the chief of police.

Doyle Sawyer had been police chief for twelve years, and he'd had occasion to work with the FBI before. When they introduced themselves he was already in cooperative mode.

"Gentlemen, ma'am, please take a seat. I think I can guess why you're here. It's about the Storm-chaser, isn't it?"

"Yes, it is," Tate said as they settled into chairs around the desk.

"Ya'll sure got here fast. As of yet, I don't have any reports that would indicate he's been here, although I heard he took out several people in Wichita Falls, Texas, and then in Tulsa," Sawyer said.

Tate nodded. "Yes, sir, and since the same storm system has been recycling itself every few days, we thought it prudent to follow up. As you know, I-44 runs straight to St. Louis from Tulsa, making it a convenient road for him to travel."

The chief nodded, somewhat excited to be part of such a huge ongoing investigation.

"What do you need from me?" he asked.

"Right now, I'd ask you to seal off the scene and notify any one of us immediately should the M.E. identify a body as being a murder victim, rather than a victim of the storms."

The team pulled out their cards and handed them to the chief. He glanced at them, and then looked up and smiled.

"Husband-and-wife team here?" he asked, indicating the two Lucketts.

"Not anymore," Jo said, and then realized how defensive that sounded, but it was too late to take back her words. She kept her gaze on a photo mounted on the wall just behind the chief's head rather than look directly at him.

"Sorry," Sawyer said quickly, and dropped the cards in a drawer. "Where will you be staying?"

"Don't know yet," Tate said. "We just got here, so we'll have to find a hotel that's not already filled up with storm victims needing a place to stay."

"If there's anything you need while you're here, my department is at your disposal."

"Thank you, Chief Sawyer. We appreciate your help," Tate said, and pulled a file out of his brief-case. "I have pictures of Hershel Inman, along with an artist's rendering of how he might look with burn scars. And we recently identified the make and model of the pickup he's driving, along with the license tag. We would appreciate it if you would distribute these among your officers."

"Of course," Sawyer said, and walked them out.

Once they reached the parking lot, they paused by their SUV. Jo was still embarrassed that she'd spoken up so quickly and wanted to clear the air.

"Wade, I'm sorry about my knee-jerk response to the chief's question," Jo said. "It was unneces-sary, but I can't take it back."

He glanced up, both surprised and pleased by her consideration.

"It's no big deal. Besides, it was the truth, so don't give it a second thought."

"Thanks," she said.

"What next?" Cameron asked.

"I vote for breakfast or lunch or whatever you want to call it," Wade said.

Jo stifled a smile. Some things never changed, one of them being Wade's insatiable appetite.

"We'll eat as soon as we find lodging, my friend. Do you think you can hold off that long?" Tate asked.

"Yeah, sure, just adding my two cents," Wade said.

"You're always hungry," Cameron muttered as they began getting back inside the vehicle.

Jo had been riding in the back all the way from Tulsa. Part of the time Cameron was her seat partner. Part of the time it was Tate. Wade had driven the entire way, and she didn't know whether it was so he didn't have to sit by her or if that was their usual protocol. Several times he'd caught her staring at him and each time, rather than acknowledge it, she'd quickly looked away, but she'd seen the tension on his face and guessed part of it had to do with her. She knew what she'd done to him but didn't know how to fix it, or if she should even try.

* * *

Wade got into the driver's seat again and turned on the engine so the car could cool off. Tate was scrolling through hotel listings on his phone. Cameron was reading a text and smiling. Wade guessed he'd heard from Laura Doyle, who was still with the Red Cross in Tulsa. And Jo was looking out a window. The sadness in her eyes when she thought no one was looking was unmistakable.

Damn it. They needed to talk, if for no other reason than to clear the air between them. The only question he really wanted answered was a big one. Why had she turned on him when their baby died? He needed to understand how she'd channeled her grief into a rejection of him.

Tate got on the phone and started checking room availability. The first hotel he called was already full up. The second one had a suite available. One room had two double beds. Another room had a king-sized bed. They would be short a bed for Jo again, and there was no adjoining room this time. They had to settle for one across the hall.

Jo heard them discussing the arrangements and appreciated that they were looking out for her privacy. The initial meeting between her and Wade had launched a whole raft of memories she'd spent three years trying to forget, and it wasn't going to get better anytime soon.

What they didn't expect was the waiting media when they arrived at the hotel. Somehow the news crews had already gotten wind of their presence in St. Louis, and now they were clamoring for footage.

Wade frowned as he drove up to the front of the hotel to let the others out. "What the hell? We haven't been in the city long enough for this to happen."

"We were at the police department. There's always a media snitch somewhere. All it would take was one phone call to the right person, and then they'd stake out a few hotels," Jo said.

Tate nodded. "She's right."

"So do you still want to get out here, or should I park first?" Wade asked.

"They'd just follow us. The rest of us will get out here and deal with them," Tate said. "We'll get your bags. Just park the car. I'll text you our room number so you won't have to stop at the desk."

Wade nodded, then glanced up in the rearview mirror to gauge Jolene's mood.

She caught the look. "What?" she asked.

"Nothing. Maybe I just like looking at you," he

said, and then was mad at himself for pushing her buttons when he saw her flush.

"And on that note…" Tate said, then opened the door and got out. He met the media head-on, leaving Cameron and Jo to signal a bellhop with a luggage cart and get everything inside.

Wade drove out from under the canopy and then directly into the underground parking. He glanced up in the rearview mirror to make sure the media wasn't following him, and then, as was the team's usual habit, parked beneath a security camera in a well-lit area. He gathered up his cell phone and briefcase, got out, locked the door, and then started toward a side entrance into the hotel. He was almost at the door when two men, one of them carrying a camera, came running in from the street.

"Agent Luckett? You *are* Agent Luckett, right? We're with CNN. We saw you at one of the crime scenes in Tulsa. Is there anything new you can tell us?"

"Agent Benton is our team leader. He's out front giving an interview. You need to talk to him."

"We heard a new member has been added, an agent by the name of Jolene Luckett. Are you two related?"

Wade's heart sank. Again, he wondered what the hell the Director had been thinking to put her on their team, given the personal connection. Even though the killer's initial interest in Nola had begun because she'd witnessed him murdering three of her neighbors, he'd taken delight in knowing Tate had a personal interest in her. Wade didn't want to think about Jolene becoming the Stormchaser's target, too.

"No," Wade said, and kept walking.

"That's not what we were told," the reporter said.

Wade just kept walking.

"Jolene Luckett is your ex-wife, isn't she?"

Wade was inside the hotel now, and the reporter was right behind him. But before he could push the interview any farther, hotel security headed him off and sent him and his photographer packing. Wade just kept moving across the lobby, looking for the elevator signs as he went.

His phone suddenly signaled a text. He checked it. They were on the seventh floor. He kept moving, but with every step he took his instincts were telling him that when that footage aired—and it would, of that he had no doubt—it was going to set Hershel Inman off all over again.

Hershel had pulled into a truck stop on the outskirts of the city and was eating his first real food in nearly eighteen hours. The parking lot was packed with 18-wheelers, as well as dozens of other vehicles.

The dining area was larger than he'd expected and as busy as he'd predicted, but they seated him at a small table at the side of the room facing the front. He caught a few curious glances as he followed the waitress, but it was to be expected. His bandages were fresh, but his clothes were pretty rank. He wanted a burger and fries in the worst way but ordered soft foods instead, catering to his sore face and jaw. When the brown beans and corn bread he'd ordered showed up, they were as tasty as a rib-eye steak.

The waitress stopped by to top off his coffee, eyeing his bandages at the same time. She refilled the cup and then paused. "Don't mean to be nosy, mister, but did you get caught in the twister last night?"

He nodded.

"I'm real sorry you got hurt," she said quickly, and moved on to the next table.

He nodded, more interested in soaking chunks of corn bread in the beans than in her concern, when he noticed that one of the televisions mounted on the wall was airing footage of the storm. The sound was off, but the closed captioning was scrolling across the bottom of the screen.

He didn't pay much attention until they suddenly switched from footage of victims walking among the debris to a scene outside a hotel. His heart skipped a beat as he recognized Agent Benton from the FBI. They'd gotten here fast. Any other time that would have interested him, but right now he felt like he'd failed to offer them anything new. He also realized he hadn't checked to see if his phone still worked. A lot of his stuff had gotten wet inside his bag. If that phone was ruined, he'd lost his only safe means of contacting the agents.

As he was reading the text, he realized the cameras were now on a reporter in the crowd, and then he caught a glimpse of the CNN microphone the reporter was holding and smirked. He was definitely in the big time. As he was reading the text of the reporter's question, he nearly choked on his corn bread and reached for his iced tea to wash it down.

According to the reporter, a fourth agent had been added to the team: a woman by the name of Jolene Luckett. Wade Luckett's ex-wife. Hershel couldn't help but wonder what would prompt the FBI to do something like that, and then he wondered how he could use it to his advantage.

But as intriguing as the news was, it also made him leery. He began thinking of little safeguards he'd let lapse, and one of them was changing the license tags on his truck. As soon as he finished eating, he was going into the big gift shop and picking up a pair of sweatpants and a T-shirt to change into, and then he was going to steal a new license tag from some unlucky vehicle in the parking lot. Without camping equipment, he needed shelter, but with his face all bandaged up, he could safely choose about any place he wanted. And then there was that problem of no Stormchaser victims. Tonight he would do something about that, too.

Wade unpacked, set up his computer equipment, and then checked the room service menu before suggesting a change of venue.

"Let's go downstairs and eat in one of the restaurants. We can do room service tonight. Okay?"

"Sounds good to me," Tate said. "Cameron, you up for it?"

"Sure, whatever. What about Jo?"

"I'll go ask her," Wade said, then patted his pocket to make sure he had his key card and left.

Cameron glanced at Tate. "This feels like déjà vu."

"What do you mean?" Tate asked.

"This is pretty much how you and Nola danced around each other last year."

Tate smiled. "Oh, that."

"I'd like to see Wade and Jo back together," Cameron said. "I think Wade would, too."

"You have to remember we're just bystanders here, so whatever you do, don't take sides. We have to work together," Tate said.

"Absolutely. Just making an observation."

Across the hall, Wade knocked on Jo's door.

The moment she opened it, he began to explain his presence, as if he needed an official excuse to be there.

"We're going to go down to one of the restaurants here in the hotel to eat. Do you want to come, too?"

Her hand automatically went to her hair, as if checking her appearance.

"Yes. Give me a second to get my purse."

He stood in the doorway, watching as she walked back to the bed. She'd been unpacking. Her underwear and a makeup bag were lying next to the open suitcase. Once upon a time his things would have been there, too. When she turned around, he made a point of looking elsewhere.

"I'm ready," she said.

He stepped aside as she came out and then

quickly opened the door to the suite across the hall to let her in.

Tate looked up as she entered.

"Good, you're coming, too. I stopped at the front desk and got an extra key for the suite. No need for you to knock. You work in here, too."

"Thanks," Jo said as she dropped the key in her purse.

"So, are we ready to go?" Wade asked.

Cameron rolled his eyes. "Lord, yes, we're ready. Let's get some food in this man before he withers away."

"Good idea," Jo said. "We can't have *People* magazine's Sexiest Man losing his good looks."

Tate blinked. "What's that mean?"

"The other day two girls thought Wade was Channing Tatum and asked for his autograph," she said.

Wade glared at her for bringing it up.

They were still laughing as they rode the elevator down to the lobby.

Hershel found a room at a Motel 6. It was on the backside of the building, away from the eyes of cops in patrol cars and with access to a quick escape via an alley. He'd found a Walmart and stocked up on some clothing to replace what he'd lost. He'd also discovered that while the battery in his cell phone was down, the phone itself was okay. It was a relief to know he hadn't lost his best means of contact with Benton.

His belly was full, and he'd finally had a bath, being careful not to get his facial bandages wet. Now he was lying on the bed in his underwear, watching the news. This was a huge relief compared to living in the tent. He was getting too old for roughing it. The local news came on, and he saw the same footage he'd seen in the café. Agent Benton sidestepped nicely when asked if there were any new victims here in St. Louis, he'd answered, "We're not sure."

Hershel snorted lightly. What he meant was, none had been identified, and Hershel knew that unless he did something about it, none would be.

He put his hands behind his head and closed his eyes, letting his mind relax. Obviously most of those who had survived last night had already been found, so he had no viable options here. He needed to think about how to proceed, but a solution would come to him. Of that he was sure. The room was quiet and cool, and he was so tired and drifting closer and closer to sleep.

What happened to your face?

Hershel flinched and then sighed. He should have known this was too good to last.

"I got caught in the tornado last night."

It wouldn't have happened if you had stayed home.

"And done what? Lived in shame knowing how I'd let the government get away with killing you?"

The government didn't kill me. Diabetes killed me, because of a hurricane, neither of which was the government's fault.

"If they'd rescued you in time, you wouldn't be dead."

Listen to yourself. There were thousands of us in peril, and only so many available to help.

"Go away, Louise. My face hurts, and I want to rest."

What does it look like?

He frowned. "I don't know. It's bandaged up."

Aren't you curious? I mean, you're going to have to live with the results, just like the burn scars.

"Go away," he said. He tried to find that restful zone, but she'd put a bug in his ear that wouldn't stop buzzing. Finally, muttering beneath his breath, he rolled out of bed and headed for the bathroom.

He'd purchased some fresh bandages and tape, and he laid them on the counter in case he couldn't get these back on properly, then looked up at himself in the mirror and frowned. Hiding behind the white gauze had given him a false sense of security. Taking the bandages off was suddenly scary. His hands were shaking as he reached up for the first piece of tape and began to pull. One by one, he removed the squares of gauze and the pads beneath until his face was revealed.

He gasped.

"What the fuck?"

Every place where the doctor had dug out debris had either a black stitch with tiny ends sticking up like mini-rabbit ears or tiny butterfly bandages holding the skin together. It looked like he had cactus spikes embedded in his face, and, coupled with the old burn scars, he was a monster straight from a horror movie.

He watched the blood drain from his face as shock set in, and then all of a sudden he was hanging over the commode, throwing up. He puked and gagged until there was nothing left, and finally staggered back into the bedroom and collapsed.

"I shouldn't have asked God to save me. I'd rather be dead," he muttered.

It's punishment for your sins.

He closed his eyes. "Shut the fuck up, Louise. Can't you see how I'm suffering?"

I have no sympathy for you. The people who

*pulled you out of the storm didn't have a Taser
and a rope waiting to choke the life out of your
body, now, did they? This is your punishment. Deal
with it.*

"Shut up! Shut up! *Shut up!*" Hershel screamed,
but Louise was gone.

Just like a woman to throw down the last word
and run out before anyone could respond. As soon
as he could pull himself together, he got up, went
back into the bathroom, and began doctoring the
wounds and then putting on new bandages. They
weren't as professional looking as what the doctor
had done, but his face was covered, and that was
all that mattered. The release papers were lying
in the sack with the meds. He picked them up and
read them again, pausing when he got to the last
line.

See your local doctor in seven days for
removal of stitches.

"I'll take the damn things out myself," he said,
and stuffed the meds back in the bag with the bandages, popped a pain pill and went to bed. "It is
what it is," he said, and closed his eyes.

He had to rest now, to be ready for tonight.

Seven

Wade was still up watching television after the others had gone to bed. Spending the day with Jolene had pretty much shredded his composure. What he was trying to come to grips with was how a man could still feel something for a woman who'd cut and run as fast as *she* had.

He needed to get some sleep, but right now going to bed would be futile. All he could see when he closed his eyes was the blood all over her body when they'd brought her into the E.R., and all he could hear was the EMT yelling out she was pregnant.

They'd tried so hard that afternoon to save the baby, but the bullet that had gone through her had gone through their unborn son, as well. When he died and Jolene lived, she never forgave herself.

Wade shoved his fingers through his hair in

frustration. He wasn't the kind of person who hid from a job that needed to be done, and yet he'd let her run their marriage into the ground, too damn afraid to fight for her for fear she would come the rest of the way apart.

He slowly became aware of a *beep beep beep* sound and realized it was a weather alert. He upped the volume, listening to a forecaster giving the latest news on the approaching storms. Meteorologists predicted lightning, thunder and the possibility of small hail, but no circulation in the clouds, which meant no tornado cells were building. He thought of the people who'd been trying to clean up today and knew the additional storms would delay their progress. It was a bad situation all around, but nothing anyone could control.

So far five bodies had been recovered after last night's storm, and all day he and the others had expected to get a call from the police, but at least so far, none of the deaths had been attributed to the Stormchaser.

Wade wanted to think the guy was gone, but he knew better. If God was into payback, it would have been justice to find Hershel Inman's body among the dead. But that hadn't happened, either. Still, this was only one day, and there were still people unaccounted for.

He got up and moved to the windows, fascinated by the wild play of lightning shooting across the sky. He could hear the faint rumblings of thunder, and then moments later heard someone at the door.

He turned to see just as Jo came in looking a little sleep-tousled and anxious. He guessed the oncoming storm had awakened her and she'd panicked, because she was still in pajama bottoms and a T-shirt, and her feet were bare.

"I knew someone was up. I heard the television."

"I couldn't sleep," Wade said.

She sighed. "The storm woke me up. I wanted to make sure it wasn't a tornado."

"Do you want something to drink?"

"Do you have any Diet Dr Pepper?"

He smiled. "On ice?"

"Please."

She sat down at one end of the sofa and curled her feet up beneath her as she waited for him to come back with her drink. Normally she would have been fixated on the television weather map, but right now watching the muscles flex in Wade's back as he put ice in her glass and poured her drink was better. She still had anxiety, but on a different level.

Wade came back with her drink, a Coke for himself and a package of peanut butter crackers.

"Thank you," she said, opening the package and, without thinking, handed him half.

Wade's hand was shaking, but she didn't see it as she dropped the little sandwiches into his palm. Just for a moment it had been business as usual between them, sharing cold pop and crunchy crackers in the middle of the night.

As usual, he put one whole cracker in his mouth.

"Don't forget to chew," Jo said absently, and then looked up with a startled expression on her face. "Sorry. That came out before I thought."

He wanted to laugh but felt more like crying.

"Old habits and all that," he said, and swallowed, then chased the cracker with a sip of Coke.

Jo was staring at the screen. "It's going to storm again, isn't it?"

"Not anything that will hurt us. Just a lot of wind and noise. Maybe some hail."

"Okay."

He ate his last cracker without tasting it because he was watching Jo. She felt his gaze, and when she turned her head, she was lost. Her eyes welled. Her chin quivered. When the first tear rolled down her cheek Wade felt like he'd been kicked in the gut.

"Why are you crying?" he asked.

"This is hard."

"Being here with me?"

She nodded.

"Why did you come, then?" he asked.

She wiped away the tears with an angry motion.

"You know why! Women in the Bureau can't be weak. Working with an ex-husband should not be a deterrent, and refusing a job is like asking to be fired."

He sighed. "I'm sorry you're so uncomfortable. I'm sorry you're so mad at me. If I knew how to help you, I would."

Jo was stunned. "What do you mean, mad at you? Why would I be mad at you? I'm not mad at you."

Wade frowned. "Then why the hell did we get a divorce?"

"Because I killed our baby. I saw the anger in your face every time I looked at you, and I couldn't take it anymore."

Wade was stunned. "What the fuck, Jolene? You didn't kill our baby. I never once thought it was your fault. Where did you get that stupid-ass notion? Every time I tried to get close to you, you pushed me away and looked at me like I was the perp who'd pulled the trigger."

She covered her face with her hands. "You told me not to go to work, and I did anyway. I put my career ahead of our baby's welfare."

He couldn't believe what was coming out of her mouth, and crawled across the sofa and took her in his arms. She was trembling so hard it scared him.

"No, no, I suggested you call in sick because you *were* sick, don't you remember? You were getting the flu. It was going around the whole office. People were dropping like flies. Everyone was using up sick days like crazy."

"No, I don't remember it like that. You said don't go, and I did. I did, and I went out with my partner on a call, and he and our baby died. If I hadn't been trying to be a superwoman..." The sobbing took over, and she couldn't even talk.

"Sweet Lord," Wade muttered, and just let her cry.

There had been so many misunderstandings between them. They'd been great together in bed, but their communication skills as a couple were obviously appalling. At first he'd been so scared he was going to lose her as well as their baby, and when she recovered, he didn't realize what was happening until it was too late.

"I'm so sorry. I was so relieved you survived that I never thought you would feel guilty. You never mentioned any of this when we went to counseling."

"I know, I know," she said, still sobbing. "I think I was a little bit crazy back then. I'd lost the baby, and I could see I was losing you, too. The only thing I had left was the job, and I hung on to it with everything in me."

The thunder was coming closer. He could hear rain beginning to blow against the windows.

She sat up, wiping her eyes with the sleeve of her T-shirt, and began a slow physical withdrawal from his arms.

But it was the emotional withdrawal that hurt Wade most.

"We should have said all this three years ago," he said.

"Three years ago I couldn't have had this conversation. I was way too close to a nervous breakdown for logic."

He reached for her again, but she pulled away.

"Thank you for listening," she said, and stood up.

Wade followed. "Well, hell, Jolene, is that all you think I was doing? Just listening?"

"No, but—"

He shook his head. "It's late. We're tired. This has been an emotional breakthrough for both of us, but I want you to sleep on *this*. I never wanted a divorce. You weren't the only one who lost a child, and you never acknowledged my grief. When you said you were divorcing me, I had to face losing you, too. It was like you died anyway, because first you were there, and then you were gone. I don't know how you feel about me anymore, and I know I'm still pretty mad at you for dumping my ass, but I didn't stop loving you, okay? So if you're even remotely interested in a relationship with a slightly used ex-husband, I would probably be available."

Thunder rattled the windows.

Jolene eyed him curiously, almost as if she didn't trust what he was saying.

"Are you serious?"

"As a heart attack," he said. "Got your key?"

She picked it up from the side table.

"I'll see you to the door," he said, then opened it wide and waited until she was inside her own room.

She looked back. "I'm interested," she said, and closed the door.

Wade took a deep breath, then stepped back inside the suite, shut the door and turned the dead bolt.

He was so stunned by the night's revelations that her last comment barely registered. It wasn't until he crawled into bed and closed his eyes that he let it all sink in.

She was interested—interested in seeing what they could do about being a couple again.

That might be the best news he'd ever had.

Hershel woke up just after the sun went down and for a few tranquil moments forgot about the storm and his face, and that he was starting all over again. He reached up to scratch his chin and felt the bandages instead, and everything came rushing back.

He rolled over to the side of the bed, turned on the television, and then headed to the bathroom. When he was finished, he added another piece of tape to one of the bandages and then took another pain pill.

His anger at what had happened to his face was on the back burner as he went to get dressed. He was taking the tags off a new pair of jeans when he heard the newscaster talking about another round of storms in St. Louis and he raised the volume. No tornadoes were predicted, but it was going to storm, which would give him the cover he needed to put out a little present for the FBI.

As soon as he was dressed he began checking his weapons. The new Taser was charged, and he had cut one of his new ropes into shorter lengths. He was hungry but wasn't in the mood to face the stares that would come with eating in a public place, so fast food it would be. He grabbed his new poncho and carried it and his duffel bag out the door. It was time to go hunting.

After a burger and fries from one fast-food place, and an ice-cream sundae from another, Hershel was feeling a little more human. Until he stopped to get some gas.

When he went inside to pay, the clerk behind the counter openly stared.

"What's the matter?" Hershel snapped.

"Sorry," the man said. "That'll be forty bucks even."

Being reminded that he looked like a science experiment gone wrong pissed Hershel off. He slapped two twenty-dollar bills on the counter, but when he turned around to walk out he saw his reflection in the glass and flinched. It wasn't a pretty sight, and once again his mind was in free fall, placing blame everywhere but on himself.

When he braked for a red light the cup with his leftover drink slid off the dash and into his lap, getting his clean pants wet and sticky.

"Damn it all to hell!" he yelled, and slapped the steering wheel with both hands.

Don't curse, Hershel. It's unbecoming.

"Go away, Louise! I'm not in the mood."

It wouldn't have happened if you had cleaned out your truck when you stopped to get gas.

The light turned green, and he drove through the intersection, screaming, "You are right, you are right, you are always right!"

He drove without thought, just staying on the move to keep from thinking about his situation, until even he had to admit the trash inside his truck was getting on his nerves. He didn't know where he was, but there were boarded-up storefronts and half the streetlights were out. He saw an old woman pushing a shopping cart piled high with her worldly goods, and on the next street corner a flashy black car slowed to a stop. He saw someone come out of a building, saw the window roll down. So there was a drug deal going down. It had nothing to do with him, and it was starting to rain.

The wind was rising when he wheeled into an alley, drove right up to the Dumpster and got out. The moment the wind hit his face, the loose-fitting bandages blew off. He grabbed at them, but it was too late. Whatever, he would put new ones on later. He'd just lifted the lid to toss in his trash when a dark, shapeless figure came out of the shadows, muttering and cursing.

"You get on out of here," the man said, waving his hands. "This is my spot. You got no business here."

Hershel frowned. The crazy bastard. Someone needed to put him away.

Lightning flashed, momentarily illuminating the alley where the two men stood, and when the man saw Hershel's face he took a giant step back.

"Get away from here, freak! You have a disease. I don't want your disease. Get away! *Get away!*"

Rage washed over Hershel so fast it took away his breath, and when the guy began chucking rocks and empty bottles at his head, he lost it.

He grabbed the Taser from the front seat, spun and fired it at the bum's face so fast he never saw it coming. The electrodes were stuck in the man's cheeks, just like the little whiskers from the stitches in Hershel's face, and all of a sudden his mission was suddenly clear.

The guy was on the ground, immobilized and twitching. As the lightning flashed again, Hershel saw the fear in the bum's eyes. He grabbed a rope, yanked the electrodes out of the man's face and strangled him where he lay. By the time the man's body went limp, Hershel's euphoria was peaking.

"Worthless piece of shit," he muttered, and quickly tossed his Taser and the rope back in the truck.

Rain was falling hard and fast, and the wind whipping through the alley was blowing the drops sideways. He tossed the body into the back of his truck and drove away, straight toward the tornado-ravaged area of the city. He passed a police car going in the opposite direction and laughed out loud, then kept on driving until he found what he was looking for. After a quick glance around to make sure he was unobserved, he turned off his lights and dragged the body up into debris and stripped off the bum's clothes. Lightning flashed again just as he laid out the body. He caught a quick glimpse of the wounds from the electrodes in the bum's face, and in a fit of rage, he picked up a piece of broken crockery from beside the body and stabbed it over and over into the flesh until the dead man's features were obliterated.

He was still shaking from the adrenaline rush as he got back in the truck and drove away. His wounds were wet and stinging, and his hands were bloody, but the pressure in his chest was gone. He felt nothing but relief.

He drove away from the tornado damage, and then found a street that led to I-44 and drove east.

He was outside the city before he took out his phone. It was time for the Stormchaser to welcome the feds to St. Louis.

Change is painful, but justice is like water. It eventually finds its own level.

He smiled as he hit Send, and then turned off the phone, found an exit and drove back into the city. Even if they tracked the call to the nearest cell tower, it wouldn't lead them to where he was.

It took him almost an hour to find his motel, and he made a mental note to get a map of the city if he decided to stay. The rain was beginning to let up by the time he got to his room. He turned on the lights, dropped his wet clothes by the door and walked naked to the bathroom. His hands were scratched from holding the broken crockery, but they didn't really hurt. He patiently cleaned his wounds with alcohol, then poured some on his hands as well, cursing softly beneath his breath as the burn made the hair on the back of his neck stand up. He finished up with a fresh dose of medicine on his face, left off putting on new bandages and popped a couple of antibiotics before he went to bed. This time when he closed his eyes, it was with a feeling of satisfaction for a job well-done.

* * *

Wade woke up before daylight, bathed in sweat despite the air-conditioned room, and sick to his stomach with fear. It took him a few moments to realize he'd been dreaming, and that everything he'd dreamed was three years come and gone.

"God Almighty," he whispered, and staggered to the bathroom, trying to keep quiet and not wake Cameron, who was still asleep in the other bed.

One cold shower later, he'd washed the bloody memory down the drain and was remembering Jo's parting words. She was interested. So was he. They just had to find a way to work through everything they'd done wrong.

As he returned to the room, Cameron was rolling out of bed.

"Morning," Cameron muttered. "I smell coffee. Don't drink it all before I get there." Then he stumbled into the bathroom.

Wade sat down to check his messages and spent a few minutes answering the most pressing ones, then went to get dressed.

Cameron was out of the bathroom by then and dressing quickly.

"I hope Tate already ordered breakfast, because I'm hungry," he said.

Wade grinned. "That sounds like my line."

* * *

Jo's rest was fitful, and by the time the sun was up, so was she. She dressed for work and went across the hall before 6:00 a.m. as if she was going to the office, guessing she would be the first one up. She found the coffeepot and started it brewing, and then made an executive decision and ordered food. She'd fed these men enough when she and Wade were still together to know their likes and dislikes, and she ordered enough extra that every man could have what he wanted. Next she booted up her laptop and got to work. She was trying to find out how Inman was funding his killing sprees. He had to have money stashed somewhere under another name. If she could find it, it might be the key to catching him.

She'd been working for almost an hour when there was a knock at the door. That should be breakfast. After a quick glance through the peep-hole, she opened the door to a smiling waiter and a cart full of food.

"Just put it all on the table," she said, and stood aside as he unloaded their meal. After she signed for the food, she locked the door behind him and then poked around until she found the bacon and scrambled eggs she'd ordered for herself, chose a bagel over a sweet roll, and topped off her coffee, leaving the fresh pot from the cart for them.

She was sitting down with her feet up, watching the morning news while she ate, when she heard someone moving around in another room. She'd finished her eggs and gotten up for some fruit when Wade and Cameron came in.

"Smells like you've been cooking up something good," Cameron said. "I hope you ordered plenty."

"I've fed all of you before. I think I ordered enough to soothe the savage beasts," she said, and slid a couple of slices of melon onto her plate.

Cameron laughed as he started removing the food covers to see what was on offer.

Wade was already downing a piece of bacon as he checked out the rest of the choices, but instead of digging in as he usually did, he stopped.

"Hey, Jo, thanks for the French toast," he said.

"No problem," she said, but she was secretly pleased that he'd noticed she'd chosen one of his favorite breakfast foods.

They were still eating when Tate came out, and they could tell by the look on his face that something was wrong.

Wade swallowed the bite in his mouth. "What?"

"We got a text," Tate said.

"Well, hell," Cameron muttered. "I was half

hoping the little bastard had blown away in the storm."

"We couldn't be that lucky," Tate said. "Listen to this. 'Change is painful, but justice is like water. It eventually finds its own level.'"

Jo frowned. "What does that mean?"

"I'm not sure, but I can guarantee he left a body somewhere."

"I never get used to how crazy people can be," Jo said, and put aside the fruit. Her appetite was definitely gone.

Tate saw the food and smiled at her. "Thank you for this."

"No problem. I'm still trying to track down Inman's funding. I had a couple of ideas and wanted to see where they went, so I was up a little early."

"It's just as well," Tate said. "I need to call the chief. I won't be long, and then I'll be back for my eggs and bacon."

Eight

This was the first time the team had been able to see a crime scene before the body was removed, but their purpose here wasn't to ascertain who'd done it. That was a given. What they didn't expect was the nature of the victim or the condition of the body.

"What the hell?" Wade said as they walked up on the scene.

Tate stared.

Cameron shook his head in disbelief.

"Is this what he meant by a painful change?" Jo asked.

"Who found the body?" Tate asked.

The officer standing guard pointed to a teenager sitting on the curb across the street next to a ten-speed bicycle. The boy was obviously very shaken up.

"Hell of a thing for a kid to see," Tate said. "Do you have an ID on the vic?"

The officer shook his head. "No, but I'd guess he's homeless. The clothes lying beside the body are in rags."

"Then what was he doing all the way out here? Have you been having problems with the homeless trying to scavenge for food or clothes?" Wade asked.

"No. They usually stick to the poorer neighborhoods. My guess is this guy would have been holed up somewhere taking shelter from the rain, not out prowling miles from his usual route," the officer said.

"What's the kid's name?" Tate asked.

"Bryce Lewis."

"Wade, you and Jo go talk to him," Tate said.

Jo followed Wade across the street, leaving the other two at the scene. They stopped in front of the boy and flashed their badges.

"Bryce Lewis?" Wade asked.

The boy looked up. "Yes, sir."

"We're from the FBI. We need to ask you some questions, okay?"

"Yes, sir," Bryce said, and stood up, quickly wiping his face and nose with the tail of his shirt.

"So what time did you find the body?" Wade asked.

"A little after seven," Bryce said.

"Why were you out here so early in the morning?"

Tears ran down the boy's face as he pointed across the street.

"That's where my house used to be, and I was looking for Mutt."

"Is Mutt your dog?" Jo asked.

He nodded. "We weren't home when the tornado happened. My mom and I got a call from my older brother about what happened, and we just got into town this morning. We're staying at his place, so I borrowed his bike and rode over first thing to see if I could find her. That's when I found the body."

"Did you see anybody else around?" Wade asked.

"No, sir. I called the police first, and then I called my mom, but she and my brother are at the hospital with my dad."

"Your dad was in the house?" Wade asked.

"Yes. He couldn't get time off of work, so he stayed behind. He has head injuries and isn't awake yet," the boy said.

Jo could hear the fear in his voice.

"Did you recognize the victim?" Wade asked.

The boy shuddered. "No, sir. I just want to go back to my brother's house. Can I leave now?"

Wade patted the boy's shoulder and glanced at Jo. "Get his personal information and then let him leave."

Jo began taking down the info on her iPad as Wade left. The boy was a trooper, trying to pull himself together and answer like a man, but she could tell he was shaken.

She soon finished her questions, but she hated to send him off with something so brutal on his mind.

"So you have a dog named Mutt. What kind of a dog is he?"

"She's not any one breed. It's why we named her Mutt. We got her from the pound over four years ago. She sleeps with me at night."

"Do you have a picture?" Jo asked.

He pulled out his phone and then scanned his photos until he found one to show her.

"This is Mutt last Christmas. I always take a picture of her with a Christmas bow on her head. Mom says we should have named her Queenie because she wears that thing like a crown until it falls off."

Jo smiled. "That's a great little dog. She looks like she's part Yorkie."

"Could be, ma'am," Bryce said.

"So, are you going to be okay to bike back to your brother's house on your own?"

He nodded.

"I hope your father gets well really soon," she said.

"So do I," he said, and got on the bike and rode away.

She walked back across the street, dodging patrol cars and officers as well as the crime scene techs who were still there.

The day was getting hotter by the hour. Coupled with the humidity from the rain the night before, it would be miserable outside until the sun went down. She unbuttoned another button on her tailored shirt for circulation and tossed her jacket in their SUV as she walked past. When she saw movement from the corner of her eye and realized it was another news crew, she slipped on her sunglasses. They weren't much to hide behind, but she had no intention of becoming fodder for the media just because she was Wade Luckett's ex.

"Did you get everything?" Tate asked as she walked up.

"Yes." She eyed the body bag on the stretcher. "Do we have a time of death?"

"Best guess was sometime around midnight, but we'll have a more thorough report soon enough."

"So he's no longer using a Taser?" Jo asked.

"No, we think he is," Wade said. "The M.E. saw what looked like burn marks on his cheeks where the electrodes would have hit."

Jo thought back. "He started using the Taser when he kidnapped Nola, right?"

Tate nodded.

"And he's continued using one. It means he has to be closer to the victim, but it also means he can disable them instantly," Jo said.

"I'm leaning toward the theory that something has physically changed for him, and that he needs that edge to take them down. He could have been injured more severely in that boat explosion than we first thought," Tate said.

"But this is the first time he's mutilated the face. Why do you think he did that?" she asked.

"I have theories, but at this point they'd just be conjecture," Tate said.

"One thing is obvious," Wade said as he walked up. "This was personal. Inman might not have known the guy, but he was mad at him. What he did to that homeless guy came from pure rage. Maybe something to do with his own facial scars."

"I have to agree," Tate said. "Inman's scars might be worse than we imagined, because that type of damage is overkill."

"Are we done here?" Cameron asked.

"Yes. They're going to send copies of the crime scene photos to my computer," Tate said. "And I'm waiting on a callback to get a location on where Inman's text message came from."

Jo was listening to them talk, but she was also hearing something else off in the distance. She did a one-eighty, giving the area a thorough look, but saw nothing to explain what she was hearing.

"Hey, guys, do you hear that?" she asked.

They stopped talking.

"Hear what?" Wade asked.

"I hear a little dog barking."

"Yeah, so do I," Wade said.

"I hear it, too," Cameron put in.

She turned away from the scene and started walking through the debris field, past the lot where the house once stood, and then moved slowly down the block, stopping every few yards to listen. The sound was getting louder, and on a hunch, she stopped and called out, "Hey, Mutt! Come here, Mutt. Where are you, little girl?"

The moment she said the name, the dog began to bark again in earnest.

Wade was right behind her. "Where is that barking coming from? There's so much crap around here, it's no wonder we can't see the dog."

She pointed. "Somewhere over there, I think," she said, and kept moving.

She stopped at a pile of debris nearly five feet high, a combination of broken lumber, chunks of insulation and Sheetrock, someone's rocking chair and part of a kitchen table. There were soggy sofa cushions ripped to shreds, a drapery panel as well as books and broken dishes strewn around it.

She could still hear the small dog whining.

"Hey, Mutt! Hey, little girl! Are you in there?"

The dog yipped once, then whined again.

"Wade, I think the dog is in that pile somewhere," she said, and grabbed a sofa cushion and tossed it aside.

Wade lifted the rocking chair from the stack, and she reached in and pulled back a slab of Sheetrock. Within seconds, the barking resumed, only louder.

Jo pulled back some more debris and then leaned in so she could see down into the hole. She saw a fuzzy little face and shiny black eyes looking back at her.

"Look, Wade! It's Bryce Lewis's dog."

"How can you be sure?" he asked.

"He showed me a picture. Help me get her out."

They began moving debris faster now, and finally Wade leaned in and picked up the dog.

The little dog was whining and licking Wade's fingers as he pulled her out.

Wade grinned. "I've got you, girl. Yeah, yeah, you're welcome," he said as she kept on licking him.

But Jo was in assessment mode. She'd noticed dried blood on Mutt's fur and was looking for the source.

"Oh, no, bless her heart! Look, Wade, her paw is cut, and there's a big gash on her side." She picked up the torn drapery panel and wrapped it around the dog's body; then Wade put the dog in her arms. "Poor little girl. Poor little baby. Did you think you were lost forever? Bryce came looking for you, yes he did. I think he loves his little Mutt."

The moment she said the name Bryce, the little dog yipped again.

Jo laughed. "Yeah, you know who that is, don't you?" Then she looked up and caught an expression of such longing on Wade's face that it made her weak. "Wade?"

He blinked, trying to focus on anything but what he was thinking. "Uh…yeah? What?"

"Someone needs to call Bryce and tell him we found his dog."

"You have his contact information."

"It's on my iPad," she said, and shifted so he could get it out of her shoulder bag. Then she began walking back to the crime scene with the dog, leaving Wade behind searching for the information.

As soon as he found it, he gave the boy a call.

"Hello?"

"Is this Bryce Lewis?" Wade asked.

"Yes."

"Hey, Bryce, this is Agent Luckett. We just spoke, remember?"

"Yes, sir, I remember."

"Would you like some good news?" Wade asked.

"Yes, sir."

"The agent who took your information just found your little dog."

The elation in the kid's voice was immediate.

"Aw, man, are you serious? That is so great! Is she okay? Is Mutt okay?"

"She's got a few cuts, but it doesn't look like anything life-threatening."

"This is great! So great! My brother just got home. He'll bring me right over. Will you wait?"

Wade smiled. "Yeah sure, Bryce. We'll be waiting," he said, and then hurried to catch up with Jo, who was already the center of attention back at the crime scene.

Tate was patting the dog's head, and Cameron had already checked out the cuts. A crime scene tech walked up to take a look and saw the dog's little pink tongue hanging out.

"Hey, I'll bet she's thirsty," he said, and immediately poured some water from his bottle into a paper cup from his work kit, then set it down on the ground.

Still holding the dog, Jo knelt so Mutt could drink.

"I'll bet she's hungry, too," Jo said. "She's been trapped in there since night before last."

"Hey, I have a piece of a sausage biscuit in my cruiser," an officer said, and headed for his patrol car. He ran back with what was left of his breakfast-on-the-go and handed it to Jolene.

Mutt's little black nose was twitching as Jo broke the bread and meat into small pieces and fed them to her one bite at a time.

"Poor girl," she kept saying. "Poor baby... Did

you think the world forgot about you? I know how that feels. Scary, huh?"

Wade couldn't take any more. He stuffed his hands in his pockets and walked away.

Tate started to say something, then let it go. Whatever was happening between them was theirs to deal with on their own.

By now the media that had already been there covering the discovery of the latest body was fully invested in the rescue. They'd been filming Wade and Jo from the moment they walked away on their own, zooming in and catching the entire event from start to finish.

The news crews wouldn't have been surprised if the agents had found another body, so they weren't expecting a little dog, and a live one at that. Now they were thrilled to have a feel-good story in the midst of sadness and disaster. They couldn't have asked for anything better.

And when Bryce Lewis and his brother came driving up in a Jeep less than ten minutes later, and the reporters caught the boy in tears and calling Mutt's name, they knew this was going to be the perfect footage to end the piece.

The moment Mutt heard Bryce's voice, she began wiggling and yipping. Bryce dropped to his knees beside Jo and picked Mutt up in his arms.

She was licking his face, and Bryce couldn't quit laughing and crying.

Jo stood and brushed the dirt off her knees and hands, trying not to cry with him.

"This is turning into a good day after all," she said.

Tate put a hand on her shoulder and gave it a quick squeeze.

"Yes, it is. Good job, Agent Luckett."

She glanced up at him and then looked around for Wade. He was at their SUV. She walked down to where he was standing and pointed at a container of wet wipes sitting on the dash.

"I could use a couple of those," she said.

He hadn't heard her approach, and jumped at the sound of her voice.

"Oh! Yeah, sure thing," he mumbled, and gave her the container.

"That felt good, didn't it?" she said.

"Yes, it did. Good ears, Jo."

She smiled absently, still wiping at the grime on her hands, then pulled one more wipe from the canister to finish the job.

"So what happens now?"

He was pretty sure she didn't mean what was going to happen between them, and shrugged.

"It's Tate's call, but unless we get a lead on

Inman's tag, or get a good location off a cell tower to tell us where he was when he sent the text, we're back in a holding pattern."

"This is crazy," she said.

"Well, it's for damn sure *he's* crazy," Wade said, then took another wipe and gently swiped it down the side of her face. "Puppy kisses."

The pain in her chest was surely emotional. If it wasn't, then she was dying from a heart attack. She felt like Mutt, only the debris beneath which she was lost was emotional. She needed Wade to rescue her, just like he'd rescued the little dog.

He'd offered help. She'd held up her hand to let him know she was drowning. Now it was up to him to throw out the lifeline.

"What do we do now?" she whispered.

"You mean about us?" he asked.

She nodded.

His eyes narrowed against the sunlight as a bead of sweat ran down the back of his neck. The erratic pounding of her pulse was visible in the vein at the base of her neck.

He knew she was scared, but so was he.

"I think we take this one day at a time. I'll do counseling with you, if that would make you feel easier."

She sighed. "I haven't had one easy day since I was shot."

He frowned. "That's mostly your fault. I tried to be there for you."

She wanted to be insulted, but if this was going to work, honesty had to come first. "I know. I'm sorry."

Wade frowned at himself. "That sounded petty and defensive. I shouldn't have said it. Sorry."

"Truth only, Wade, or this doesn't work."

He hesitated and then held out his hand. "Want to shake on it?"

She smiled. "Yes, I think I do."

His grip was firm.

Her fingers curled around his palm.

It was as pure a bargain as the day they'd said "I do."

Tate walked up just as they moved apart and couldn't resist the urge to tease them. "Got that introduction out of the way, did you?"

Jo blushed.

Wade frowned. "We just made a deal, that's all. Where are we going from here?"

Tate began ticking off his plan. "I'll drop Jo off at the hotel so she can resume her investigation into Inman's finances. I'm going to the morgue. The M.E. has agreed to rush this autopsy for us.

Cameron is going to ride with a police officer to the impound yard. I was just informed that the police located an abandoned vehicle with Inman's tag number and had it towed in to the crime lab. Problem is, the vehicle is a car, which means he's swapped tags."

"What do you want *me* to do?" Wade asked.

"The Missouri State Bureau of Investigation is loaning us an SUV. I'll drop you off to pick it up. Working on the assumption that our latest victim was homeless, I want you to head down into the area with the heaviest concentration of homeless. Show Inman's picture around and see if you get any hits. The Stormchaser's M.O. has morphed. There has to be a reason why he chose a victim who wasn't a disaster survivor, disfiguring the face and dumping the body in the storm's debris."

"Will do," Wade said.

One of the perks of Hershel's chosen motel was the free breakfasts. He'd picked up some doughnuts and coffee from the dining area early on, and was back in his room eating at his leisure.

He was watching live coverage of the Stormchaser's latest crime scene, riding the high from once more being the media darling. It was interesting watching how the addition of a fourth team member changed their dynamic. The cameras followed Wade and his ex-wife as they walked across the street, and Hershel could tell by the way they were together but not looking at each other that they were both uncomfortable. He knew exactly how he could work this to his advantage.

He finished his second doughnut and was starting on the third when he saw the woman suddenly turn and walk away from where the body had been found. The media followed her exit as if she was some Hollywood starlet walking the red carpet. It pissed him off.

"This isn't about some agent's ex-wife! This is about me and *my* wife!" he yelled, and threw a pillow at the television screen.

He watched as the two agents began digging through a pile of debris, wondering what the hell they were doing in there when it should be all about the body he'd given them, when all of a sudden they were pulling out some muddy ball of fur.

"A dog? Are you kidding me? You saw the face on that body! You saw what I did to him, and all you care about is the rescue of some stray?"

When the camera followed the female agent all the way back, homing in on the way she was cradling the dog in her arms, he felt just as helpless as the day Nola Landry escaped. Hershel could feel his power slipping away.

"By God, I'm putting a stop to this shit before it goes any further. *I'm* the one in control!"

He stuffed the last of the doughnut in his mouth and then headed for the bathroom to clean up. He knew where they were staying and needed to stake out the place, find their weaknesses and then make his move. He stopped in front of the mirror, staring at his face and trying to judge his best options. If he bandaged himself back up, no one could tell who he was, but it would call attention to his presence. On the other hand, if he left his face uncovered and tried to move around in public, he might as well put a target on his back.

After doctoring the wounds, he opted for the bandages again, took another pain pill and went to get dressed. It was hot as blazes outside, so he settled on blue jeans and a cotton T-shirt, put on the brown mullet wig, packed his Taser and rope, and headed for his truck. He didn't know how long it would take for them to show up back at the hotel, but he would be waiting when they did.

Tate talked on his Bluetooth with the Director all the way to the hotel, so Jo didn't have to worry about conversation. Her energy level had spiked, as if she'd been asleep for three years and was just now coming out of an emotional cocoon. She hadn't felt optimistic about anything for so long she was afraid it wouldn't last. But she trusted Wade, and if he said he wanted to work on their relationship, then she knew he would give it his all. She had to be ready to meet him halfway. Before she knew it, Tate was off the phone and they were at the hotel.

"There's a camera crew," Tate said.

"Crap," she muttered.

"Don't worry," he said. "I'll drive into the parking garage and let you out inside. You can go into the hotel from there, okay?"

"Perfect," she said, and began gathering up her things.

"Got everything?" he asked.

Jo put her jacket over her arm, slung the strap of her purse over her shoulder and patted her hip to make sure her weapon was secure. "I'm good to go."

"I don't know when any of us will be back, so if you get hungry later on and we're not there, don't wait on us."

"Okay."

"If anything comes up, just give me a call," he said. He signaled as he took the turn up into the hotel drive, then proceeded into the parking garage.

"See you later," he said, and braked.

"Good hunting," she said as she got out and then stepped back as he drove away.

When Hershel saw Agent Benton's SUV pull into the parking garage where he was waiting, he smiled, and when he recognized the passenger, his smile widened. Jolene Luckett! When Benton slowed down to let her out and he realized the woman he was after was suddenly on foot and only yards from where he was parked, he took it as a sign. He grabbed the Taser and a length of rope, and when Benton left the parking garage, he slipped out of his truck and started after her.

The Luckett woman was taller than he'd expected and looked very fit. He couldn't delay or she would be inside the hotel and out of reach.

He began walking faster. Between the traffic sounds coming in from outside and the soft soles on his tennis shoes, his steps were virtually soundless. He was within spitting distance when she suddenly turned, and when he saw the gun in her hand, he panicked.

Jolene had shifted the purse strap on her shoulder to a more comfortable position and started walking, keeping her head up, taking mental note of everything around her.

She was passing a big car with tinted windows when she caught the reflection of movement behind her. At the same moment she caught the slight sound of shuffling feet and labored breathing, and that was when her instinct for survival kicked in.

All of a sudden she was three years in the past, walking beside her partner up to an apartment to interview a witness when they heard footsteps running up behind them. She was the first to turn around, but he was the first one shot. The bullet hit him in the back of the head, and he was dead before he hit the ground. She was returning fire even as the bullet hit her. She'd been shocked by how fast a life could end, and now it was happening to her all over again.

She pivoted quickly, her weapon already drawn, and was taking aim at the man coming at her on the run. She saw what she took to be a weapon in his hand, and when he aimed it at her, she fired.

Hershel fired the Taser only a fraction of a second before she pulled the trigger, and when the electrodes hit her in the chest, it was enough to throw off her shot.

He ducked as the shot went over his head and

watched as she went down on her side. Her muscles were seizing, and there was a guttural moan coming from between her clenched lips, but she was looking at him with such hatred that it startled him. He hadn't scared her. He'd made her mad, and he couldn't finish her off, because the gunshot would have been heard.

"Fuck you, bitch. You don't belong here," he whispered, yanked the electrodes out of her chest, spun and ran.

Even though Jo's shot had gone wild, it had echoed through the underground parking as though a dozen guns had been fired at once. She couldn't see anything but brown shaggy hair and eyes beneath the bandages as he bent down and yanked the electrodes from her chest. She was still immobile, jerking from the electrical shock, when he disappeared from view. A moment later she heard the screech of tires on pavement.

He was getting away, and she couldn't even move.

All of a sudden she heard the sound of running feet and people shouting. She was trying to catch her breath when her eyes rolled back in her head, and then she was gone.

Nine

Wade had just picked up the loaner car from the Missouri State Bureau of Investigation when his Bluetooth began to ring. It was Tate.

"What's up?" Wade asked.

"Get back to the hotel. The Stormchaser just attacked Jolene."

Wade's heart nearly stopped. He hit the brakes, made a U-turn in the middle of the busy street and headed back to the hotel, still talking.

"How bad is she hurt? What did he do? Damn it to hell, I knew bringing her on to this team when there was a link between us was a bad idea!"

"All I know is she's talking and they're taking her up to the suite. I'm on my way there. Just don't have a wreck coming back."

The line went dead. Wade stomped the gas, only one thing on his mind. If Jolene lived through this again, he wasn't wasting another day without telling her what was in his heart.

Hershel was in shock.

He'd underestimated Jolene Luckett, and it had nearly gotten him killed. He'd had her down, but he couldn't finish her off without the danger of getting himself caught, and she knew it. Even as he turned and ran, he imagined he could hear her laughter, knowing that she'd bested him. He jumped in his truck and drove out of the garage, laying down rubber as he went, taking the back streets to his motel. On the way he realized they would have caught the make and model of his truck on the hotel security camera, and probably the tag number. Even though the tag wouldn't be registered to Hershel Inman, they had all they needed to find him.

Now, because of one bad decision, not only had he failed to get rid of her, he had to get something else to drive. He drove through the city until he found a street that got him onto the I-55 and headed south out of St. Louis toward a more rural area, fuming as he went. This was not the outcome he had hoped for.

The day was hot, and he had the air conditioner turned up full blast, cooling his body but doing nothing for his temper. It didn't help his attitude when Louise suddenly decided to pop in.

See! See what happens when you act all crazy! You nearly got yourself shot, Hershel Inman.

"Keep your opinions to yourself, Louise. I do not need a backseat driver."

That wasn't an opinion. That was a fact. You have lost your way, Hershel. You don't even know why you're killing people anymore. It's no longer about me or what happened to me. You're just killing for the sake of killing.

He clenched his jaw, willing himself not to answer. She didn't have a dog in this fight, so she needed to keep quiet.

You are wasting all of our retirement money and my inheritance money on murder. You are ruining everything we planned to do.

He threw back his head and laughed.

"What do you mean, ruining what we planned to do? You did that when you went and died, Louise! There is no retirement plan anymore. You're gone! Our home is gone! The world went on without us. They didn't care. No one cared. But I'm *making* them care!" he screamed. "Now shut up! I need to think."

Our money won't last forever. You're going to need your retirement and Social Security money that's accumulating in the bank back home. And there's the insurance settlement from when our house was flooded. Only you can't get to it without giving yourself away.

He thought about the money that came in monthly to Hershel Inman, deposited directly into his bank back in New Orleans, but right now there was nothing he could do about it, so he kept on driving.

Wade told himself all the way to the hotel that Jo was going to be all right. Tate had said she was talking. He'd said they were taking her to the suite. That had to mean she was okay, otherwise she would be on her way to a hospital.

But when he finally reached the hotel, the street in front of it was crawling with media, and the lobby was crawling with cops. He could only imagine how pissed the hotel management was going to be. Having a guest attacked in the parking garage was not good for business. He made his way through the lobby to the elevators and got off at their floor running. The door to their suite was ajar. He hit it with the flat of his hand and was immediately stopped by a uniformed officer.

"This is my room," Wade said, flashing his badge.

Tate was on the phone talking to their boss when he heard Wade's voice and quickly ended the call. "Sir, I need to call you back."

When he saw Wade come in with his hands doubled and a wild look on his face, he could only imagine the hell his friend had been through just getting here.

"She's going to be okay," Tate said.

"Where is she?" Wade asked.

"I had her moved into my room. The EMTs are with her."

"What happened?"

"I dropped her off inside the parking garage and left. She was on her way into the hotel when he ran up behind her. She heard him coming and grabbed her gun. He used his Taser on her. She got off a shot. He got away."

Wade wiped a shaky hand across his face. "Lord. Please tell me we caught all of that on a security camera."

"We did, and there's already an alert out on the vehicle and tag, which, by the way, is not the same tag that was on the truck back in Tulsa, which explains the abandoned car that was towed in with his old tag on it."

"But it *was* him, right?" Wade asked.

"Jo said his face was heavily bandaged, which

might explain the mutilation to his latest victim's face. If he's marked in such a way that he can't hide from us again, then by destroying his victims' faces, in effect he's hiding *them* from *us*. With every failure he experiences, he believes he's losing his power."

"Crazy bastard," Wade muttered, and headed for the bedroom at a lope.

An EMT was treating the electrode burns just below Jo's collarbone, and there was an ice pack on her belly for the localized spasms that had yet to stop. The friction burn on her chin looked painful, and there was a bleeding cut on her forehead that they'd closed with a small butterfly bandage. The moment she saw Wade's face, she knew what he'd been reliving.

"I'm okay, I'm okay," she said.

"I'm not," he said shortly, and grabbed her hand.

If the EMT hadn't been in the way, he would have crawled into bed with her and taken her in his arms. He glanced down at the ice pack, saw the scar on her belly instead, and felt sick all over again, remembering why it was there. At that point Tate walked up behind him with a bottled sports drink packed with electrolytes.

Tate set the cold drink within reach of where Jo was lying.

She was still in shock, but she looked mad. Wade considered that a good sign.

The EMT took her blood pressure again, then checked her heartbeat one last time.

"I think you're good to go," he told her. "Your vitals are stable."

"Finally some good news," Jo said as she gave Wade's hand a quick squeeze. "Help me sit up, will you? I need to start drinking that blue stuff you brought. These spasms are both painful and annoying."

But Wade didn't just help. He physically lifted her, then tucked a couple of pillows behind her back.

"Thanks," she said, and plopped the ice pack back on her stomach and reached for the bottle, pausing momentarily to eye the contents, then sighed. "Oh, great. My tongue and lips are going to be blue," she said, and wrinkled her nose as she took a big gulp.

Wade waited until the officers were out of the room and the EMTs were gone before he turned on Tate like a pissed-off parent at a PTA meeting.

"Did you tell the Director what happened?"

"Yes."

"Well? Is he ordering her back to D.C.?"

"No."

Wade's temper blew. "Why the hell not? Doesn't he get what's going on here?"

"Look, this isn't my call, and we don't question the Director, or don't you remember?" Tate said.

Jolene rolled her eyes and then threw the ice pack. It sailed right between them, hitting the wall.

Their surprise was evident, but now she had their attention.

"I realize Agent Benton is in charge of this team, and I realize Agent Luckett has my best interests at heart. But will the both of you please shut up! This is *my* assignment. I got off a shot and came this close to ending the whole mess in the parking garage of this hotel. I do not *want* to go back. I will be pissed beyond words if that happens. Inman put Cameron in the hospital back in Louisiana. Did anyone offer to send *him* home?"

Neither one of them would look at her.

She snorted softly. "That's what I thought. He shouted something at me as he ran away. He said I didn't belong here, which I'm guessing explains why he tried to get rid of me. For whatever reason, I don't fit into his game." Then she grabbed her stomach and groaned as a new ripple of muscle spasms rolled through her. "Somebody hand me that ice pack."

Wade picked it up, started to carry it back, then saw the gleam in her eye and tossed it instead.

She snagged it in midair and settled it back on her belly, wincing when the cold pack hit warm flesh.

"Thank you. That's better. Now, Agent Benton, would you please go put out some media fires so I can talk privately to Wade for a few minutes?"

Tate nodded. "You did a good job today, Jo, and you're right. You came damn close to putting an end to the Stormchaser case. I'd bet real money that the reason he says you don't belong is because you weren't here at the start. In his mind, he's developed a relationship with the three of us, and you're an unknown. Hershel doesn't like change."

"Does that mean he'll try to kill me again?" she asked.

Tate glanced at Wade and then shrugged. "No way to tell, but I wouldn't put it past him. We'll just have to be extra vigilant where you're concerned. Now that we have the security footage from the hotel parking lot, there's a new BOLO out on him. He'll be on the run again, and maybe this time we'll get lucky. In the meantime, I'm out of here."

Wade walked closer, stopping at the foot of the bed.

"Come sit by me," she said, and patted the mattress as Tate left the room.

Wade was still trying to come to terms with the firebrand she'd become. The past three years had given her an edge she didn't have before.

"Are you going to throw ice at me again?"

"Not unless I have to," she said.

He sat. "There's something I need to say, and I'm going to ask you to hear me out before you argue."

She wanted him to hold her, but after the fit she'd just had, turning into a crybaby wasn't in the cards.

"I'm listening."

"All I heard when I got that phone call was that you'd been attacked, but I made a promise to myself that if you survived this, then you need to know my truth."

Suddenly she was holding her breath. This sounded scary, and she wasn't sure if it was scary good or scary bad.

He slid his fingers along the length of her jaw, tilting her chin until they were eye to eye.

"The truth is that I still love you, and I want

you back in my life. I'll even grovel and take you on any terms you're willing to offer."

"But—"

"Wait! Just hear me out first, okay?"

She nodded, but her heart was suddenly hammering.

"I'll go to counseling with you. I will do whatever you need to feel safe with me again. And I'll work through all my own crap, as well. We got a divorce because we were too sad to fight. Well, I'm not too sad to fight with you anymore. I'll fight with you, and *for* you, for as long as it takes until you say yes."

"Now can I talk?" she asked.

He sighed. "Yeah. Now you can talk."

"I say yes."

"Yes? You said yes?"

She clutched his hand. "I say yes to everything. I want you back. I'll do whatever I have to do to make up for shutting you out. I did this to us. I need to be the one to fix it."

Wade frowned. "No, Jolene. We do this together or not at all."

"Together, then," she said softly.

He leaned in and kissed her; without foreplay, without promises, without fanfare. She still tasted the same, and it made him ache with anticipation.

He was a lustful man with the things he liked, and he liked the way she looked, the way she felt—even the way she smelled. He loved making love to Jolene. One day soon they would do *that* again, too.

Jo felt light-headed again and then remembered she needed to breathe. For a brief moment today she'd thought she was going to die, and she'd been so pissed that she'd never told Wade she was sorry. Now she'd been given her life back, and she was never going to waste a second of it again.

"I'm sorry for everything," she said.

"So am I, sugar. So am I." He picked up the sports drink. "A toast to better days."

"I'll drink to that," she said.

And he laughed because there was finally something in life to rejoice over.

As Hershel drove, he watched in the rearview mirror for any cop cars in pursuit while looking for a state highway that would take him away from the heavily populated areas and in the general direction he wanted to go.

Sometime later he turned onto State Highway 21, breathing easier as he continued to put more and more distance between himself and the city. It was midafternoon when he stopped at a little station on the outskirts of the Mark Twain National Forest to get something to eat and some gas. He hesitated to show his face, but there was no way around it. If they had put out a bulletin on him, the description would be of a guy in bandages, so he needed to get rid of them.

He sat in the truck, using the rearview mirror to see what he was doing, and one by one removed the bandages until he was bare to the world. The stitches were still there, little black barbs poking out of his face like porcupine quills, but the wounds were healing. His face wasn't as red, and the skin beneath the stitches was dry. There was no sign of infection, which was good. A few more days and he could take the stitches out. He dug through his duffel bag, pulled out a blue bandana, rolled it up and tied it around his head.

"Here goes nothing," he said, and got out to fill up the tank. He swiped his credit card and then inserted the hose.

The air was still. The sun was hot on the back of his neck. The scent of gasoline fumes was all he could smell as he waited for the tank to fill. When he went in to pay, he put a little swagger in his step. It was a sign to the world that he knew what the hell he looked like but didn't care.

The clerk stared at him when he walked in, then

YOUR PARTICIPATION IS REQUESTED!

Dear Reader,

Since you are a lover of our books – we would like to get to know you!

Inside you will find a short Reader's Survey. Sharing your answers with us will help our editorial staff understand who you are and what activities you enjoy.

To thank you for your participation, we would like to send you 2 books and 2 gifts – **ABSOLUTELY FREE!**

Enjoy your gifts with our appreciation,

Pam Powers

SEE INSIDE FOR READER'S SURVEY

For Your Reading Pleasure...

YOUR READER'S SURVEY
"THANK YOU" FREE GIFTS INCLUDE:
▶ 2 FREE books
▶ 2 lovely surprise gifts

▶ DETACH AND MAIL CARD TODAY! ▶

PLEASE FILL IN THE CIRCLES COMPLETELY TO RESPOND

1) What type of fiction books do you enjoy reading? (Check all that apply)
○ Suspense/Thrillers ○ Action/Adventure ○ Modern-day Romances
○ Historical Romance ○ Humour ○ Paranormal Romance

2) What attracted you most to the last fiction book you purchased on impulse?
○ The Title ○ The Cover ○ The Author ○ The Story

3) What is usually the greatest influencer when you <u>plan</u> to buy a book?
○ Advertising ○ Referral ○ Book Review

4) How often do you access the internet?
○ Daily ○ Weekly ○ Monthly ○ Rarely or never.

5) How many NEW paperback fiction novels have you purchased in the past 3 months?
○ 0 - 2 ○ 3 - 6 ○ 7 or more

YES! I have completed the Reader's Survey. Please send me
the 2 FREE books and 2 FREE gifts (gifts are worth about $10) for
which I qualify. I understand that I am under no obligation to
purchase any books, as explained on the back of this card.

191/391 MDL F45L

FIRST NAME | LAST NAME

ADDRESS

APT.# | CITY

STATE/PROV. | ZIP/POSTAL CODE

quickly looked away, but Hershel felt the stares when the guy thought he wasn't looking. He gathered up some doughnuts and a cold drink, then stopped at the deli counter and pointed at some already prepared food behind the glass.

"How about fixing me up with some of those chicken strips and potato wedges, and add a couple of bean burritos and some hot sauce for later on."

"Sure thing," the clerk said.

When Hershel got to the counter to pay, the clerk's curiosity won out.

"What happened to your face?"

"Oh, man, I got caught in the St. Louis tornado. I'm lucky to be alive."

The clerk's eyes widened. "Well, I'll be damned! I reckon you're a real lucky man. That'll be something you won't ever forget."

"That's for sure," Hershel said, and counted out the money to pay.

The clerk slipped the money in the till as Hershel picked up his sack and cold drink and headed out the door. He was eating a chicken strip as he drove away, still looking for a new ride. He was thinking he might like a van. In a pinch, he could even sleep in it.

A few miles farther down the road he saw a junkyard with a sign that said We Buy Your Junk, and across the road from the office there was an old house with a van parked on the side of the road with a for-sale sign on it. He considered it a signal that he was on the right path.

"Well, lookee there," Hershel muttered. "A van. Just what I wanted. Ask and ye shall receive."

God isn't giving you any signs to go about your killing, Hershel Inman, so you can get that out of your head right now.

Hershel jumped. Louise's voice was so loud it had startled him.

"My God, Louise. Don't be yelling in my ear. You could have caused me to have a wreck!"

I had my say. You don't have to like it...like it... like it...

He frowned. There she went, echoing again.

"Well, that's good, because I damn sure *don't* like it," he muttered, but Louise was obviously done for the moment, because he heard nothing more.

He stopped at the house and got out to look at the Chevy van. Within moments a little old lady came out carrying an umbrella over her head against the sun and her purse over her shoulder. She stared at his face and then shifted focus to the van.

"Howdy! You lookin' to buy my van?"

"I might," he said. "What model is it?"

"It's a 2003. Got about ninety-seven thousand miles on it. My man, Billy, died last month, and I don't drive. Reckoned as how I'd just sell it rather than let it go to rust. I got the key right here. We can start it up. It runs like a top. Uses a little oil, but that's all."

Hershel got in, rolled the windows up and down, turned on the heat and then the air conditioner to make sure everything worked, and then popped the hood and started the engine, then looked at the engine to check for leaks. It sounded good, and he didn't see any oil in the grass underneath, or around the engine.

"Reckon I could take it for a drive?"

"Yep, but you'll take me with you. No offense, but I don't know you, mister."

Hershel liked the old woman. "None taken," he said. She got in, and he drove out of the yard and up the road to the crossroad at the first section line, and then turned around and drove back. It ran smooth. He parked and killed the engine.

"What do you want for it?" he asked.

"I was thinking fifteen hundred dollars."

Hershel knew how much money he had in his wallet, but it wasn't that much.

"Give me a few minutes to think it over," he said, and handed her the key.

He got in his truck and drove across the road to the junkyard, then went into the office. A man came out from behind a curtain in the adjoining room wearing a Roll Tide T-shirt and a pair of dirty jeans. His hands were as greasy as his hair, but at least he had some, Hershel thought. Once again he got a startled look. He couldn't blame them. He pretty much looked like hell.

"I'm Bill. How can I help you?"

Hershel pointed at his truck. "It runs good, but it got tore up in the tornado just like me, and I don't have insurance on it, so I can't get it fixed. What would you give me for it?"

Bill frowned. "This isn't a body shop."

A younger man walked into the office, wiping his hands.

"Hey, Daddy, I just pulled that carburetor Willis is coming after. It's on the back step." Then he eyed Hershel carefully, trying not to stare. "Looks like you and your truck had a bit of an accident," he said.

"He got caught in the St. Louis tornado. He wants to sell me his truck," Bill said, then glanced back at Hershel. "That's my son, Terry."

Hershel saw interest on Terry's face. "It runs

good, and I was thinking of buying that van across the street if I could make a deal here first."

The young man's eyes lit up.

"He wants to buy Grandpa Billy's van, Daddy. We'd be doing Granny a favor, and I'd get me a truck. I can fix those dents, and we got a new windshield out in the yard. I could paint it and it would look like new."

Bill was torn. Now that he knew his mother would profit from the deal, he was giving it some thought. He eyed Hershel's face, and then looked at the beat-up truck in front of the office.

"Go start it up," Bill said, and then he and Terry followed Hershel out the door.

Hershel got in the truck. It started up like a charm.

"I just filled the tank," he added.

What do you want for it?" Bill asked.

"It's a 2009 GMC, and I got the title right there in the glove box. I was thinking a couple thousand dollars. It's worth every bit of that, and it's got four-wheel drive to boot."

Bill frowned. "It'll cost a thousand just to fix it up."

"It's worth at least five thousand resale," Hershel countered.

"Come on, Daddy. I can fix it up. It's just hail damage. Not a wreck."

"I'll give you seventeen hundred," Bill said.

"I need nineteen, at least," Hershel said.

"Eighteen-fifty," Bill countered again.

"Deal," Hershel said, and held out his hand.

They shook on it, Hershel went out to get the title, and Bill went to get the cash. Hershel glanced at the title. He was going to have to sign Lee Parsons, which was the name he'd been hiding behind. But he had no choice. He could switch over to another one later. He went inside and laid the title on the counter to sign, and then squinted.

"I can't see which line I'm supposed to sign on. Could you turn on some lights?"

"We haven't had power since day before yesterday."

That means they don't know about me, Hershel thought.

Terry leaned over and pointed.

"You sign on that line," he said.

"Younger eyes," Hershel muttered, signed over the title, pocketed the money and then glanced at the kid.

"If you'll drive me over to the van so I can unload, I'd appreciate it," Hershel said.

Terry jumped in behind the wheel, excited to

drive their new purchase, and drove across the road to his grandmother's house. She came right back out with her umbrella and her purse again.

"Well, hello there, Terry. What are you doing driving this man's truck?"

"We just bought it, Granny. And he's gonna buy your van."

She began to grin.

"You boys made a deal that turned out as handy as a pocket on a shirt for me. I got the title right here."

"And I have your money," Hershel said.

The old woman signed over her title.

Hershel handed her the money and then began unloading his things into the back of the van while the boy visited with his grandmother. He went through the truck twice, making sure there wasn't a shred of paper left behind that would tie him to the truck or it to the killings.

"I got everything out," he said. "You have a nice day." Then he got into the van and drove away. Now he could get back to St. Louis, but not until he disabled the dome light. He did too much night work to have a spotlight come on every time he opened the door. After he was through, he took out his phone and sent Benton a new text.

* * *

Tate had just come from a news conference. There was a text waiting from Nola, and he could only imagine what she was thinking. She knew who Jo Luckett was but had never met her. However, she was plenty sympathetic to what had happened. He read her text and smiled.

Tell Jo Luckett I said "Girl Power Rules." I hate Hershel Inman. I miss you. I love you. Be careful and come home soon.

He was about to get on the elevator and go back up to their suite when his phone signaled another text. And when he saw who it was from, he hated to open it. This communication between them, while helpful to their case, also played in to Hershel Inman's delusion that they were all in this together. Still, he had no other choice.

You didn't tell me about the new team member. I don't like surprises. You changed the rules. Now I changed the game.

"Well, crap," he muttered, then dropped the phone in his pocket.

Ten

Cameron was back in the suite when Tate walked in.

"I saw the news conference. Good job," Cameron said.

Tate shrugged. "Thanks, but there's no way to put a spin on what happened. Now Jo's a target, and we know it. Where is she, by the way?"

"Jo is asleep on your bed, and Wade is running an errand. Something about balancing electrolytes?"

"She came damn close to putting an end to this case," Cameron said.

"Yes, she did, and saved her own life in the process. If she hadn't gotten off that shot, I hesitate to think what might have happened."

"What's going on between her and Wade?" Cameron asked.

Tate smiled slowly. "I'd say that they're in the process of mending fences."

Cameron grinned. "Fantastic!"

"Yeah, pretty much what I thought, too."

"So listen. I just got a text from Inman," Tate said, but before he could pull it up, they heard someone at the door.

It was Wade. He tossed the sack he was carrying onto the table.

"Do we know anything new?" he asked.

"Yes. We got another text from Inman."

"Was it about me?" Jo asked.

"You're awake," Wade said as she walked into the room. "How do you feel?"

"Sore. Pissed. Like someone tried to fry my brain. What did the text say?"

Tate pulled it up and read it aloud. "You didn't tell me about the new team member. I don't like surprises. You changed the rules. Now I change the game."

"I told you what he told me...that I didn't belong, remember? That warning can't be good," Jo said.

Wade frowned. "If he changes everything, including his M.O., it'll be like starting over."

"But we know who we're after, and we know what he looks like...more or less, and that's more than we could say when we got to Louisiana last year," Tate said.

Wade pointed at the cabinet. "I brought some more electrolyte stuff for you to drink." Jo looked in the sack, saw it was in powder form and not another sports drink, and went to mix up a glass, but he was still stuck on the danger she was in. "So she stays, but how do we protect her? For that matter, how does she protect herself? Look how close we came to losing Nola, and she was living with the three of us."

Tate frowned. "A thing I remember all too well."

"Seeing as how Inman gave me a concussion in Louisiana, I'd like to pass on getting another, so why don't we bug her?" Cameron said.

Jo looked up from the drink she was stirring. "I'm down with that, but what would we bug? It has to be something that's with me all the time. Something I would never be without."

Wade stared at her for a few moments and then offered up one more solution. "We could bug *you*."

Her eyes widened. "As in…on my person? Like a chip implanted under my skin? I didn't think those things worked except in the movies."

"I didn't say we'd buy it on the open market," he drawled.

"Oh. You're talking CIA toys, aren't you? I like it. Let's do it."

"I'll talk to the Director and have him send someone ASAP," Tate said.

Jo arched an eyebrow at Wade. "I hope you aren't thinking this is going to be a lifelong opportunity to keep tabs on me."

He grinned. "It never entered my mind."

The extreme heat of the day continued, but the warnings were already up. The weather centers were predicting the possibility of severe weather. When it began to cool off, the storms would fire up, and if the Stormchaser was still in the city, all hell would break loose for someone somewhere. It was maddening to have to wait for a body to show up, or for the man to be sighted. There were no preventive measures to be taken other than what had already been done. The city knew the Stormchaser had been there. The authorities knew what he looked like, and they knew what he drove. The St. Louis Police Department had patrol officers on the lookout for the vehicle with orders to pay particular attention to the area of the city where most of the homeless population lived, since that was where he'd picked his last victim. Other than that, all they could do was wait.

* * *

Hershel got back to his motel about sundown, wheeling into the parking space in his new van like he owned the place. He was still wearing the mullet wig and blue bandana, and when he got out, he carried in a sack of groceries. After the day he'd had, he was ready to get his mojo back.

Inside, the room was blessedly cool and the bed still unmade, which was exactly how he'd expected it to be. He'd left the do-not-disturb sign on the outside of the door. For obvious reasons, he didn't want anyone inside his room.

After a quick trip to the bathroom, he began sorting through his purchases. Tonight's dinner was in there somewhere, a can of Vienna sausages and a box of saltine crackers. For dessert he had powdered doughnuts, a messy but favorite treat. There was a coffeemaker in the room, and he started a pot brewing, then sat back to catch up on the news, which was all about his faux pas. It pissed him off no end that he'd been thwarted, and again at the hands of a female.

Well what did you expect, Hershel? She's a trained FBI agent. You always underestimated women. It's a failing of yours.

"I didn't underestimate *you,* Louise. You were a fine woman and an amazing wife."

Yes, I was.

He frowned. "Not very holy of you to brag on yourself."

I didn't brag, just stated a fact. A fact is allowed.

"Whatever. The female FBI agent still doesn't belong. She's as bad as that damn female witness who nearly destroyed everything I've been working toward."

The sooner you accept that you're the one making the mistakes, the better off you'll be. If you failed, it's your fault. If you get caught, that will be your fault, too, and no more than you deserve.

"Shut up, Louise. I don't need any negative comments here. I need you to be supportive. One day we'll be together again, and I'd like to think you'll be happy to see me."

We won't be together, Hershel. You will be going to a place of rehabilitation and then coming back in another life to make amends for what you've done in this one.

Hershel frowned. Louise always had her weird beliefs about life and death, even though their pastor had not approved. "Are you saying that I'm going to Hell?"

That's not what we call it. It's a place for spirits who lose their way.

"That's bullshit."

*You do not curse God's plans...God's plans...
God's plans...*

"While we're at it, what's up with this echo?"

Louise didn't answer. She was already gone.

"Fuck that," he muttered, then poured himself
a cup of coffee and sat down to eat just in time to
catch a rerun of the news conference Agent Benton had held.

By the time it was over, he was livid. Everyone's focus was on the agent who'd nearly taken
him down, which exacerbated his frustrations. The
news anchor padded the story with an update on
the incoming weather and a reassurance to the cit-
izens of the city that the police were on the street
looking for the killer and his vehicle.

Hershel snorted. "Only they'll never find me
or that vehicle," he said, and kept eating until he'd
emptied the Vienna sausage can and eaten nearly
half a sleeve of saltine crackers. He finished off
dinner with the powdered-sugar doughnuts, drank
another cup of coffee and then leaned back on the
bed to rest. Once the storm came in, he would
use it as a cover to find his next victim, and this
time when those smart-ass feds saw the body, they
would remember he was the man in charge.

All of the agents, Jo included, were in a holding
pattern, checking and rechecking data, trying to

find the source of Hershel Inman's money. Wade kept pacing, unable to settle down and focus. Just knowing there was another severe thunderstorm warning for the area was an open invitation to Hershel Inman to do his worst. They wanted to think Inman had left the area, but sound reasoning and serial killers rarely went hand in hand.

The closer the storm came, the more antsy they felt. Finally Jo gave in to exhaustion and began gathering up her things.

"I'm going to bed, guys. If anything comes up, you know where to find me."

Tate hit Mute on the remote and got up.

"I'll happily trade beds with you, Jo. You can have the king-size bed in here, and I'll take your room across the hall."

She waved off the offer. "I'm not afraid Hershel Inman is going to show up at my door."

"Well, you're more certain of that than I am," Tate said. "He warned us that he's changing his game, and we don't know what that means."

"It doesn't matter," Wade said. "I'm staying with her, because I *am* afraid, and I won't sleep a second over here on my own."

Jo stifled a grin. "You always did talk a good game, Luckett. Okay, go get your jammies and bring your pillow. I'm not sharing either one of mine."

Cameron laughed out loud.

Tate smiled.

Wade set his jaw and went to get his things. When he came back, he had a pillow under his arm and a frown on his face.

"See you in the morning," Jo said to the others, and then headed for the door. "By the way, thanks for everything today."

And then they were gone.

Cameron looked at Tate and laughed again, then went to make a fresh pot of coffee. With the storm coming, no one would be doing much sleeping until they knew for sure there wouldn't be any tornado warnings.

Across the hall, Jo dumped her laptop on the desk, took the ponytail holder out of her hair and rubbed the back of her neck. Her chest was sore where the Taser electrodes had hit, and she felt as though she'd been coldcocked whenever she opened her jaw too wide.

Wade threw his pillow on the bed, dropped his bag near the chair and then stood there, watching her.

"What can I do for you, honey? Do you hurt? I've got some stuff for headaches in my bag."

She glanced up into the mirror over the desk and saw the concerned expression on his face. The thought crossed her mind that he did look a little bit like Channing Tatum, only better, but she shook her head.

"I'm okay. I just can't settle down. I know that storm is coming. I'll never be able to sleep, but I've had enough company for one day."

He looked stricken. "I'm sorry. I didn't think of what you might want. I was just thinking about how *I* felt. Would you rather be alone?"

She turned around just as he approached and, without thinking of the consequences, walked into his arms and laid her head on his shoulder.

"You aren't company. I'm just so tired," she said softly.

Wade began rubbing her back in a slow, soothing motion and swallowed past the lump in his throat, grateful beyond words that they were back at this place in their lives.

"Why don't you take a hot soaking bath? That used to be your favorite way to unwind," he suggested.

"I'm afraid I'd fall asleep in the tub. I *am* going

to shower, but when I come out, will you just lie down with me?"

"Yes, I will just lie down with you."

"Thank you," she said, and stroked the side of his cheek, somewhat shocked that after three lonely years she was standing in a room again with the only man she'd ever loved. She kept remembering how good they'd been together, but not tonight. She was so damned tired she couldn't think. Then she dropped her hand and kicked off her shoes.

"I won't be long," she said, and walked away.

Wade had seen the want in her eyes, but he also knew she was exhausted. There would be time enough later for making love. Tonight would be for just settling in.

Gunner liked living inconspicuously. It was why he'd opted for life on the streets, but since all this killing stuff began happening, there was too much going on. Having cops in his neighborhood made him nervous. They weren't after *him,* but they *were* after information. They had been all over the place trying to identify the body of the homeless man who'd been found dumped amid the wreckage left by the storm. They were flashing pictures of the man, with his face blocked out, in the hopes someone might recognize him by the clothes he was wearing. Gunner had been dodging them all day because he was afraid he might know who it was and he didn't want it to be true.

When Teacher never came back to their shelter that night he feared something had happened, but never in a million years would think his friend had been murdered. And he'd heard what they were saying, that the victim's face had been mutilated. He didn't want to see that. It wasn't the way he wanted to remember Teacher.

Still, knowing what had happened made him extra wary. He finished all his panhandling long before it began to get dark. By the time the street-lights came on, he was only a few blocks from his place. He didn't need a television and a fancy weatherman to tell him what was coming, either. All he had to do was look up.

Gunnar was moving as fast as his crippled knee would take him when he passed the Salvation Army's secondhand clothing shop. He walked with his head down and the sack with the food he'd scavenged well hidden beneath his coat. It didn't matter that the weather was too warm for the clothing he was wearing. For the homeless, it was a case of use it or lose it.

All of a sudden there was a wind at his back. He increased his stride and was barely inside the abandoned warehouse he called home when the heavens opened and the rain came down.

Hershel had been cruising the area where the homeless population was largest when the first raindrops began to fall. All the stores were closed. A few had security lights, but most were just darkened interiors beyond the heavily barred windows.

He kept looking down alleys and around Dumpsters, but the weather had driven everyone indoors. Down the street he could see the neon lights of a neighborhood bar, and he decided to park just up the block. The windows of the van were tinted, which gave him extra protection from being spotted, and if any cops cruised by more than once and noticed the van hadn't moved, they would just assume he was inside the bar.

He'd only been there a few minutes when the thunder and lightning arrived, followed by rain, then pea-sized hail. He was cursing the fact that once again his vehicle was getting dented when the hail abruptly stopped. The rain was coming down so hard he couldn't hear himself think, when all of a sudden he saw two kids come running down the street and then into the bar.

Within seconds they came back out again with a very drunk man between them. They were holding his hands and pulling at him as they went, trying to keep him upright.

He frowned. Some damn woman must have sent the two kids down to the neighborhood bar to get their father—in this kind of weather and in a place they had no business being.

You have no room to talk, Hershel Inman. You're sitting out here looking for someone to murder. Shame on you...shame on you...shame...

"Louise, would you quit with the damn echo?"

She did, but only because she was already gone.

He glanced up and down the street, and was thinking of driving away when he saw a cop car turn at the intersection and drive down his way. He sank down in the seat and watched them pass, and told himself if they swung back by this way again he was driving away. But they didn't come back. The wind grew stronger, and he watched trash come up out of an open Dumpster as though there was some kind of suction making it happen. He shivered, remembering the tornado he'd been caught in, started the engine and drove away.

He was about ten blocks down and taking a turn to the south when he saw a woman huddled up beneath the overhang of an empty building. He could tell by the way she was dressed that she was a prostitute. The first thing that went through his mind was why God would let someone like that live yet take his sweet wife. The thought fed his anger, and his anger fed his need, and seconds later he pulled up beside the curb and rolled down the window.

"Hey, honey. You wanna party?" she said.

Hershel grunted. "Yeah. I wanna party. Get in."

He sat with his face in the shadows, and when she opened the door, the dome light didn't come on.

It was to her credit that she hesitated.

"Why didn't your light come on?" she asked.

"Burned out," he said. "Come on. Get in before you drown."

It was the water in her shoes and the rain in her face that made her ignore caution.

"Yeah, okay," she said, and jumped up in the van and closed the door.

She wiped the water from her eyes and pushed the wet, stringy strands of hair off her forehead as she began to recount her wares.

"I don't do anything kinky, and I get twenty-five bucks for a blow job. If you want to fuck me, it's fifty bucks and you have to wear a condom, so what's your pleasure?"

His Taser was between the console and his leg. He saw a flash of panic in her eyes as he reached down, but it was too late for her to react. He fired at point-blank range straight into her face.

He immediately smelled urine and knew she'd just wet herself. He shoved her into the floorboard and pulled out a wet wipe. Grateful the van had leather upholstery, he calmly cleaned off the seat where she'd been sitting, then, just for the hell of it hit the Taser one more time and gave her a second jolt. Her eyes were rolling back in her head and her body was seizing as he drove away.

From inside the warehouse, Gunner had seen Proud Mary huddling beneath the overhang of the old cigar shop. He knew her pimp and knew she was afraid to go home without making her quota. She was nearing forty years old and way past her prime. She'd been there for almost an hour when he saw headlights appear, and heading in her direction. He was making bets with himself as to whether the guy was trolling for drugs or sex, so when he pulled up to where Proud Mary was standing, he guessed it must be sex. He watched as she darted out into the street and over to the light-colored van. When she opened the door he expected to at least get a glimpse of the guy behind the wheel, but the light never came on. Then she hesitated.

"Don't do it," he muttered. "Don't do it, don't do it. Don't get in the van."

When she did, he frowned. He kept his eye on the van as it drove away, but it was raining too hard to be sure about the color, let alone make out the tag number. He watched until the taillights disappeared, and then he moved away from the gap in the wall where windows used to be and curled up in a corner, away from the blowing rain.

The old warehouse was spooky enough on still nights, but tonight, with the roar of wind and rain, it was worse. Old Nick himself could sneak up on him tonight and he would never hear him coming. He missed Teacher's company, but in a way he was actually envious, too. Old Teacher didn't have to mess with this life anymore if he was already dead. He'd gone on to a better place.

The television was still on when Jolene fell asleep, giving Wade just enough light to look his fill at the woman by his side.

The butterfly bandage on her head was a little bloody. The scrape on her chin looked red and raw. He knew the burns from the electrodes Inman had shot into her chest were uncomfortable, too. He kept thinking how close he'd come to losing her again, and how bad he wanted to put his hands on

Hershel Inman. The man was a walking, talking monster who needed to be put down.

When the storm finally hit, Jo began to get restless. Fearing she was going to wake up, Wade moved closer, slipped his arm beneath her neck like he'd done so many times when they'd been married, and held her close.

When she sighed and then rolled toward him, throwing her arm across his chest, he closed his eyes. This was the way people who loved should always sleep: as one.

Along toward morning, Jolene woke up with her nose squished against Wade's bare chest and her hair caught beneath his arm, and groaned.

He woke instantly.

"Are you okay? What do you need, Jo?"

"I need to go to the bathroom, but my hair is caught."

"Oh, sorry!" he said, and quickly moved to free it.

She rolled over to the side of the bed and sat up, then groaned again.

"Sweet Lord, I am sore in every muscle in my body," she said.

"Compliments of the Taser. Muscles don't like getting a jump start. Do you need help?"

"No, I'm okay. Just complaining," she said, and hobbled off to the bathroom.

Wade got out of bed and went to the windows to look out. There were puddles on the lower level of the hotel roof, and the streets below looked glassy, still wet from rainfall, although the sky was clear.

It was just after daylight, and he was suddenly hungry. He turned on the bedside lamp and fumbled around until he found the room service menu, scanned the breakfast offerings and grunted. Good. They started serving at 6:00 a.m.

When Jo came out of the bathroom, she found Wade on the phone. Fearing it was some kind of bad news, she almost laughed out loud when she realized he was ordering pancakes and sausages for two. She eyed the play of muscles across his broad back as a flash of heat shot through her belly. How easy it was to still want him, even when they hadn't done the homework to make peace with how they'd hurt each other.

Finally he hung up, then realized she was sitting on the bed behind him.

"Do you feel better since you moved around a little?" he asked.

"Yes." And she added, "You know Tate and Cameron will most likely order breakfast for all of us later."

He shrugged. "It doesn't matter, I'll be hungry again by then anyway."

"You have a tapeworm," she muttered.

He frowned. "No, actually, I just have a healthy appetite." He leaned down until they were nose to nose and then added, "For all things tasty."

He watched the color rise up her neck and into her cheeks, and once he was satisfied he'd gotten under her skin, he went to the bathroom, leaving her to consider the ramifications of what he'd just said.

Jolene sank against the pillows behind her, watching his sexy strut as he left the room. There had been a time when she would have called him on that taunt. Instead, she rode the little shiver that coursed through her body and tried not to think of how it felt when they made love.

Hershel got back to the motel just as the storm was winding down. He'd dumped the redhead's body amidst the debris at a storm site that had yet to be cleared, then finished off by stripping off her clothes and mutilating her face postmortem.

He was soaked to the skin and wanted nothing more than to take a hot shower, doctor his face and go to bed. He wouldn't send a text to the FBI team tonight but would let his handiwork speak for itself.

When he got inside the room and saw that his bed had been made and clean towels put out in the bathroom, he almost turned around and ran. He looked around outside for the do-not-disturb sign he'd left on the door and finally saw it out in the parking lot, lying in a puddle of water. It had blown off in the storm.

He ran back inside the room, frantically checking to see what, if anything, had been moved, but as far as he could tell, his bag with his disguises was still in the closet and untouched, and the only things different were clean sheets and towels, and a freshly scrubbed bathroom.

"Damn it to hell!"

Now he was going to have to move. He couldn't take the chance and assume everything was okay. He felt every day of his sixty years of living as he stared at the room.

Weary to the bone, he began packing, and soon had everything in his van and ready to go. He trudged up to the office, tossed the key on the counter and settled up with his credit card.

"Thanks a lot, Mr. Parsons," the clerk said as he handed Hershel a copy of his bill. "Safe travels, and I hope you heal up real soon."

Hershel nodded, pocketed his wallet and headed back to the van. Now he had to find another place to stay. As he drove away, he told himself it was probably for the best. No need getting too settled when the next storm could hit anywhere.

A little while later, just as Wade and Jo were digging into their first breakfast of the day, Hershel Inman was checking into a motel less than a mile from his hunting grounds. He considered it a boon to his business to be this close to a prime shopping district. He then crawled into bed and fell sound asleep.

Eleven

"Are you going to eat that sausage?" Wade asked, pointing at Jolene's plate.

"No, help yourself," she said.

He popped it in his mouth as she poured the rest of the coffee into his cup.

"Uh…Wade?"

"Yeah?"

"Before we get all busy with the day, thank you for staying here last night."

"I'm going to do it again tonight," he said, and set his empty plate aside.

"I'm sure it won't be nec—"

"Yes, it will be," he countered. "Inman threw down the gauntlet, so to speak, when he tried to take you out. He's been very straightforward about how much he dislikes your presence. You cannot take his threats lightly."

She shrugged. "So when am I going to get bugged?"

"Tate said sometime today, and…I have something to tell you."

She frowned. The quick change of subject couldn't be good.

"What's wrong?"

"I liked being back in bed with you."

She blinked.

"Okay, but why did that come out sounding like you're pissed off about it?"

"I also like making love to you. A lot."

All of a sudden she could see where this was going.

"Well, I always liked making love to you, too, so I don't understand the—"

"I just want you to know that last night could very well be the last time I'm a gentleman about being in your bed."

She started to laugh, then thought better of it and circled the table, sat down in his lap and put her arms around his neck. She hadn't been with anyone since their divorce and was suddenly very grateful. The pulse at the base of his neck was pounding against her palm, and she recognized the glint in his eyes. She leaned forward until their foreheads were touching.

"I felt really bad last night, and you were so great, but you have my permission to be a complete heel the next time the mood strikes you."

Then she centered her mouth across his lips, enjoying the scent and taste of maple syrup. Who knew pancake syrup could be such a heady aphrodisiac?

Within seconds he had her flat on her back on the bed.

"Time's up," he said gruffly, and stripped off her clothes. "I promise not to hurt you, but I swear to God, I just might die if we don't do this now."

In a way, it felt like the first time they'd made love, with more than a little desperation and an ache needing to be quelled. Foreplay was unnecessary, even a distraction. She wanted that rush, and she wanted Wade.

There had been a few moments yesterday when Wade had feared they would never have this chance again, and now that fate had spared her once more, he wasn't wasting time. She was hot and ready when he slid between her legs, and just that quickly, it could have been over before it began. He stopped, took a breath, and then focused on the woman beneath him.

"Sweet Lord, I have missed you so much…and missed doing this with you."

When he started to move, the heady heat of Jo's body wrapped him up and pulled him under.

"Look at me," he said softly.

She cupped his face with her hands. "I see you. I see you, sweetheart."

"Don't let go," Wade whispered, and began to move, going stroke after long, steady stroke until minutes had passed and their bodies were bathed in sweat.

Then Jo began breathing faster, inhaling short bursts of air, and when she suddenly arched her back and wrapped her legs around his waist, he knew she was coming. Just like the first time they'd made love, she began to cry. Then it had scared him. Now he knew he was doing everything right.

As for him, he'd lost his mind somewhere between the gasp and the moan, and collapsed on top of her, shaking in every muscle.

"Oh. My. Lord," Jo said.

Wade had no words. He was waiting for sanity to come back with his vocabulary. He buried his face in the curve of her neck and took a deep breath, then exhaled slowly.

They lay motionless, holding on to the feeling and each other as long as they could. All too soon the reality of why they were in St. Louis would rear its ugly head and they would be back to chasing a killer.

The bedside phone rang.

Jo sighed.

Wade rose up on one elbow and grabbed the receiver. "Hello?"

"It's me," Tate said. "Get Jo over here ASAP. The spooks are on their way up to put that tracer in her."

"Will do," Wade said, and rolled out of bed.

"Get dressed, Jo. They're on their way up with your tracking chip."

She sat up with a groan and combed her fingers through her hair.

"Oh, great. My legs feel like rubber, and I smell like sex and syrup."

"My kind of woman!" he said, then picked her up in his arms and kissed her soundly.

They dressed with speed and without a care for formality. Wade had to put his jeans and T-shirt back on, because the rest of his clothes were across the hall. Jo grabbed a pair of cotton slacks and a fitted tank top, and then stepped into a pair of canvas shoes.

She brushed her hair and left it hanging, and he grabbed his room key as she slipped hers in her pocket.

Just before they left, Wade slid an arm around her waist, pushed her up against the door and kissed her until she was breathless.

"That's one for the road," he said softly.

They exited quickly. He used his key to let them into the suite. Two strange men were standing near the table, talking to Tate. When the door opened they turned as one, eyeing the new arrivals.

The introductions Tate made were brief.

"Good morning, Jo. Meet Mr. Windom and Mr. Garcia. Gentlemen, this is Agent Jolene Luckett, the lady in question, and Agent Wade Luckett."

Garcia and Windom nodded.

"So how does this actually work?" Jo asked. "Because I didn't think there was anything on the market that performed well."

"This isn't on the market, and all you need to know is that it does the job," Garcia said, and then smiled briefly. "I'm going to numb the back of your shoulder. It's a bit like getting an injection, only with a much bigger needle."

Jo shrugged. "Yesterday it was a Taser. Today it was a chip. Damn fine job I have."

Her sarcasm broke the awkwardness of the moment and had the men laughing; all except Wade. He saw no humor in her situation. He was focused on Windom's instructions as he put a tracking app on Wade's phone and showed him how it worked. The program was calibrated to the frequency of the chip in her back, and as long as she was within a hundred miles of his phone, they could find her.

"Can you put that same app on my phone, as well?" Tate asked. "I would hate to think that after going to all this trouble, if Agent Luckett's phone gets lost or broken we would have no way of finding her."

Windom shrugged. "Just make sure you keep this among yourselves because it isn't something we want advertised. You can thank your director for campaigning so strongly to make this happen. This particular technology is secret and ours alone, and we would hate for it to fall into the wrong hands."

"Of course," Tate said, and then glanced at Jo.

Whatever Garcia had done to her was over, and he had packed up his things.

"Ma'am, I sincerely hope you don't have to put this to use," Garcia said. "It was nice meeting all of you, and good luck on catching your killer. We'll see ourselves out." Then he and Windom left as quietly as they'd come in.

Wade shoved Jolene's hair aside to look at the injection site, but all he could see was a small strip of tape.

"Why the bandage?"

Jo shrugged. "He just said leave it on for a couple of hours and then I could take it off."

"Did it hurt?"

"A little, but not nearly as much as hitting the floor of the parking garage with my chin."

Cameron grinned. "I'd forgotten your weird sense of humor."

"I had almost forgotten it myself," she admitted.

There was a knock at the door.

"That's probably breakfast," Tate said.

"Did you order for all of us?" Wade asked.

Tate nodded.

"Good, I'm starving," Wade said, then looked at Jo and grinned.

She rolled her eyes. "I'm going to go shower and get dressed properly while you three eat."

"Aren't you hungry?" Cameron asked.

She glanced at Wade and decided not to give him away.

"If there's fruit, you can save me some for later."

She opened the door to let the waiter in with their food and then went back across the hall. Once inside, she eyed the chaos they'd made of the bedclothes, their dirty trays still on the table and the bedspread on the floor, and shivered deliciously, remembering the sexual high.

"Breakfast orgy. Every day should start that way."

She set their trays outside in the hall, tossed the bedspread back on the bed and went to take her shower.

It was almost noon before the hooker's body was found. Just like the last one, it had been left amid the rubble in one of the areas hardest hit by the tornado. Surprisingly, she was still fully clothed and had died from strangulation. And like the homeless man, her face had been all but obliterated by puncture wounds.

Wade was staring down at the body with a knot in his belly, knowing that but for the grace of God and Jo's quick thinking she would have wound up the same way.

He looked around to see where she'd gone and saw her talking to the city employee who'd found the body, then thought about Inman taking pictures at the site in Tulsa and did a three-sixty turn, eyeing all the vehicles in the area. They were either fire department or police cars, except for the usual media frenzy cordoned off several blocks away.

"What do you think?" Tate asked as he walked up behind Wade.

Wade turned around. "I think the fucker has lost what was left of his sanity."

"He's really rubbing our noses in it, which is what this is all about," Tate said. "I also think he's losing focus on his original quest, because none of this is triggered by natural disasters anymore. It's becoming more about one-upping us rather than getting back at the authorities in general."

Cameron was a short distance away on a phone call, and as soon as he finished, he joined them.

Tate eyed the frown on Cameron's face. "Everything okay?"

He sighed. "More or less. That was Laura. They were going to send her down here to help set up some new shelters, but I told her not to come. The last thing we need is for him to see her here again, catch on to the fact that we're a couple and target her next."

"Was she upset?" Wade asked.

"Let's just say she didn't argue."

The trio shifted their gaze to Jo.

"She's one tough lady," Tate said.

Cameron's eyes narrowed angrily. "Since we have a new body, he's obviously still in the area, so why haven't we gotten a hit on his truck?"

Wade shrugged. "He's good at changing license

plates to stay under the radar, so he's probably changed vehicles, as well."

"It's this endless money supply that keeps him moving. If we could only get a handle on where it is and cut it off, it might bring him out in the open," Tate said.

"Jo says he's got to have at least one alias besides the Bill Carter name he used back in Louisiana, but she can't find anything," Wade said.

"Remember, he was in that mental hospital for over a year after he had his nervous breakdown," Tate said. "That gave him all kinds of time to plan for extenuating circumstances."

"For a crazy man, he's crazy smart," Cameron said.

"The scariest ones usually are," Wade said. "So, are we done here?"

Tate nodded. "There's nothing more we can do until we get the autopsy report and see if anything new turns up. Chief Sawyer is sending some of his men out to talk to some of the working girls...see if any of them went missing last night. The victim's clothes are noticeable, and there's an odd snake ring on her left hand that someone might recognize. It would help us to get an ID. So far we have two unidentified victims. He feels something needs to stay hidden, so I think the mutilation is to hide their identities from us, since his is no longer unknown. It has to make him nervous, losing his anonymity."

"We can analyze the man six ways to Sunday, but it's still not helping us find him. I'm going to tell Jo we're ready to go," Wade muttered, and strode off to where she was standing.

"We're done here for now, anyway," Tate said, and headed back to their vehicle.

Gunner had been panhandling on a street corner when the first cop car went by. He'd watched them park and get out with a handful of pictures, and ducked his head and walked the other way. They were always looking for runaways down here. When would they get it through their heads that the young kids didn't hang out with people like him? Most of them were holed up in some flophouse getting high or had already been picked up by some pimp. They weren't walking the streets scrounging for food and a dry place to sleep.

Now it was late evening. He was on his way back to the warehouse when he heard that they'd found a woman's body, and he immediately thought of the man in the van who'd picked up Proud Mary. He wondered if it was her. He knew he could go to the police station and look at the pictures to find out, but he didn't want to get involved.

Once he reached the warehouse, he went in through a back entrance rather than the front, just in case someone was lying in wait for his arrival, then went up the stairs to the second floor. After a quick look around, he crawled into his packing crate with a half-eaten sandwich and some bruised fruit he'd picked out of a Dumpster behind a restaurant, and ate. He didn't let himself think about where the food had been, only that it was filling the perennial hole in his gut.

It was long after dark when he heard the sound of shuffling footsteps down below, and then someone coming up the stairs. He told himself maybe it was Teacher, finally coming back from wherever he'd been. But then he heard a grunt, a belch and a groan, and knew whoever it was, he was most likely drunk, which left Teacher out.

"Anybody up here?" someone shouted.

"Yeah!" Gunner yelled out.

"I jus' wanna place to sleep. Won't bother no one."

"Who is it?" Gunner asked.

"It's me, Fish."

Gunner relaxed. "Gunner here."

"Oh…hi, Gunner. Damn shame about Proud Mary, ain't it?"

"I haven't heard. What happened to her?"

"They found her body over on the other side of town, close to where they found the other one the night before. Someone said her face had been all cut up so she couldn't be identified, but the cops were showing pictures of the body, and one of Little Reggie's girls recognized her ring."

"Shit," Gunner said. He lay there for a few minutes, thinking about Teacher and feeling guilty for not checking on him. "Did you see Teacher around today?"

But Fish was already snoring, passed out on the floor.

Gunner took the old chair cushion that was his pillow, rolled it up under his neck and tried to sleep, but he couldn't get past his guilt over ignoring what he'd seen. Maybe tomorrow, if he saw those cops back on the street, he wouldn't run away.

After spending half a day at the library, Hershel was lying low in his new motel room tonight. Without the cover of a thunderstorm, he couldn't safely find a new victim and dump the body without the danger of being seen.

He'd been at the library on one of their public computers all afternoon trying to find a man he'd once known named Conrad Taliaferro, whom Hershel had called Connie. They'd been on the same floor in the mental hospital.

Unlike Hershel, who'd walked in on his own and had been free to walk out the same way, Connie had been committed by relatives after a lengthy court battle, and could only be dismissed after being cleared by a court-appointed examiner. But that didn't suit Connie, and one day he told Hershel that he was going to be leaving soon, then hacked into the hospital computers, issued his own dismissal papers and waited for the doctor to come tell him he was free to go. He'd packed his bags, winked once at Hershel as he was leaving the building, and then walked out into the sunlight and disappeared.

Hershel remembered how time and again Connie had talked about wanting to live in the Florida Keys. He'd done a Google search on him and checked the online White Pages looking for a Conrad Taliaferro anywhere in Florida, but to no avail.

Before any more time passed, Hershel needed to find a way to get his money transferred out of the New Orleans bank without alerting the police that it was gone, and if anyone could pull that off, it would be Connie.

He finally went to bed, frustrated by his lack of progress, and decided to go back tomorrow and do some more research. He was almost asleep when he thought maybe the reason he couldn't find Conrad was because he was no longer alive. Tomorrow he would expand his research to death certificates and see what popped up.

For the FBI team, getting the identity of the second victim so quickly was the first positive thing that had happened since they'd come to St. Louis. She had been a prostitute who went by the name of Proud Mary. It took a little digging, but they soon learned her real name was Janet Good, originally from Dayton, Ohio, the missing wife of a man named Elton Good, who'd been publicly accused of her murder over fifteen years earlier. Even though the police hadn't had enough evidence to take him to trial, he'd been shunned by friends, family and neighbors for all those years. Proud Mary's death had absolved Elton Good of any wrongdoing and put an end to any lingering questions as to what had happened to his wife. He'd even gone so far as to offer to bury her once the police were through with her body.

Wade had been riding a high all day from the pure joy of having Jolene back in his life. And there was the added relief of knowing that if she suddenly disappeared, they had a way to find her.

Jo was back on the computer, trying to link the Bill Carter alias to any of Inman's financial records. If she could find a money link between Hershel and Bill, then she might be able to find a link from Bill to another alias. They all knew there had never been a hit on his flagged New Orleans bank account, so he had to have money, a lot of money, somewhere else.

The team came back to the suite late in the afternoon and found her still working. She had notes spread out all over the table, along with three empty water bottles and a half-finished can of Diet Dr Pepper. She'd started a sandwich at lunch and abandoned it after two or three bites, and then forgot it was even there.

Wade leaned down and kissed the back of her neck, then whispered in her ear, "Are you going to eat that?"

She blinked, then leaned back and laughed.

"What's so funny?" Wade asked as he picked up the sandwich, smelled it and then took a big bite.

"The sweet nothing you just whispered in my

ear has nothing to do with me and everything to do with your stomach."

He grinned, leaned down and whispered in her ear again, then delighted in the deep flush that rose up her cheeks.

Cameron grinned. "What did you say that time?"

"It had nothing to do with food," Jo said, and punched Wade on the arm.

This time they all laughed, which lightened the mood considerably.

"How's it going?" Tate asked, eyeing the stack of notes she'd been making.

"It's not. Either Hershel Inman is a freaking genius at hiding his tracks, or I've clearly taken one too many knocks on my head."

"It's been said before, but it bears repeating. The man had a long time to plan his revenge. There's no telling how many false trails he's laid," Wade said.

"Well, it's making me crazy," Jo said. "I've never run into so many dead ends. The only way anyone can hide assets this completely is by creating complete identities. I'm talking Social Security numbers, fake birth certificates, driver's licenses, health and car insurance in other names, ATM cards—a complete background. And it takes a lot of money to set up accounts in multiple names in different parts of the country. Someone remind me, what the heck did Hershel Inman do for a living before he retired?"

"He was a steelworker in his youth," Wade said, still working on Jo's sandwich.

"And he worked for the railroad at one time, too," Cameron said.

"He was a plumber when he retired," Tate added.

Jo rolled her eyes. "No wonder he has money. Plumbers charge big bucks just to unclog a sink. Anyway, I made sure the flag was still on his New Orleans account. Money keeps going in, but none is going out. There's a lot in there, too. Something close to $475,000—about half of which came from insurance on the house he lost in Katrina. Then he has monthly direct deposits from Social Security and two retirement funds."

Wade tossed a piece of wilted lettuce into the trash, went to get a cold bottle of water and unscrewed the cap. "We found out last year after he was finally identified as the Stormchaser, that his wife had inherited a pretty big sum of money from her parents some years before, and that he'd withdrawn it six months before he began killing, along with more money from another account that his banker said he'd called a vacation fund."

Jo sighed. "See, even then he was setting up money he could access under other names. I need another piece of the puzzle before I can go any further."

"No one ever said this job was simple. Stop worrying about it. We've been at this for over a year, and we're still spinning our wheels. If you go and solve this too quickly, think how bad you'll make us look," Wade said.

"I'm done for today," she said, then hit Save and began powering down her laptop. "I'm going to shower. Are we going anywhere for dinner?"

"We've been relying pretty heavily on room service and there are some great Italian places here," Wade said.

"How much time do I have?" Jo asked.

Wade glanced at his watch. "Can you get ready in thirty minutes?"

"Let me guess. You're starving?" Jo said. "Thirty minutes is fine."

"It takes fuel to run a body this fine," he said.

Laughter followed her out the door. She was still smiling when she got in the shower, but true to her word, she was dressed and street-worthy in just under thirty minutes.

Twelve

The restaurant was packed and noisy, the perfect place to blend in. The team was following their hostess to a table when a little boy came barreling around the end of a banquette. He ran right into Wade's leg, then ricocheted backward so fast he would have fallen and bumped his head if Wade hadn't reacted quickly. He caught the boy as he was falling, then lifted him up in his arms, laughing at the look of surprise on the toddler's face.

"Hey, Speedy, where are you going so fast?"

At that moment a harried young woman ran up.

"I am so sorry! Squirt got away from me."

Wade grinned at the little boy, who was giving him the evil eye now.

"Is your name Squirt?"

The little boy frowned. "No, I Todd."

"Well, hello, Todd. My name is Wade. I think

you need to tell your mama you're sorry you ran away, okay?"

Todd frowned as Wade dumped him into his mother's arms.

"Sowwy, Mama."

The woman rolled her eyes. "As you can see by the frown on his face, he is less than sincere. Sorry again," she said, and hurried off.

Wade was still grinning when he realized Cameron and Tate had already been seated a couple of tables away, and Jo was looking at him with an expression of such sorrow that it was all he could do not to hug her, a move he knew she would not appreciate. Instead, he held out his hand.

"Hey. No. Don't go there," he said.

She quickly looked away, but he could see the tears in her eyes. Damn it. One step forward. Two steps back.

He put a hand on the curve of her back as they moved to their table. The moment they were seated, he began talking to give her time to recover.

"Are we ordering appetizers? If we are, see if they have fried ravioli. I love that stuff."

"I have yet to find a food you don't like," Cameron muttered.

"He doesn't like eggplant," Jo said, and then picked up a menu and started reading.

Tate gave her a quick glance and then looked at Wade, who frowned and shook his head.

"She's right about that," Wade said. "It's a texture thing."

The conversation kept moving, and within moments Jo had recovered herself enough to join in. By the time their appetizers came, outwardly she was fine. But she couldn't get the image out of her head of Wade holding that little boy and laughing. Their son would have been that age, and, if he'd turned out anything like his father, about that wild.

When no one was looking, Wade slipped a hand under the table and patted her leg, as if to say, "I get it, and it's okay."

As soon as she felt his touch, she looked up.

He winked and smiled, and she remembered how good-natured he was about almost everything—until someone cheated or lied, and then he was all business and in your face. That endearing quality was one of the reasons she'd fallen in love with him. He was an almost-too-good-to-be-true kind of man.

The conversation slowed considerably as their entrées arrived. By the time they were back at the hotel, everyone was comfortably sated, and Jo was exhausted both emotionally and mentally.

"Is there anything pressing we can't leave till morning?" she asked as they paused in the hall between her room and the team suite.

"Not that I know of," Tate said.

"Good, because I'm beat," she said. "I'm going to bed, but if anything comes up, just give me a call."

"I'll see you in a few," Wade said. "I need to check email and grab some clean clothes."

She swiped her key card to open her door and then handed it to Wade.

"Here, come in when you want. I might already be asleep."

He took the card, kissed her cheek and gave her a long, serious glance that the other men couldn't see.

"I'm fine," she said softly.

"As a liar, you suck," he said, and kissed her again.

Her smile was a bit lopsided as she closed the door between them.

Wade followed the others into the suite and went straight to his laptop. Tate did the same, and Cameron went to change. The weather was clear and life went on, whether someone died or not.

* * *

Jo had been dozing when a click at the door woke her. She was reaching instinctively for her weapon when she saw Wade's silhouette as he came inside.

"It's just me. Sorry I woke you. Go back to sleep," he said softly.

She began pushing herself into a sitting position. "No. I wanted to talk to you and fell asleep waiting."

He laid the clothes he was carrying on a chair, kicked off his shoes and pulled his T-shirt over his head. The night-light from the bathroom illuminated the room just enough for her to see the play of rock-hard muscles on his belly.

"Light on or off?" he asked.

"Off. It's going to be hard enough to talk about this," she said. "To borrow a quote from my grannie, who has long since passed, I had a come-to-Jesus moment when you picked up that little boy at the restaurant. It's what made me cry."

"Look, honey, you don't have to—"

"No. I do have to. If we do this again, there needs to be total honesty between us first. In a nutshell, here's what I need to say. In all of my guilt and grief, I never shared yours. I know you were sad. I saw you crying at the funeral just like me. But I never held you when you cried. I never talked about what you'd lost. It was all about me."

A sudden wash of sadness caught Wade off guard. It happened so fast there were tears in his eyes before he knew it.

"I appreciate that," he said. "I also understand it. You didn't *just* lose a baby. The baby was murdered. And *you* nearly were, too. I was so scared that night in the hospital, afraid I was losing you both. Every time someone came to update me on your surgery, they were so cautious about what they would even say that I felt you slipping away. I needed to be with you, and they wouldn't even let me see you."

Jo threw back the covers, crawled over to where he was sitting and put her arms around his neck. He pulled her into his lap and kept talking, his voice shaking as he remembered that day.

"They told me that the baby was gone, but I'd already accepted that, because I'd seen them bringing you in. When I saw where you'd taken the bullet, I knew there was no way he could survive. So, in my heart, my son was already dead, and the sorrow that went through me was visceral. From the day we found out the baby was a boy, I'd had all these images in my head of the years to come. Teaching him to swim and ride a bike, how to play ball, and when he was old enough, giving him my Hot Wheels collection. It's at Mom and Dad's, and you didn't even know about it. Afterward, it didn't matter. I sat in the waiting room with Tate and Cameron, with the Deputy Director and his wife, with our friends, fielding frantic phone calls from my parents, who lived too far away to get there, and all I could think about was what would I do if I lost you, too?"

Jo was clutching his hand, too moved to speak as she swallowed back tears.

"When they came and told me you'd made it through surgery, my prayers had been answered. I expected your grief. I expected you to have all kinds of PTSD issues. What I hadn't expected was your anger. But I dealt with it, because I understood how you could be mad at what fate had done to us."

Jo lifted his hand to her lips and kissed the palm, then held it to her heart.

"I'm so sorry," she said. "It took me nearly a year after we were divorced to fully understand what I'd done. I was so bathed in guilt I stayed defensive. My partner was dead. My baby was dead, and every time I looked at your face, I imagined I saw accusation and anger. As much as I dreaded this assignment, it was the best thing that happened to me, because it made me face you again. I quickly realized how mistaken I'd been in what you were going through. It's what my therapist kept trying to tell me, but I wouldn't listen. It's survivor guilt. I lived and they didn't, therefore everyone who loved them is probably mad at me. I just flat-ass shut you out, and I'm sorry."

Wade wrapped his arms around her and tucked his cheek against the side of her neck, rocking back and forth in a slow, steady motion.

"I love you, Jolene. I will always love you. I want you back in my arms every night, back in my life forever. I don't care how long it takes for you to be ready for that again. I'll wait because that's how much you mean to me."

She began to cry. "I don't want to wait for anything, but I also don't want to go back. I want to go forward, where happiness isn't just something other people have. When it's time, I want to be your wife again. I will *do* better, *be* better. I want us to have another baby. Is that too much to ask?"

Now Wade was crying, too. "We will have *all* that again. I promise."

Jo crawled out of his lap, then took off her T-shirt and held out her hand.

"Make love to me, Wade. It makes me feel whole."

He stripped and stretched out beside her. He wiped away her tears and began leaving butterfly kisses all over her face, and then moved down her neck, then to the valley between her breasts, and then her belly. When he slid his hands beneath her hips and traced the scar with the tip of his tongue and then moved beyond, she moaned.

Everything they did that night, they did slowly and together. From whispers of sweet love words to arousing all the pleasure spots on each other's bodies, they gave and they gave, healing the rift that had opened between them, until there was nothing left but their building passion.

Jo's heart was hammering so hard, all she could hear was the rush of her blood.

Wade was so caught up in the rhythm of their dance that when he felt her climax coming, he let go and rode it out with her. When it was over, they fell asleep, motionless and exhausted in each other's arms.

Hershel got up before daylight and showered. Despite the burn scars, he still needed to shave parts of his face, but at this point, there was no way he could run a razor over his skin.

He poked at the little stitches. They looked dry

and healed, but the straggly-looking whiskers among the stitches looked terrible. He frowned.

"You're never gonna be pretty, Hershel, so get over it," he muttered.

He heard something clatter outside the bathroom window and shoved the blinds aside to look out into the alley. Some bum was digging through the Dumpster. This was definitely the seedier part of St. Louis. As he eyed the guy a little closer, he realized it wasn't a man after all, but a woman wearing men's clothing. From the filthy rags she was wearing to a ratty old fedora, she was a worthless piece of humanity. If it had been nighttime, he might have been tempted to put her out of her misery. But it wasn't, and she'd just lucked out.

He dropped the blinds and went to get dressed. Today was a day for making things happen. He needed to find out if Connie Taliaferro was dead. Today was also a day for staying under the radar, which meant choosing a wig and mustache. He opted for red curly hair, and a bushy little handlebar mustache to match, then made sure to attach them securely. He dug through his meager assortment of clothing, opting for a pair of jeans and a Coors beer T-shirt, and put them on as he watched the morning news.

To his surprise, the police had already identified the hooker he'd killed. Proud Mary, aka Janet Good, had been a runaway wife and fifteen years long gone. Her murder by the Stormchaser had not only added cachet to her demise but apparently cleared her husband's name, which the newscaster went on to discuss in detail. Damn it! Once again the Stormchaser's accomplishments were taking second place to his victims' former lives.

That's because it's not all about you, Hershel Inman.

Hershel frowned. "I'm not talking to you, Louise. All you do is gripe at me."

You turned bad...bad...bad...

There was that damn echo again. He upped the volume on the TV and reached for his shoes. He wanted some breakfast, and he wanted to find Connie Taliaferro, not listen to his dead wife ream his ass out every day.

He left the motel room with a bounce in his step. Having purpose was what got him through the day. He unlocked his van and jumped in.

Gunner was poking about in the trash behind the motel when he saw the man get into the van and drive away, he was thinking about Proud Mary. It was all over the street now as to what had happened to her. The story to her life didn't surprise him. Nearly everyone on the street was running away from something. Proud Mary had run away from one man, but the irony of her so-called escape was that she'd wound up sleeping with a whole lot of strangers to get by. Still, it didn't matter what she'd done. No one deserved to die like that.

He watched the van until it completely disappeared, then closed his eyes and tried to picture the taillights on the van Proud Mary had gotten into, but he couldn't. It had been raining really hard, and he hadn't seen the driver at all. Still, it was something to pay attention to. If another storm blew through the city, he would make it a point to check out this guy's moves.

Hershel was at the library again, this time searching death records. Last night he had remembered that Connie was originally from Memphis, so he began running the name Conrad Taliaferro through the records there.

He didn't find a death certificate, but he did find a name he recognized. Roger Taliaferro. Conrad had a son named Roger. He made a note of the address and phone number, then left the building. He stopped long enough to pick up a disposable telephone, had it activated and sat in his van to make the call. It rang four times, and he was about to hang up before it went to voice mail when he heard a man's slightly breathless voice, as if he'd been running to answer.

"Hello. Taliaferro residence."

"Mr. Taliaferro, my name is Junior Wardley. Are you the son of Conrad Taliaferro?"

He could practically hear Roger Taliaferro frown. "What's the old bastard done now?"

Hershel's heart skipped a beat. Hot damn, Connie wasn't dead.

"Oh, no, no, it's nothing like that. I've been out of the country for a couple of years and just got back. Connie and I became good friends while he was in Stately Hill, outside of New Orleans, and I wanted to look him up."

Roger snorted. "Oh, you mean the loony bin?"

Hershel frowned. "He told me then that he always wanted to go to Florida. Did he?"

"No. He's back here in Memphis."

"Really? I'm in Missouri at the moment, but heading east. I would love to stop off and visit with him. Mind giving me his number?"

There was a moment of silence, and Hershel was afraid he was going to say no, and then Roger spoke.

"What did you say your name was?"

"Wardley. Junior Wardley."

"Yeah, what the hell. I can give you his number. If he doesn't want to talk, he won't answer. He's still weird, but he's harmless."

Hershel was so excited he felt like giggling. "I appreciate this," he said.

"Got a pen and paper?" Roger asked.

"Yep. Right here."

Roger read out the phone number, then added, "He's like a damn vampire. Sleeps all day. If he answers at all, it would be at night. Call him then."

"I will, and thank you again."

Hershel hung up and then glanced at the time. It was a little after noon. Restaurants would be crowded with people on their lunch hour, but he was in the mood for something besides fast food. It was a damn shame he'd had to give up using a motor home because he could have cooked something for himself. That was so much more convenient but considering his past, that would be the first thing the FBI team would look for.

Still, he had a new plan of action, and that was a good thing. He started up the van and drove away.

It was obvious to the other team members that Wade and Jo had come to some kind of an understanding. The warmth when they spoke to each other was a far cry from the uneasy truce with which they'd started.

As the day wore on, the temperature rose. Early weather reports were predicting the possibility of thunderstorms, which would cause the river running through the city to rise even more. On top of everything else, parts of St. Louis were in danger of flooding, a disaster the Stormchaser seemed to favor.

Except for the healing cut on Jo's forehead and the slight redness still on her chin, she looked fine. And after her talk with Wade last night, she felt one hundred percent better, too.

She was running the name Bill Carter through a database that could tie it to Hershel Inman's age and physical description. Unfortunately, Bill Carter was a very common name, and so were middle-aged, bald, bow-legged men. She was also rerunning searches on everything pertaining to Hershel's life prior to when he began killing, everything from the church he and Louise had attended to the yearly plumbers' union convention they attended. She was looking into where he'd grown up, the high school he'd attended, and the members of both his and Louise's extended families. It was maddening to get nowhere, and she was beginning to get nervous. If she didn't come through for the team, the chances were good the Director would pull her off the case and send her elsewhere. Not only did she not want to leave Wade again when they'd just found each other, but Tate had made it clear that no matter where she went, he was certain that if the Stormchaser could find her, he would take her again. He had a thing about failures and needing to rectify them by repeating the process until he was successful. She rubbed the back of her neck where the chip had been implanted, grateful it was there, as she kept on working.

Hershel spent the afternoon in a little park far away from his motel, sitting on a bench under a shade tree with a book in his lap and a sack of roasted unshelled peanuts beside him. Over time he'd gathered quite an audience of birds and squirrels, all vying for some of the treats. He shelled a nut for himself and ate it while shelling more for the birds, then threw still more nuts, shell and all, for the squirrels. He watched them fighting over the goodies as if their lives depended on it, even making side bets with himself as to which ones would win.

But he was beginning to get anxious again. He could almost *feel* the rain in the air, although the impending thunderstorm was still several hours away. The large white puffy clouds made shadows on the ground as they passed overhead, and every time he felt one move between him and the sun, he shuddered. It reminded him of when he and Louise had been trapped on the roof after the rains had gone. The sun had come out, turning on the heat in the already flooded city and turned the floodwaters into a kind of witches' brew of floating debris, dead animals and human bodies. The news choppers periodically flew over, filming aerial shots of the massive destruction. He and Louise had waved at them, beseeching them for help, and begged the already filled up boats that passed to stop for them, as well. "We'll be back," they all said, but no one came until it was too late.

When the wind began to change, Hershel stood up, emptied the peanuts onto the ground and headed for his van. He couldn't sit there any longer with the memories. He had to move.

It was nearing six o'clock in the evening when he finally got back to his motel. He had a sack of barbecue baby back ribs and French fries for his dinner, and a liter of root beer. Tonight was a night for hunting, and he didn't need anything alcoholic blurring his senses.

He ate in front of the television, using a washcloth for a napkin, and when it became too messy, he just got up and washed it out and used it again. The local newscast replayed a clip from the FBI's last news conference, and then the rest was once again all about the hooker he'd killed and not him. They were showing clips of where Janet Good had lived with her family, and what she'd looked like. A pretty young woman with three kids and a husband, but in those old pictures the smile on her face never reached her eyes. He thought back to what she'd looked like when he shot the Taser in her face. She'd lit up then, all right, but from fear, not joy.

It pissed him off that they had only mentioned him once, and he decided if the thunderstorm and rain were severe enough, and lasted long enough tonight, he would make a statement with his victims that would not be overlooked.

Finally he finished his meal, gathered up all the scraps and went outside and tossed them in the Dumpster. Back in his room he washed his face and hands a couple of times to get rid of the barbecue smell and the grease, then eyed the ugly stitches in his face. For two cents he would take them out right now and be done with it, but he got distracted as he went in search of the phone he'd bought earlier. It was time to start calling the number Roger Taliaferro had given him and hope that old Connie picked up.

Conrad Taliaferro would have made a good survivalist, if that kind of thing had been popular in his youth. He hated the "establishment," disregarded laws he thought unjust and had nothing to do with two-faced people. Most of his family fell into that last category quite nicely.

After he'd defeated his loving family's attempt to have him committed indefinitely and get control of his money, they'd all made nice and made up. But they weren't fooling him. He knew they would do it all over again if they thought they could get away with it.

But, since he'd been born into this most disagreeable world, he had learned early on to use it against the people who ran it and made himself rich in the process.

He was a brilliant investor, an inventor of many things electronic, and the entire second floor of his home was devoted to computers and everything that went with them. He had every high-tech gadget on the market and knew how to use them, and for several years, unbeknownst to anyone but his employers, he had been writing programs for computer-controlled weapons belonging to the United States Army. He also developed, copyrighted and distributed high-tech computer games. His family had no idea how much money he'd made on those alone, and he had no intention of telling them.

So when his phone began to ring and he saw it was his son, Roger, he almost didn't answer. However, they hadn't talked in nearly six months, and getting a call out of the blue made him answer, thinking maybe someone in the family had died. If they had, he hoped it was his nephew Wayne, the one who'd come up with the concept of "having Uncle Conrad put away."

"Hello."

"Dad! Hi, it's me, Roger."

"You are my only child, therefore the only person on the face of the earth who would call me Dad, and I also recognize your voice, so the remainder of your greeting was entirely unnecessary."

"Yes, well…beyond the usual put-down, I needed to tell you something. A man called me earlier today. Said his name was Junior Wardley, and that you'd been in Stately Hill together. Said he was coming through here in a few days and wanted to visit with you. He wanted your phone number. I knew you two must have known each other at some time, since he asked me if you'd gone to Florida after you left Stately Hill, because that's where you'd told him you were going. Oh...he also called you Connie. No one calls you Connie, but I thought it might ring a bell with you."

Conrad's interest had been caught the moment Roger said Stately Hill. He'd only made friends with one man in that place, and that man was now high on the FBI's Most Wanted list—and his name wasn't Junior Wardley.

"So did you give him my number or not?" Conrad asked.

Roger cleared his throat. "Well, yes, I did, but I also told him that you might not answer, so if you see an unknown number pop up on your caller ID, it's most likely him and you don't have to answer."

"Does the fact that I have an unlisted number mean anything to you?" Conrad asked.

Roger cleared his throat again. "That's why I'm calling you now. If you don't want to talk, don't fucking answer the phone. Nice talking to you, *Father*. We must do lunch sometime."

The click in Conrad's ear was abrupt, but he had gotten the message. Roger had done something stupid by handing out his father's unlisted phone number and wanted to be absolved. Conrad snorted as he hung up the phone. If Roger wanted absolution, he could go to a priest.

But it had aroused Conrad's interest in a way nothing had in years. He had liked Hershel Inman and felt sorry for the man, even empathized with him in a way he'd never empathized with anyone before. And the man had a hatred for the establishment that went far beyond the disgust Conrad bore. If Junior Wardley *was* Hershel Inman, he wasn't frightened at all. Despite Hershel's violent method of righting the wrongs he'd suffered, he and Hershel were kindred spirits, and he couldn't wait to find out what the man wanted.

Hershel sat down at the little table in his room with his throwaway phone and the list he'd made, which consisted of the goal he hoped to achieve, his bank account number, the tracking number of the account and the phone number of the bank. He didn't know if Connie would get hostile, berate him for what he'd become and hang up, or even threaten to tell the police that he had called. But there was an outside chance he might be interested enough in sticking it to the establishment to help Hershel see this through.

He glanced at the time. Close to 7:00 p.m. They were in the same time zone, so he hoped this wasn't too early to make the call. He punched in the number, and when it began to ring, his heart skipped a beat. Moments later he heard the well-remembered sarcastic rasp of Connie Taliaferro's voice.

"Is that you, Hershel?"

Hershel gasped. "What the fuck, Connie? Have you turned into a psychic on me?"

Conrad laughed, then choked and coughed, because it had been so long since he'd laughed that it took his breath away.

"No. My son, Roger, had the good sense to give me a heads-up call to warn me that he'd given out my unlisted number to a total stranger. I never knew any Junior Wardley at Stately Hill, but there was only one person there who called me Connie. Needless to say, you *have* been busy since we last met. What the hell's going on with you? Have you lost your ever-loving mind?"

Hershel frowned. "Probably. Louise says I'm crazy."

Conrad was silent for a moment. "Uh, isn't Louise your deceased wife?"

"Yes, but she won't stay dead. She's on my ass every day for something or other."

Conrad sighed. So now he got part of Hershel's

problem. The man was not only still mad at the establishment but also slowly losing his mind.

"Sorry to hear that," Conrad said. "So, since it's hardly possible for us to go to dinner together, why the call?"

"I need a favor, and you're the only person I know who could make it happen."

Conrad's conscience told him to hang up the phone, but his anti-establishment self was curious. "What is it?" he asked.

"I'm fairly certain the government has flagged my bank account back in New Orleans, and I can't get to my money, the money I earned, my pensions and my Social Security, not to mention the insurance money on my house that washed away. I can't get even one cent of it without giving myself away. When I die someday, all that money I earned and paid taxes on will go right back in the government's pocket. Is there a way I can get it transferred somewhere without anyone knowing it happened? I'm not asking you to participate in what I'm doing, just to tell me what to do. I just want what's mine."

For Conrad, it was the "going back into the government's pocket" that turned the tide.

"What made you think I would be willing to aid and abet one of the FBI's Most Wanted?"

Hershel's voice was shaking. "I was remembering all those nights in Stately Hill when we were in straitjackets and doped out of our ever-lovin' minds."

Conrad shuddered, and then took a deep breath. "I'm going to need specific information."

"What will it cost me?" Hershel asked.

Conrad thought of the millions and millions of dollars he had stashed in the Cayman Islands.

"Nothing. Just consider it a gift from one old friend to another, and then don't ever call me again."

"Deal."

Thirteen

Hershel's elation was at an all-time high. He didn't know how Connie had made it happen, but as of thirty minutes ago, he was almost a half-million dollars to the good.

It began to rain about an hour after sunset. First just a little shower, like a heads-up notice of what was coming, but it was enough to get him on the move. He had already scouted out the places that would most likely flood, and had his rifle and ammo between the seats of his van. He'd put away the Taser. No more close-up kills or hauling bodies back to the tornado site, because they would be watching for him now, and besides, he'd already planted that field.

Since the brown mullet wig had been rained on before, it seemed like a good choice to go with it again. He got ready inside, then put a knee-length hooded poncho over his clothes and made a run for the van. As he backed up, he paused in the parking lot, gauging which way he should go, then drove south. The glow from the streetlights highlighted the swiftly growing deluge as he moved through the city streets. Soon water was running fast along the curbs and into the sewers, sweeping trash and debris along with it. A stray dog ran out of an alley and in front of his van with its tail tucked between its legs, looking for a place of refuge. Hershel frowned. No one should be allowed to have a dog if they weren't going to take care of it.

You're a fine one to start being critical, Hershel Inman, when you're out looking for someone to kill.

"Hello, Louise. I figured you'd show up today. It's our anniversary. We've been married forty-seven years today."

What did you get me for our anniversary, Hershel? Oh. Let me guess. A dead body. Is it a man or a woman this time? Never mind. I don't want it. You need to take it back...back...back...

"Louise! Can you hear yourself? What's with this echo business?"

He waited for an answer, but as usual when he had a question, she disappeared.

The rain was coming down so hard now that he

could barely see to drive, and he pulled over to the curb to get his bearings. When a flash of lightning snaked across the sky, it lit up the surrounding area enough for him to see the river. He could also see that the street leading in front of him was already flooded. The streetlights highlighted the swiftly moving water where the streets used to be, but most of the houses were dark, already abandoned in the face of the rising flood. Only a few had lights on inside, and he didn't know if that meant the residents had left the lights on when they left or if some people had refused to evacuate.

He drove as far as he dared, and then parked against a curb to watch the houses on the off chance that someone might step outside. If any laggards *were* still at home, eventually they would have to come out, because the swiftly rising water was lapping at their steps and would soon be running beneath their doors.

He turned off the engine and sat in the dark. As he waited, he calmly loaded his rifle, then attached the night-vision scope.

Thunder rattled the windows. The occasional lightning strike lit up his view. And the rain kept coming down.

It was almost an hour before he saw a door open in one of the brightly lit houses. He watched in-

tently through the downpour as someone stepped
out onto the porch. His heart started pounding as
he moved to the back of the van and slid the side
door open. Without ever getting out, he put the
rifle to his shoulder, located his mark through the
night-vision scope and without hesitation pulled
the trigger. The sound of the gunshot was less than
a pop in the downpour as the man dropped where
he stood.

Hershel waited. Moments later a younger man
came out. Hershel saw the man's mouth open as if
to scream, and pulled the trigger again. The second
body went down as quickly as the first.

And still he waited. When the third person
came out, he could see it was an older woman,
holding a child by the hand. He took aim at the
woman and, even as she was screaming, put a bullet in her mouth. The child disappeared, and Hershel didn't care whether it was in the water or in
the house.

Still riding an adrenaline high, he pulled the
side door shut, rolled the rifle up in a blanket,
shoved it beneath the seat and drove away. He left
the flooded streets and drove all the way through
the city out to the far west side of St. Louis. It was
past time to let Agent Benton know he was still
on the job. He got the phone out of the glove box

and turned it on, noted it was low on power and kept his text brief.

This isn't about killing a prostitute. It's about a good woman who died because of people like you, but no one seems to remember why this is happening.

By the time he turned off the phone, he was emotionally spent. He turned around and drove all the way back to his motel, and took the rifle inside with him. He stripped off his wet clothes and proceeded to clean the gun thoroughly, then put it back together and packed the night-vision scope inside the bag with his wigs.

Satisfied by what he'd accomplished, he took a shower, hung his clothes up to dry and crawled into bed. The last thing he thought before he fell asleep was that the media wouldn't be talking about Proud Mary anymore.

Wade was dreaming that he was standing at a curb with a toddler in his arms. They were listening to the jingle of the approaching ice cream truck when he suddenly woke to the fact that his cell phone was ringing. It was 3:00 a.m. Whatever it was, it couldn't be good.

Jo's phone began ringing, too. She turned on the light and sat up to answer.

"What's going on?" she asked as she picked up her phone.

Wade shrugged. "Hello?"

Jo echoed, "Hello?"

"Sorry, guys, it's me conference-calling to keep this brief."

"Tate. What's up?" Wade asked.

"We just got a call from Chief Sawyer. Someone killed three members of one family tonight. All three bodies were found on the porch, and there was a kid, about six years old, inside the house, hiding under a bed. He told the police that thunder did it."

"And they're telling us this because…" Jo asked.

"The M.O.'s different—all three were shot in the head from a good distance away, in the dark—but it was during the worst of the storm, on the verge of washing away."

"You mean their house was flooded?" Wade asked.

"The whole neighborhood is flooded. In fact, it's cut off from the rest of the city and they're taking people out by boat as we speak."

"And why do we think it's the Stormchaser?" Jo asked.

"He sent me another text. I found it after the chief's call. Basically, he's pissed the dead hooker got more press than he did. I'm having headquarters run a trace, but we all know how that's going to turn out. He's in the area, which we always know, but we can never pinpoint his actual location."

"Are the bodies still on-site?" Wade asked.

"No. The crime scene is officially under water. The bodies are being taken to the morgue now. I've already asked the chief to copy ballistic tests and autopsies to us. I'm going down to the morgue. Cameron is going with me."

"I'm getting dressed," Jo said as she threw back the covers. "What do you want us to do? Are there any witnesses?"

"They're taking the evacuees to a local church. I'll text you the address. I want you and Wade to go interview them, see if anyone saw or heard something that might give us a lead. We'll meet back here later."

Wade and Jo ended their calls, looked at each other, and then began grabbing clothes.

"Is it still raining?" she asked.

Wade moved to the window. "Yes, but not as hard. Damn it, what a way to wake up," he said, and finished dressing. "My raincoat is across the hall. I'm going to go get it and come back for you."

She nodded, then stopped in the middle of putting on a bra and put her arms around his neck instead.

He buried his face in the curve of her neck.

"Thank you, baby. I have a feeling it's going to be a very long day." He kissed her chin, then her lips. "I'll be right back."

"Give me five and I'll be ready," she said, and hurried to the bathroom as he left.

The evacuees were still coming into the basement of a Catholic church when Wade and Jo arrived. They identified themselves to a policeman on-site, then to the Red Cross workers who were still setting up the shelter, just to let them know what they were going to do. Then they began moving about the area, Jo on one side of the room and Wade on the other, quietly talking to people, asking if anyone had seen or heard anything or anyone suspicious.

Jo found the woman who'd called the police to report the bodies on the porch, and sat down on a cot beside her to talk.

"Mrs. Ainsworth, you're the one who called the police, right?"

The old woman nodded. "Call me Clara, and yes, I'd gone out to see how high the water was getting and saw the front door open up the street. I could see the bodies on the porch because the rain had let up and there's a streetlight right out front. It was awful. I had no idea what had happened, I just knew they were lying in the water."

"Did you see any strangers in the area, or hear the gunshots?"

"No. But the rain was really coming down, so I doubt I would have heard anything. Not to mention I'm getting hard of hearing, you know."

"Did you know the family?" Jo asked.

"Yes. It's an old neighborhood. We've all lived there a long time. I'm just sick about what happened, and worst of all, I guess Mabel's grandson saw them being shot. Terrible thing. Terrible, terrible thing."

"Yes, ma'am," Jo said, and gave Clara one of her cards. "If you think of anything else, please give me a call."

"I will, and I sure hope you all catch whoever did this. He's a beast."

"Agreed," Jo said, and patted the old woman's arm before moving away.

She went through the crowd asking her questions, heading back to the doorway whenever new people came in, but they all said the same thing. They hadn't heard a thing, hadn't seen any strangers in the area.

She met up with Wade nearly two hours later. He was drinking a cup of coffee and eating a cookie. She smiled. If she was ever going to be stranded on an island with someone, she would want it to be Wade. He could find food faster than anyone she knew.

"Want a cup of coffee, honey? The church ladies just made a fresh pot."

She nodded.

"One more coffee for Agent Luckett, if you please," he said sweetly, and the lady standing beside the huge urn smiled as she poured a fresh cup.

"Thank you," Jo said, cradling the cup in her hands.

"Oh, hey! You're the agent who was attacked by the Stormchaser, aren't you?" the lady asked.

Jo nodded as she took a quick sip. "Good coffee. Thanks a lot."

But the lady was still putting together the pieces of her little puzzle as she handed Wade another cookie.

"Then that means you were her husband, right?"

He took the cookie, winked at Jo, and then grinned. "Was once, will be again."

The lady giggled. "How romantic."

Jo moved away, anxious for that conversation to die on its own. Unfortunately, a local news crew had just arrived on the premises, and it didn't take long for word to spread that not only were the FBI already on the scene talking to the survivors, but that it was the two agents who used to be married to each other. Since there were no new leads on the killer's whereabouts, the human-interest story took center stage.

Despite Wade's best intentions, he and Jo had a camera in their faces all the way to their vehicle. The reporter was throwing questions at them right and left, and while neither one of them paused to answer, it was clear that the footage was destined for the early morning news.

It was that exact piece of film that sent Hershel straight over the edge. He was sitting on the end of the bed eating a package of mini-doughnuts and drinking a Pepsi when it aired. He had just popped a whole doughnut into his mouth as he waited for the journalist to begin describing the horror of the Stormchaser's latest kill and instead the news-reader glossed over the carnage, mentioned the child as a survivor, then showed film of the Luck-etts going to their car.

He jumped up and threw his food against the wall, then dumped the Pepsi in the trash.

"What the fuck do you have to do to get anyone to pay attention around here?"

Then he began to pace. "I've said it before, and I'll say it again. That bitch doesn't belong. She's not part of our team. She's throwing everything off. It's me and the team. We've been together from the start. That woman has no place here. I've fucked around long enough. It's time to get rid of her."

Hershel was getting rid of that woman, and he was going to do to her what had been done to his Louise. It had taken eleven days before they'd found Louise's body after she washed away in the floodwaters, and then another month to get a positive identification. Once he got his hands on Jolene Luckett, he would end her life and hide her body so deep in the woods that when or if she was ever found it would be in pieces. Just like Louise.

As Jo and Wade were leaving the church, Wade received a text from Tate letting them know that they'd gone to the hospital to interview the little boy who'd survived the shootings.

"Glad it's them and not us," Jo said. "I hate interviewing kids about stuff like this. It's bad enough that they know their family is dead without making them feel like they've failed if they don't have any information."

"Maybe he saw something," Wade said, and then wheeled into a fast-food drive-through on his way back to the hotel.

Jo frowned. "What he saw was the back of his grandmother's head explode. The Stormchaser is a good shot."

"You should hear Tate's wife talk about that. She witnessed him murder three of her neighbors in cold blood."

Jo shuddered. "I've had my own little run-in with the guy, and I hope it was my last."

Wade squeezed her hand. "I hope so, too, honey. Hey, would you please text Tate and see if they've already eaten before I order."

"Sure," she said.

A short while later, they arrived back in the suite with a sackful of breakfast sandwiches and large coffees for everyone.

Wade began to make a fresh pot of coffee for later, while Jo turned on her laptop to check her messages. A few minutes later Tate and Cameron returned, and then the team began exchanging information as they ate.

Jo had already shared her interview with Clara Ainsworth and was deep into her work, still trying to find Inman's money trail, when all of a sudden she jumped to her feet.

"No! No way!"

She dropped into the chair again, her fingers flying on the keyboard as she rechecked the data.

"What's wrong?" Wade asked.

"Just a minute," she muttered, and kept on typing, checking, and rechecking, and searching for an answer where none was to be had. She shoved her hands through her hair and looked up. "Inman's money is no longer in the bank in New Orleans, and there's no trace of where it's gone. Who flagged that account? Was it us?"

Tate couldn't believe what he was hearing. "Hell yes, it was us. If it moved, we would not only know who moved it, but where it went. Are you sure? Maybe it—"

Jo threw up her hands. "Yes, I'm sure. This is what I do. Somebody moved it. It wasn't withdrawn. It's just gone, and without a computer trail."

"There's nothing in Inman's background to indicate he had this kind of expertise," Wade said.

"Oh, Inman didn't do this. *I* couldn't do this."

Tate frowned. "What do you mean?"

"This took international hacker-gone-wild skills.

That was half a million dollars, give or take…
Plenty of money to make it worth someone's while
to try."

"That's ridiculous," Cameron said. "Inman
doesn't have connections like that."

"Is it possible this is an internal theft by someone at the bank itself?" Tate asked. "By now everyone knows Inman is a wanted man. It wouldn't
be the first time a bank employee availed him or
herself of easy pickings."

"I don't think so, but right now all I know for
sure is that the money was there last night and now
it's not. Someone needs to tell the Director ASAP.
They can get on this back at headquarters. They've
got better equipment than I have here."

Tate frowned. "Sharing bad news falls under
my job description." He walked out of the room
with his cell phone in his hand.

Jo couldn't get over what had happened. She sat
back down and began typing again, but one search
after another came back empty.

After a few more minutes Wade asked, "Still
nothing?"

"Still nothing." She paused to look up. "You
have no idea what skill it took to make that happen. I don't know anyone personally who could

do this. Isn't there anyone in Inman's background who's a computer whiz?"

"His only family was his wife, Louise. That's what makes this so difficult. Even after we found out his real identity, we never found anyone who was close to him or could give us info on anything personal. He was, and still is, an enigma."

"Well, if he's the one who took it, then he's got a half-million dollars in his pocket now."

"He can run and hide for a really long time on money like that," Cameron said.

"God forbid," Wade said.

Gunner was rummaging through a Dumpster behind a restaurant when Fish shuffled up behind him.

"Find anything?" Fish asked.

Gunner shrugged. "Some."

Fish poked his head over the side to look, but what he really wanted was a drink, not something to eat.

"Did you hear about them three people getting shot last night?"

Gunner shrugged again. "People are always dying. What's the big deal about three more?"

"It was that Stormchaser guy. The same one who killed Proud Mary."

Gunner stopped and looked up. "Are you sure?"

"Yep. Heard two cops talking about it this morning."

Gunner sighed. He hadn't thought about a conscience in years, but something was bugging him, and he wondered if that might be what it was.

"Who got killed?" he asked.

"An old couple and their son. Their grandson saw it and hid in the house."

"The killer didn't go after the kid?"

"No, he couldn't. It was dark, and the place was already flooded. They were stranded in their house, and when they went out to check the water level, he killed them one at a time. Cops said he used a rifle and probably some kind of long-distance scope."

"But the kid's okay?"

Fish frowned. "As okay as you can be after you watched your whole family die."

"Well, fuck," Gunner mumbled.

"What's wrong?" Fish asked.

"Oh, nothing. I can't find anything good here. I'm moving on."

"Yeah, okay. See you around," Fish said, and went in the opposite direction.

Gunner had just lost his appetite. Even if what he'd seen wouldn't have been enough to stop those people from getting killed, he felt guilty for not trying. He thought of Proud Mary, and then of Teacher. They never had identified that first body. What if it really was old Teach? He brushed at the dust on the front of his clothes, then gave it up as a lost cause. No amount of brushing was going to make him any more presentable. He put his head down and began walking uptown toward the nearest police station.

Fourteen

The desk sergeant looked up as the door opened, groaning inwardly as Gunner walked in.

This one is gonna stink.

And he was right.

"What can I do for you?" he asked.

Gunner could tell by the way the cop's upper lip was curling that he smelled bad, but he already knew that.

"I want to talk to someone about the Stormchaser murders."

It didn't take long for the sergeant's attitude to change.

"Hang on a second," he said, and picked up the phone and punched in some numbers. "Hey, Compton, there's a guy down here who wants to talk about the Stormchaser murders." There was a pause. "Yeah, okay," he added, then hung up. "He's on his way. Just have a seat over there."

Gunner walked to a row of chairs against the wall. Two people got up and moved all the way down to the far end of the row. He just kept staring at the door, waiting for someone to come through so he could get this over with. A few minutes later a big burly man with a thick head of curly brown hair came out. He looked at the desk sergeant, who pointed at Gunner. To the detective's credit, he never reacted as he approached the chair where Gunner was sitting.

"You wanted to talk to me?"

Gunner nodded.

"Follow me," the detective said.

A few moments later they entered a small narrow room with an even smaller table and two chairs on opposite sides.

"My name is Detective Compton. Have a seat."

Gunner sat.

"Just for the record, I need you to state your name."

"My name is Jeff Holly, but everyone on the street calls me Gunner."

"Were you in the military?" Compton asked.

"Yeah. Two tours in Iraq."

"So you have information about the Storm-chaser?"

"I might," Gunner said. "Have you identified that first body? The man with his face all cut up?"

"No."

"Do you have pictures I could look at? I don't want to see the face, but I heard the cops said he was a homeless guy. I have a friend who's gone missing, and I might recognize the clothes."

Compton's eyes narrowed trying to figure out if this was a guy who got off looking at bodies, or if he was sincere.

"What's your friend's name?"

"We call him Teacher, but his real name is Randal Foster."

"And you say you would know him by his clothes?"

"Probably. It's not like we have a wardrobe of choices," Gunner stated.

"Hang on a sec. I'll go get the file photos."

"I don't want to see his face," Gunner said again. "I heard it got cut up. I don't want to see that."

Compton left the interrogation room quickly and strode back to his desk.

"Hey, guys... I got a homeless guy in room one

who's missing a friend. We might get an ID on the Stormchaser's John Doe."

He picked up a file, checked to see if the pictures were still in it, and returned to the interrogation room as the other officers moved to a small television screen to watch the interview unfold.

As soon as Compton entered, he took out a picture, laid a piece of paper over the face and then put the photo down in front of Gunner.

Gunner stared intently. "Do you have any that show the coat better?"

Compton pulled another picture, switched out the paper over the face and laid it down.

Gunner grunted, then rubbed his eyes and looked away. "That's enough," he said. "It's Teach."

Compton frowned. "How can you be sure?"

"The buttons on his coat…those red ones. Red like apples. 'Apples for the teacher,' he would say."

"Well, I'll be damned," Compton said softly. "So he was your friend?"

Gunner nodded.

"Sorry for your loss, but you've done his family a great service," Compton said.

"He's from Springfield originally. That's all I know."

"That's great," Compton said. "We appreciate you coming in."

"That's not all," Gunner said. "I might have seen the guy who killed Proud Mary…or at least what he was driving."

Now Compton was really listening. "You witnessed the murder?"

"No. But I saw her that night from across the street. It was raining real hard and she was huddled under an overhang, trying to stay dry. I figured she hadn't gone home because she hadn't turned enough tricks, and she has…*had* a mean pimp. Anyway, I see this van coming down the street. It's raining so hard I can't see details or anything, but it stopped. Proud Mary ran out to talk to the driver, but when she opened the door the dome light didn't come on. I saw her hesitate, like she was suddenly afraid. But I guess he said something, because she got on in and they drove off. Next thing I hear, she's dead."

Compton's heart was racing. This was their first real lead. "Do you know the make of the van?"

"No. Like I said, it was raining really hard, lots of lightning and thunder. But it was a light-colored van with a sliding door on the side. I'm sorry I didn't come sooner. I just didn't think I knew anything that mattered."

"Everything matters," Compton said. "Listen, I need you to hang tight for a bit. The FBI team

who's after the Stormchaser is in town, and they're
going to want to talk to you, too. Are you okay
with that?"

Gunner shrugged. "I don't mind. I don't suppose you have anything I could eat while I wait? I
haven't eaten since sometime yesterday."

"Coffee and doughnuts coming up," Compton
said, and left the room.

By the time he got out to the office area, the
other detectives were smiling.

"Our first break in the case," one said.

"I have to call the feds. Someone take him some
coffee and a couple of doughnuts."

A small discussion ensued as to who would ven-
ture into the room with the food, considering the
small space and the odor attached to their witness,
but Compton didn't care. He called the chief, who
made the call to the feds.

Jo was in one of the bedrooms, talking to the
Director and trying not to sound defensive. Despite her expertise with computers and her efforts
to find a money trail connected to Hershel Inman,
he'd somehow managed to make off with the only
money they could directly tie to him, with nothing to show where it went. After she explained the
searches she'd made that should have immediately

turned up the transfers, he was inclined to agree with her initial assessment.

"I agree. This isn't your regular hacker."

Jo stifled a sigh of relief that she wasn't being blamed. "My first instinct says the hacker bounced a signal from an international location. Can you put some people on that?"

"Yes, of course."

"Have them check China and Russia first."

"Really?"

"Yes, sir."

"Okay. Thank you for your information, and carry on."

"Yes, sir, thank you," Jo said, and disconnected.

She walked back into the living room. "Well, I guess I still have my job."

Tate frowned. "Of course you do. It was never in question."

She shrugged. "I was being a little facetious, okay?"

He smiled. "Okay."

"Where's Wade?" she asked.

"Running an errand."

At that point Tate's phone began to ring. He glanced at the caller ID.

"It's the police," he said, and then answered. "Tate Benton."

"Agent Benton, this is Chief Sawyer. Thought you'd like to know we had a homeless man come in with some information about the Stormchaser."

"What kind of information?" Tate asked.

"He identified our first victim and witnessed the second getting into a van during the storm."

"Keep him there. I'm on the way."

"Will do," Sawyer said.

Tate hung up. "Grab your stuff. We've got a witness down at the police station."

Jo began looking for her iPad and shoulder bag as Tate went to get Cameron.

Hershel gassed up his van at a local gas station, bought a map of the area, a sandwich, a MoonPie and a cold bottle of Pepsi from the deli, and drove away. He stopped at the same park he'd gone to before to eat an early lunch while he checked out the map. He was looking for a heavily wooded area, preferably a place with wildlife. He didn't know what kinds of animals were common to the area, but he hoped they had sharp teeth.

After circling a couple of spots that looked promising, he headed west out of St. Louis. Once he exited the city he turned north, angling toward one of the destinations he had circled, but there were too many homes around to suit, so he backtracked to I-44, then angled south before cutting back to the west again into Robertsville State Park. The farther he drove, the better he liked it. Yes, there were marked trails and camping areas, but it was the remote, off-the-trail areas he was looking for, and this place had them.

He drove until he ran out of road and then backtracked, but he was confident this was the place. He wanted Jolene Luckett to know she was lost and at his mercy. He wanted his face to be the last thing she saw as he choked the life out of her.

He made a note of the road he was on and how many miles into the park he'd driven, then headed back to St. Louis. All he needed now was to get her alone.

Gunner was getting anxious. He'd eaten the food and been accompanied to the bathroom, and still the FBI team had not arrived. The little room they'd shut him in was making him sweat, but the one time he'd tried the door it wouldn't open, and now he felt like he was a prisoner.

He'd yelled once that he wanted out, but no one had answered. By the time the agents arrived, he was fit to be tied. When the door suddenly opened he bolted to his feet and tried to run out.

Cameron was in front and caught the brunt

of the smell and the contact. "Hey, hey, what's wrong?" he asked.

"I need to get out of here, but no one will let me out. I wanted to do a good thing, and they've locked me up."

"Oh, no, I'm sorry, but that's not it at all," Cameron said. "We just want to talk to you about your friend."

"About Teach? You want to talk about Teach?"

"Absolutely, and about the second victim. You knew her, too, right?"

"Yeah, Proud Mary," Gunner said, and reluctantly backed up and sat down as the agents introduced themselves.

"I'm Agent Winger," Cameron said.

"I'm Agent Benton, and this is Agent Luckett," Tate added. "Thank you for agreeing to talk to us."

Gunner began to relax. "Yeah, sure. Just don't know anything more than what I already told the cops."

"So tell us, in your own words, what you saw the night Proud Mary was murdered."

So Gunner told the story again, from start to finish. It was less than they'd hoped for, but more than they'd had before they came in.

"If we showed you some pictures of different

models of vans, would you be able to identify the one you saw?"

Gunner shook his head. "It was too dark and raining too hard. All I know is that it wasn't a junker, and it was a light-colored van with a dome light that didn't work."

Tate pulled some pictures out of a file.

"These are pictures of the Stormchaser. His real name is Hershel Inman. This one is a DMV photo, and this is an artist's rendering of what he might look like today."

Gunner stared at the two images, then eyed the one with the burn scars closer, trying to remember if the guy he'd seen get into a van at the motel had scars. "I can't say as how I've never seen either one of them," he said.

"Okay," Tate said, and handed the man his card. "If you think of anything else, or if you see the van again, please give us a call."

Gunner thought for a second about mentioning the man at the motel, but he hadn't noticed any scars, and so what if it was a light-colored van? They were all over the city.

"Can I go now?" Gunner asked.

"Yes, and thank you for coming in," Tate said.

"I'll walk you out," Jo said, and led the way through the station to the front door. She opened the door and then followed him out into the sunlight. "Mr. Holly, I'm sorry for the loss of your friend, but because of your concern, his family will have the blessing of knowing what happened to him. You did the right thing. Thank you."

Gunner looked away as his eyes suddenly filled with tears. He hadn't allowed himself to feel emotions in so long it scared him. He was through talking for today.

"I'm gonna leave now," he said, and put his head down and started walking.

Jo felt sad for him as she watched him leave. According to the info they'd been given on him, he'd served two tours in Iraq. She couldn't help but think how wrong it was that someone who'd served his country in time of war would wind up in this situation.

Her phone rang as she was waiting for Tate and Cameron to come out. It was Wade.

"Hey, where is everyone? I called Tate, but he didn't answer."

"We're at the police station. There was a witness of sorts who showed up with info on the Stormchaser. We'll fill you in on the details when we get back. Are you at the hotel?"

"I'm on the way."

"What have you been doing?" she asked.

"Picking up some electronics for Tate."

"See you soon," she said.

"Love you, honey," Wade said.

"I love you, too," she said, and disconnected.

It felt good to be able to say that again. She glanced up, saw a light-colored van driving past the police station and frowned. Then saw another, and across the street another one parked in front of a business. All of a sudden their big break in the case didn't seem so big anymore.

Wade was already in the suite when they got back to the hotel.

"Did you get the stuff?" Tate asked as they walked in.

"Yes. I went to the MSBI for most of it. They told me where to get the rest."

Jo frowned. "What's at the Missouri State Bureau of Investigation that we would need?"

"Some basic tracking equipment," Tate said. "It's apparent that the Stormchaser's M.O. has evolved until there's no predicting what he'll do next, although one thing hasn't changed, and that's his fixation with the three of us. And that means you're still at risk, Jo."

Wade dumped the stuff out onto the table.

"These can go on our cell phones. They look

like a decoration, but each emits a signal that we can track from the app I downloaded to my iPad."

"So you guys are in danger, too?" Jo asked.

"Not that I know of," Tate said. "We're part of the team…his team. But he's become such a wild card, I'm just playing it safe."

The men sat down at the table and began opening packages, while Jo picked up her laptop and moved to the sofa. She couldn't get over the fact that she couldn't find any trace of how that money had been moved or where it had gone.

"Hey, Tate, what about the bank manager in New Orleans?" she called over. "What was his explanation for what happened?"

"Supposedly he didn't know anything until we contacted him. I mean, once the flag was removed, it was just a simple computer transaction, after all. The challenge was in removing the flag without alerting the FBI, then in making the transfer trail disappear."

"Somebody will probably get fired over that, which is too bad, because there isn't a single thing they could have done to stop it," she said. "It happened overnight, when the bank was closed, and I can guarantee when our people begin looking, they're going to find out the initial move came from China, or maybe Russia."

Cameron frowned. "You mean someone from China was helping Inman?"

"No. I mean the hacker bounced a signal that made it look that way, which means this is not your average virus-uploading cybercrook. This is espionage-level stuff. Are we one hundred percent sure there's no one in Inman's background with those kinds of skills or contacts?"

"We're sure," Wade said.

She couldn't let it go. "He never worked with anyone with those skills?"

"He didn't have friends he hung out with. It was just him and Louise, and then she died and it was just him."

She sat there for a few minutes, remembering the files she'd read. "He was in a mental hospital for a while, right?"

Wade nodded. "Some place around New Orleans called Stately Hill, I think."

"What about the people who were there with him?"

Tate turned, then looked at Jo and slowly smiled. "And that's why new eyes on an old case always help."

"What do you mean?" Jo asked.

"Wade, did we run a check on the names of

the other patients who were in Stately Hill with Inman?"

"I didn't."

"Neither did I," Cameron said.

"I'll do it," Jo offered.

"Let me know if anything pops up," Tate said.

She nodded, already online and looking for a contact number.

It took a search warrant and a face-to-face visit from an FBI agent in New Orleans to get the list, which the agent promptly scanned and sent to Jo.

Slightly daunted that there were upward of two hundred names to check, she settled in at her computer and did what she did best, slowly but surely eliminating possibilities. Too deep into researching the backgrounds of the people on the list in the hopes that someone would pop, she begged off dinner, and the men went downstairs to the hotel restaurant to eat without her.

About one-third of the way through the list she came to the name Conrad Taliaferro. Just as she had with all the others, she typed in the name to see how many, if any, links popped up, but when they did, she leaned back, staring in disbelief.

Reclusive billionaire. Owner/CEO TriDine Corp.

A picture of him on the front of *Time* magazine, and the list went on and on.

She ran a search on the TriDine Corporation, only to find out it was an umbrella name linked to at least six more corporations, but she kept digging deeper and deeper. When she finally confirmed that Conrad Taliaferro was not only an investment shark but the developer and copyright owner of several dozen very popular computer games, she knew she'd found a very promising link. She kept searching, gathering all the information she could find, when all of a sudden she hit a wall.

"What the heck?" she muttered, and tried again, searching from a different angle, and not only was the info blocked, but her screen suddenly went blank. "Oh, shit," she said softly, and picked up her cell phone and sent Wade a text.

Don't order dessert. You guys are going to want to see this.

Less than five minutes later, Wade and Cameron came hurrying back.

Wade kissed the side of her neck and set a plastic fork and a to-go box down near her coffee cup. "It's cake. If you don't want it, I'll eat it," he said. "What's up?"

"What did you find?" Cameron asked.

"Where's Tate?"

"He got a call. He'll be here shortly."

"I'll wait," she said, then picked up the plastic fork and opened the cake box.

"It's Italian cream cake," Wade said. "With cream-cheese icing," he added.

"Sounds wonderful," she said, and popped a big bite into her mouth, chewed and swallowed. "Mmm, tastes wonderful, too." She handed him the rest.

"Are you sure?" he asked as he happily took it out of her hands.

"I'm sure, but thank you for thinking of me."

At that point Tate came in. "What did I miss?" he asked.

"I waited to tell all of you at once," Jo said.

"So you found a link?" Tate asked.

"Not just a link. I'm pretty sure I found the hacker, but I'm equally sure we'll never prove it."

"What? Why not?" Tate said.

Wade leaned over her shoulder, reading from her notes. "Hey, I have that computer game on my Xbox."

"I'm not surprised," Jo said. "He's done dozens. Here's the name. Conrad Taliaferro. He's an older guy, nearly seventy. He's a billionaire investor who just happens to have mad computer skills. According to my searches, among many other things he designs and creates computer games for one company, then markets and sells them with a second one, then hides the ownership of both under the umbrella of something called the TriDine Corporation."

"So he would have the knowledge to do what needed to be done to move Inman's money?"

She nodded. "But you're never going to prove it happened."

Wade frowned. "Why not?"

"Because when I dug deeper, not only did the sites block me out, but the last one wiped out my entire search and my screen went dead."

"Oh, my God! He works for the government, doesn't he?" Wade asked.

"Yes, I'd bet my last dollar on it. And if I'm right, our fearless leader here will be getting a phone call from the Department of Defense any minute, telling him to cease and desist whatever he's doing."

Tate blinked. "You're serious."

"As a heart attack," she said.

They stared at each other, waiting, and within moments Tate's phone began to ring. He looked down at the caller ID and then back at Jo.

"Blocked number."

She shrugged. "I'd answer it anyway if I were you."

He picked up the call, and the first time they heard him fire off a firm, "Yes, sir," they knew Jo had been right.

"Wow. So how do you think Inman made this happen?" Cameron asked as Tate walked into one of the bedrooms for privacy.

She shrugged. "It doesn't matter, and I'm betting that whatever Taliaferro does for the government trumps a serial killer getting his own money out of the bank."

Cameron shoved a hand through his hair in frustration. "That's right. Nothing was stolen. The money *was* legally his."

"Yes, and the powers that be are willing to look the other way at removing the flag and all traces of the transfer."

"But Taliaferro aided and abetted a felon," Wade said.

"I told you. You'll never be able to prove it," Jo said.

Wade set what was left of the cake aside, his appetite suddenly ruined. "Well, hell. Now we have a serial killer with access to a butt-load of money to fund his sick fantasies. I hope whatever this Taliaferro does will save lives, because he's sure going to cost some other people theirs."

Tate walked back into the room and then made a point of looking straight at Jo. "You are commended for your abilities, and officially ordered to cease and desist."

She arched an eyebrow. "What did I tell you?"

"What does this guy do?" Wade asked.

"We don't have the clearance to know," Tate said.

Cameron frowned, but knew better than to comment. Orders were orders.

"So my job here is done," Jo said. "Are they ordering me back?"

Tate glanced at Wade and then nodded. "They want you back in D.C. by Friday."

She shrugged, disgusted but not surprised. "That's the day after tomorrow, which means if I'm ever going to take a ride up inside the Arch, tomorrow would be it."

"Damn it," Wade said. "I was just getting used to sleeping in the same room with someone who didn't snore again."

"I don't snore," Cameron said.

"I'll be there when you get back," she offered, then eyed the half-eaten cake. "Are you going to eat that?"

All three men looked at her and then burst out laughing.

"See what happens when you hang around Luckett too long?" Tate said. "You turn into him."

Wade handed her the cake. "You earned it."

Jo sat down in his lap and finished it off while he held her. His silence said it all.

Ever since Gunner had identified Teacher's body, he hadn't been able to get it out of his mind. Even though he hadn't seen his face, he'd heard what had happened. Teach didn't deserve that. Nobody deserved to die like that.

He kept thinking about that light-colored van at the motel and the glimpse he had of the driver. He knew the driver was still staying there, because he'd gone over to check, so he took off walking. The van was there when he arrived, and he even waited around, hoping he would see the man come out so he could get a closer look, but nothing happened. Hours passed and it got dark, and he was about to start the long walk back when a pizza delivery car drove up near the guy's room.

Gunner stopped, and when he saw the kid with the pizza knock on the door, he moved into the shadows so he could get a little closer.

The kid knocked again, and a few moments

later the door opened just a little, as if the man inside was checking to see who was there, and then, when he saw the kid and the pizza box, he stepped out on the threshold, right below the security light.

Gunner stared. The man's face was all marked up, and it took him a few moments to realize what he was seeing was a mix of stitches and scars.

The hair rose on the back of his neck as he slowly backed deeper into the shadows.

The man handed the kid some money, took the pizza and disappeared. The kid jumped into his car and drove away, and Gunner walked closer to the motel. He stopped directly behind the van and stared at the tag number, then looked around, hoping to find a pen or something so he could write it onto his arm, but all he could find was a bent nail behind another car. He picked it up, then shoved his coat sleeve up far enough to bare some skin. He jammed the nail against his flesh, gritted his teeth and scratched the number into his arm, then started running.

His arm was stinging. He knew he'd drawn blood and wondered if he would get infected, but what was done was done. He kept on running, thinking he hadn't run like this since Iraq, and before long his side was hurting and there was a pain in his chest. He slowed down just enough to catch his breath, and then hastened his stride again and didn't stop until he'd crawled into the packing box that was his bed and pulled his worn blanket up over his shoulders. It was a very long walk in the dark through some bad parts of the city to get to the police station. And since he didn't want to end up dead like his friends, his news would have to wait until daylight.

The night was hot, but Gunner's arm hurt, and he couldn't stop shaking. He'd seen the devil tonight, and now he was afraid that the devil might follow him home. He lay with his back against the wall of his box and his gaze on the stairs while the night shadows danced and the rats ran across the floor in front of him.

All he had was a hunk of scrap iron for a club, and he wished to God for his army-issue rifle. He never once closed his eyes, and when the sun finally rose on the city of St. Louis, he crawled out of his box and went to look out the window. People were beginning to move around down below, and traffic was beginning to flow. He peed off the second floor balcony onto the floor below, and as he did his belly growled, reminding him of how long it had been since he'd eaten. He shoved the sleeve up his arm and saw that the numbers he'd scratched on it last night were all red and puffy.

Even after he left the warehouse he stopped at the Dumpster behind a local bakery for something to eat.

He found some day-old rolls that the rats hadn't finished off, pocketed two and took one with him, eating as he began a return trip uptown to the police station.

Fifteen

Morning came far too soon for Wade. He'd spent half the night making love to Jo and the other half watching her sleep. Despite the dread with which they'd begun this journey, it had all been for the good. Nothing had been left unsaid, and there was every reason to hope for a happy future. Considering how Inman had fixated on her, he had to believe getting her out of St. Louis was a good thing.

Then, just after seven-thirty, Tate sent him a text.

Our witness is back at the police station with something more.

Wade rolled out of bed, and when he did, Jo woke.

"What's going on? Where do we need to go?"

"Not you," Wade said. "Go back to sleep. You have flight plans to make today. You're officially off the clock and due back in the office tomorrow, remember?"

She frowned. "I could still go."

"Did Tate send you a text?"

She looked. "No."

"Then you're not invited."

She sighed. "Fine. But it doesn't take all that long to make flight plans. What am I going to do with myself? Isn't there something I can do for you guys here?"

"Not that I know of," Wade said. "We're in a holding pattern. Maybe the witness will have something new. You made a joke about going up in the Arch, so check it out. I hear you get quite a view from up there."

"Maybe. I'll text you if I go."

He leaned over and kissed her soundly, and groaned beneath his breath.

"No more of that or I'll be late," he said, then rolled out of bed and went to shower.

Jo stretched back out, put her hands beneath her head and began planning the day.

It was just after 6:45 a.m. when Hershel woke. His sleep had been restless. He blamed it on the pizza he'd eaten, which had given him heartburn, but that wasn't all of it. He was getting too complacent. He needed to move to a new location, but first he was getting rid of his stitches. He'd looked at that face all he could take. Yesterday he'd stopped at a pharmacy and picked up a small free-standing magnifying mirror, a tiny pair of manicure scissors, tweezers, alcohol and cotton balls. Now he had those and the antibiotic ointment the doctor had given him all spread out on the counter. He washed the sleep out of his eyes, picked up the little manicure scissors, tilted the magnifying mirror so he could see the stitches and took the first snip. Then he picked up the tweezers, got a good grip on the stitch and pulled.

The stitch came out with hardly more than a twinge, leaving a neat little scab that would soon peel off. Satisfied it was safe to keep going, he began removing all the other stitches, until every one of them was gone. The relief of being able to run his hands over his face was huge as he poured some alcohol into his hands and then splashed it on like aftershave.

"Oh, shit, shit, shit!" he yelped as the alcohol seeped in and around the tiny scratches, and set his face on fire. It didn't last long, but it was enough to take his breath away. Once that was done, he put a thin layer of the antibiotic ointment all over the skin, then stepped back for a better look.

He didn't look good, but he no longer looked like a monster. It was enough to satisfy his vanity as he began to pack. As he did, he also began to plan his day. Today he would begin tailing the team, and the moment he got a chance to grab Jolene Luckett, he was getting rid of her, then moving on.

Louise hadn't argued with him once about the decision, which made him think she was down with the idea, too.

He dressed in jeans and a clean black T-shirt, picked out a salt-and-pepper gray wig and mustache, and then added a St. Louis Cardinals baseball cap to give himself the appearance of a local guy supporting the hometown team. He began carrying his things out to the van, and once he was certain he'd left nothing behind, he checked out at the office and drove away.

It was just after 7:20 a.m.

His plan was to go to the hotel and find a secluded place to watch the agents' movements. His Taser was charged. Duct tape was on the floorboard. His rifle was wrapped up in a blanket between the seats. He was a rolling murder weapon, looking for a woman to kill.

He found a fast-food place on his way to the hotel and picked up a couple of breakfast sandwiches. Once he arrived, he made one circuit through the parking garage, located both cars the feds were driving, which meant they were all still inside, and then drove right back out again. He found a place to park where he could see cars exiting the structure and settled in to wait.

It was a few minutes before 8:00 a.m.

He unwrapped one of the sandwiches, salted the egg inside, then replaced the top and took a big bite. The bread was warm, the bacon was just like he liked it—done, but not crisp—and the egg was tasty. He would have liked a little salsa on it, too, but he ate it as-is, washing it down with coffee.

He was working on his second sandwich when a dark SUV came out of the parking garage and turned left. It looked like the feds' car, so he sat up for a better view. It *was* them, but he only counted three heads, not four. Who wasn't there? Was it the woman, or had one of the men stayed behind? He cursed the tinted windows and shifted into a better position to see what happened next.

About twenty minutes later he saw another dark SUV coming out. He sat up again, this time looking closer. It was the feds' other car. And when it passed, he saw the perfect outline of a woman's head with a ponytail sticking out behind.

"Hot damn," he said softly, started up the van and drove off, taking care to stay a couple of cars behind her so she wouldn't spot the tail.

Gunner was chowing down on fresh doughnuts and hot coffee as he waited for the feds to show up.

Detective Compton had a cup of coffee at his elbow but was waiting for it to cool. He watched Gunner eat and drink without hesitation and wondered if there were any taste buds left on his tongue or if he'd burned them all off drinking coffee that hot.

"I'll go see if there are any more doughnuts," Compton said, and got up.

"I'd like some more coffee, too, if it's all the same to you," Gunner said.

Compton nodded and left the room. When he came back, three FBI men were with him. He set the hot coffee down near Gunner's hand.

Tate quickly made eye contact. "Good morning, Mr. Holly. I hear you have some more news for us?"

"Yeah. Yeah, I do. There's a guy who's been staying at the Riverside Motel, which is right in my neighborhood. He drives a light-colored van. I never got a good look at his face and didn't think much about it. I mean, there are dozens of light-colored vans all over, right? But after I saw what had happened to Teacher and you showed me pictures of that Stormchaser guy, I thought the least I could do was try and get a better look at his face."

Wade's heart suddenly skipped a beat. He could feel what was coming, even before Gunner spoke again.

"Was it Hershel Inman?" Tate asked.

"I finally got a good look, but I had to stake out the room to do it. It's number 112, by the way. I waited and waited for him to come out, but he never did, and then it got dark. I was getting ready to leave when a pizza delivery guy drove up and went to his door. I waited for him to come out, and when he did, I finally saw him."

"Was it him? Was it Inman?" Wade asked.

"Well, it was a middle-aged guy who was nearly bald. He looked like hell. There were scars on one side of his face and what looked like little stitches all over it. But I'd say he looked a whole lot like your guy."

"What's the name of the motel again?" Tate asked.

"Riverside Motel." Then Gunner pushed his sleeve up, revealing the angry red marks. "My memory's not so good since the war, and I didn't have anything to write down the tag number, so I scratched it on my arm with a nail."

The men were momentarily silenced by the deep scratches the man had purposefully put in his arm, and sympathetic to the fact that Gunner must have known it would get infected but did it anyway.

"That's amazing," Wade said softly.

Gunner shrugged. "Teacher was my friend."

"You need some medicine on that," Tate said, as he wrote down the numbers. "It looks like it's getting infected."

Compton got up again. "We've got a first aid kit. I'll be right back."

"The guy probably won't be there," Gunner said. "He goes out early and comes back late."

"How do you know this?" Wade asked.

"The Dumpster behind that motel is on my route," Gunner said.

The matter-of-fact way the man had admitted he ate garbage was shocking to Wade. He glanced at Cameron and then looked away.

"Thank you for the information," Tate said. "This is invaluable."

"You gonna go get him?"

"If he's there, he'll be in custody within the

hour," Tate said, and thought about the man sleeping the night away right under their noses.

"Why didn't you call us last night after you saw it was him?" Tate asked.

Gunner frowned, patted his pockets and then stared straight into Tate's eyes.

"Well, I'll be. I must have left my cell phone in my other pair of pants."

"Sorry. That was a thoughtless comment," Tate said, belatedly realizing he'd given his card to a man without a phone or the money to use one.

"Until you've walked in these shoes, you have no idea of the things you learn to do without."

Compton came back with another officer, who was carrying the first-aid kit.

"This officer is going to clean up your cuts and then show you out," Compton said, then glanced at the men. "Gentlemen, if you'll follow me..."

Less than a half hour later, the team was in the car, with Wade behind the wheel, following a quartet of cop cars all heading to the Riverside Motel.

As soon as Wade left her room, Jo got up. She made her plane reservations online and went to get dressed. She had one pair of jeans with her, and added a blue cotton T-shirt to go with it, put on her tennis shoes for comfort, and pulled her hair back into a ponytail before heading out the door.

She got coffee and a sweet roll down in the coffee shop in the lobby, and after picking up a city map from the concierge, she went down to the parking garage. As she drove out, she glanced up at the sky and frowned. It looked like rain. She was going to have to hurry if she wanted to get any sightseeing done.

She ate as she drove to the Arch. It wasn't until after she made her first sweep past it that she realized wherever she parked, she would still have to walk. She circled the area twice before she found a lot and pulled in.

Hershel braked and took the turn into the same lot a short distance behind her, and when he saw her suddenly wheel into a parking space, he tapped the brakes, waited until she was looking down to gather up her things and pulled up right behind her. He bolted out of the seat with the Taser in his hand and went out the sliding door on the side of the van.

The woman was getting out when she stopped and suddenly looked back inside the car. She was leaning in just as Hershel fired the Taser.

* * *

Jolene's heart nearly stopped when she felt yet another charge from the electrodes of a Taser, this time right between her shoulder blades.

In her head, she was screaming, "No, not again," but no words were coming out. The phone she'd been about to retrieve was on the seat right in front of her, but she couldn't move to pick it up. She was slumped over the steering wheel, her muscles seizing, her mind in free fall, silently screaming, screaming, screaming, but no one could hear.

When he grabbed her around the waist and dragged her across the concrete and into the van parked behind her car, her body felt like lead. She kept asking herself why she hadn't seen him. This didn't need to be happening. She was leaving tomorrow. She wanted to tell him, but she still couldn't speak. He slammed the door shut, and she watched in horror, unable to move, as he stripped the jeans off her legs, yanked the electrodes away and then pulled the T-shirt over her head.

Her head was spinning. Was she going to become yet another naked body tossed in with the storm debris? Still immobile, she could only watch in horror as he duct-taped her ankles together and then taped her hands behind her back, leaving her on her side and trussed like a Thanksgiving turkey. Then he got behind the wheel and drove away.

* * *

Hershel wouldn't look at her this time until they were safely out of the city and she was completely at his mercy. Before, he'd seen the unexpected hate and challenge in her eyes, and he had no desire to see that again. And while he hadn't seen a gun on her, he had no way of knowing for sure if one was there until he stripped her.

He drove cautiously, unwilling to call attention to himself by speeding or cutting into another lane without signaling. Traffic was heavy, but he took his time. In fact, he had all the time in the world today. There was nothing else on his agenda but making sure this woman's death mirrored what had happened to Louise as closely as possible.

When the first drops of rain suddenly hit his windshield, he was startled. He hadn't even noticed the sky getting dark. He quickly turned on the radio to check the weather and relaxed when he learned it was nothing but some rain moving through the area. His eyes narrowed angrily as he remembered Hurricane Katrina. He already knew he wouldn't melt. He'd been wet before.

"Somebody text Jo and tell her we have a good lead," Wade said as they followed the police cars through the city to the Riverside Motel.

"I already did," Cameron said. "She didn't answer."

Wade frowned. "Probably still asleep," he said, but it bothered him. Maybe she was in the shower. She would text back soon, of that he was certain.

When their motorcade reached the motel, the police cars split up, blocking both ways out of the parking lot. The cops spilled out of their cars and took a defensive stance behind their vehicles, their weapons drawn. Even though the van wasn't there, Detective Compton and two officers approached the door to room 112 and knocked.

"St. Louis Police! Open up!"

The motel manager came out of the office on the run. "What's going on here?" he yelled.

Wade stopped him before he got any closer. "We're looking for the man in room 112. Do you know where he went?"

"He checked out early this morning. Didn't say where he was going," the manager said.

Wade didn't bother to hide his frustration as he ran toward the others to pass on the bad news.

Compton groaned, while Tate stifled his disappointment. So close and once again the bastard had escaped.

"We're heading back," Compton said. "More paperwork for nothing," he added.

Wade was still uneasy that they hadn't heard from Jo, and it was beginning to sprinkle. He glanced up at the clouds and then headed for the SUV. As soon as he got in out of the rain he pulled up the tracking app to look for Jo's location. Almost immediately she popped up as on the move but still within the city limits. So she was sightseeing, as he'd suggested.

Tate got in the front seat, while Cameron slid in the back.

"Heard from Jo?"

Wade shook his head. "According to the app, she's still in the city, driving to judge by her speed. She talked about going sightseeing, but she isn't answering, and she said she'd text me when she left." He glanced down at the blip. Nothing alarming registered to make him think she was in danger. He sighed. "I guess I'm overreacting. I'll check in with her again in a few minutes."

"What's our next step?" Cameron asked.

"The police have a BOLO out on the van and tag number, although it didn't come up as registered to Hershel Inman. DMV says it belongs to some guy named Bill Blaine. This is his information," Tate said.

"Want me to give him a call?" Cameron asked.

"Yes, and we'll head back to the hotel to follow up."

Cameron made the call, and the phone rang and rang but no one picked up.

"No answer," he said, and hung up as Wade drove out of the parking lot and headed back to the hotel.

The rain was really coming down now. The windshield wipers were swiping as fast as they could, but Hershel's view of the road was still fuzzy. He hated driving in the rain.

You did it again, didn't you, Hershel? Just couldn't leave well enough alone.

His fingers tightened around the steering wheel as the whine in Louise's voice tore right up his spine like a zipper caught on his flesh.

"Shut up, Louise. Can't you see I'm trying to drive here? It's raining. You know I don't like to drive in the rain."

You're hurting me. I want you to stop. You have to stop. Everything bad that you do hurts me. I loved you, Hershel, and you're breaking my heart.

"You *still* love me, Louise. You know you do. We married for better or worse, remember? It's not my fault that things got worse."

Your fault...fault...fault...

"Louise! Why the hell do you echo?"

Because every bad thing you do pushes me farther away. If you don't stop, one day you won't hear me at all.

"Don't say that!" he snapped. The fear of losing her permanently horrified him. Dead and still nagging was better than silent and gone. He kept driving through the city, slowly edging his way west.

He was losing his grip on reality. Between the rain and Louise's threat of leaving him forever, everything was getting mixed up in his mind. Half the time, he didn't even remember he had a hostage.

Every muscle in Jo's body was spasming. Even though the electrodes were gone, she couldn't shake the tremors. He'd wrapped the duct tape so tightly around her wrists that her fingers were nearly numb. She tried to speak, but her tongue was stuck to the roof of her mouth, and Inman was talking nonstop, as if his dead wife was right beside him. From what she could tell, Louise was berating him for what he'd done, and he was trying to justify it to her.

She closed her eyes, praying Wade would wonder why she hadn't checked in after promising to text him when she left. Surely he would check the tracking app before it was too late. She didn't want to die.

Even when she finally regained some muscle control, she stayed as quiet as possible so he wouldn't realize it. She knew the chances of getting free were slim. Still, she had to try.

She arched her body backward until her fingers could reach the duct tape around her ankles. For the longest time, she couldn't find a place to start peeling the tape back, because her fingers were so numb. When she finally felt a rough edge and then something sticky, she dug at it over and over until she had an entire corner loose. Her arms were trembling, and she was willing herself not to blow this as she got a tight grip and pulled. The ripping sound nearly stopped her heart, but Hershel apparently didn't hear it, because he was still talking to himself.

Jo needed to cover up the sound and began moaning as if she was beginning to regain her speech, and to her surprise Hershel thought it was Louise and nearly swerved off the road before he got the van back under control.

"Louise? Honey? What's wrong? Do you hurt?"

Jo got a firmer grip on the duct tape and moaned again as she gave it a pull. Protected by the sound of the rain on the roof and Hershel's growing mania, she began to make headway.

Hurt? Of course I hurt. You hurt my feelings. You hurt my heart.

Jo moaned and pulled.

Hershel was almost in tears. "I'm sorry. Even when I talk nasty to you, you know I don't mean it, don't you? You're everything to me."

Jo's ability to speak was returning, but she wasn't sure if she should try to say something or just follow Inman's lead. When Hershel took a curve too fast and the van suddenly slid sideways, she took advantage of the noise to rip the rest of the tape from her ankles.

The elation of being even halfway free was heady, but the most important part was freeing her hands, otherwise she would never be able to fight.

Hershel was crying now. "Look what you did, Louise! Talking mean to me like that. I almost had a wreck. I can't think when you're upset, and this rain is loud…too loud…just like the night we climbed up on the roof. Do you remember that? I never knew you wouldn't be around to climb down."

Jo moaned again as she scooted herself into a sitting position against the wall behind his seat. Her hands were still behind her back, but she was about to turn herself into a human pretzel. The first thing she did was lean back hard against the wall and push her body up from the floor just enough to pull her hands underneath her backside. When she sat back down again, her hands were beneath her knees. She leaned forward as far as she could go so she could slide her hands under her backside, then leaned back, folded up her legs and slipped them through the loop of her arms. Her wrists were still taped, but at least they were now in front of her.

Afraid he would look up in the rearview mirror and see what she was doing, she rolled back onto her side and began using her teeth to tear the duct tape from her wrists.

Sixteen

Tate and his team were back in their suite, following up on trying to find the original owner of the van. Wade had called the number twice more and was about to give it up as a lost cause when he tried it one last time. When he heard it pick up and then a man's voice, he almost forgot what he'd been going to say.

"Hello?" the man said.

"Hello, I'm Agent Luckett with the FBI, calling to speak to Bill Blaine."

"This is Bill Blaine."

"Mr. Blaine, are you the owner of a tan 2003 Chevrolet van?"

"Oh, you must mean my father. I'm Bill Blaine, Junior. My dad was Billy Blaine. He owned that van, but he died. My mother recently sold it."

"Could you tell me the tag number, and the name of the man who bought it?"

"Yeah, sure can." Bill rattled off the tag number, then added, "Matter of fact, we bought the guy's truck off him. It had gone through the tornado that hit St. Louis, and so had he. He was really beat up. Had stitches in his face and everything. His name was Lee Parsons. We bought his truck, and he bought my mother's van. I gave the truck to my son, and he's fixing it up to drive. Please tell me it's not stolen. The title was in his name, and everything seemed on the up-and-up. The man cleaned it out from top to bottom, and then my son took it and had it detailed."

"No, no, that's not why I'm calling. Would you please describe the man?"

"Middle-aged, face all messed up like I said. Wore his hair in a brown mullet, oh, and bow-legged as all get out. Don't think I've ever seen legs that bowed."

"If you see him again, call one or both of these numbers." He gave them the number of the St. Louis police, as well as his own cell number. "His name is not Lee Parsons. He's a serial killer by the name of Hershel Inman. They call him the Storm-chaser, and he will be armed and dangerous."

"Oh, sweet Lord!" Bill cried. "My little Mama

could have got herself killed. She actually went for a ride with that man while he tried out the van."

"Thank you for your information," Wade said, and as soon as he disconnected, he jumped up with a grin. "We have a name! Inman's been living under the alias Lee Parsons. Now we might be able to actually track some of his money to other aliases. I need to call Jo."

Cameron had gone to get some ice and was coming back into the room as Wade was relaying information.

"What's going on?" he asked.

"Looks like we have an alias Inman has been using."

"That's amazing!"

Wade was still smiling as he put in the call to Jo, but when she didn't answer, he frowned.

"Have either of you heard from Jo today?"

Tate shook his head. Cameron followed suit.

Wade's heart sank. "Something's wrong."

Just as he said it, there was a knock on the door.

"That's her!" he said, and ran to answer, but it wasn't. It was Detective Compton, and the look on his face was grim.

"Is Agent Jolene Luckett here, by any chance?"

Wade felt the floor shift beneath his feet. "No, why?"

Compton held up a purse in one hand and a phone in the other.

"Her purse was on the street beside the open door of a black SUV, and this phone was on the seat."

"No, no, no," Wade mumbled as he grabbed his phone and quickly pulled up the locator app. "Oh, God… Oh, no… She's not in the city anymore. Wait! Where did you find the SUV?"

"Close to the Arch."

Wade said, "Tate. Get the keys. According to this, she's close to thirty miles outside of the city. He's got her. Inman's got her."

Compton frowned. "Are you saying your serial killer has her?"

"He said she didn't belong," Wade said, rushing to grab his jacket and weapon. "Hurry up, damn it. We've got to get moving!"

Compton looked at the phone. "You mean you can track her with this?"

Tate asked Compton another question instead of answering. "Can you tell where they are?"

Compton frowned. "Looks like that blip is somewhere in Robertsville State Park. Parts of it are pretty rough. You need to know where you're going or you'll get yourself lost pretty fast."

"Call the state police. Give them my name and phone number, and have them meet us there."

Compton handed them Jo's things and pulled out his phone as he left.

Wade tossed Jo's belongings on a chair and ran out the door, with Tate and Cameron right behind him.

Seventeen

Hershel was lost. He'd missed the turn to the location he'd found yesterday and was driving aimlessly, momentarily oblivious to why he was even in the park or the fact that Jolene Luckett was in the van.

All of a sudden a man shot out of the trees on an ATV and sped across the road in front of him. Hershel slammed on the brakes and in the process hit his head on the steering wheel. The pain seemed to bring the world back in focus as he grabbed his forehead, cursing every other breath.

"Stupid-ass four-wheeler shouldn't even be allowed. Nobody paying a damn bit of attention and—"

He glanced up in the mirror, saw Jolene's half-naked body all curled up with her back to the seat and grunted. It startled him to realize he'd completely forgotten he had her.

And just like that, he was back on task. He looked around at where he was, vaguely remembered the dead tree up on the right and knew he'd driven too far. But the road was narrow and the shoulders all mud, so there was no place to turn around. The last thing he wanted to do was get stuck, so he took his foot off the brake and started driving, looking again for a place where he could drive far enough off the road to dump a body.

Jo knew his focus had shifted. He was all business again, no talking to himself or conversations with Louise. She had been pulling at the duct tape around her wrists in desperation, but now the sounds could alert him to what she was doing. There was only one layer of tape left, and she didn't know if she was strong enough to pull it apart with her wrists, but she was about to find out.

She was almost ready to try when the van swerved off the blacktop, and began slipping and sliding down an unpaved road. Panicked that he was going to stop at any second, she began straining as hard as she could, trying to pull her hands apart.

Hershel caught her moving in the rearview mirror and hit the brakes. He was in the back and straddling her when she rolled over onto her back and kicked him hard in the groin.

Hershel screamed, then dropped to his knees with his hands on his balls, afraid if he let go they would fall off in his hands.

"I'm gonna kill you for that!" he shrieked.

Jo was still trying to get her wrists free. She was tearing at the tape with her teeth and pulling as hard as she could. Hershel opened the sliding door, and even as she was kicking, grabbed her by the foot and dragged her out into the rain.

Her head hit the side of the van as she fell out and hit the ground. Hershel's curses were lost in the downpour as he tried to grab her arm, but she swung her hands upward and caught him under the chin with both fists.

He staggered backward, grunting in sudden pain. It was obvious he couldn't best her without a weapon, so he realized he had to get back to the van for the Taser. Just as he turned her loose and leaped, the duct tape on her wrists came free. Jolene was on her feet when he turned and aimed.

"Oh, hell no, not again!" she cried, and bolted. Her legs didn't want to work right, but she ran anyway and was soon out of range.

Hershel raged as he threw the Taser back in the

van and got the rifle out instead. He slammed the door shut, pocketed his keys and took off running, following her muddy footprints through the trees.

Wade drove because he wouldn't have been able to sit quietly. About ten blocks from the hotel Tate got a call. When he hung up, his mouth was grim.

"Watch for the first cop car. They're running hot to help get us out of the city faster."

Despite the rain, Cameron had the window down to listen for the first siren. "There!" he shouted, pointing at the patrol car that shot out into the intersection and then turned sharply so it was now in front.

Wade accelerated, riding the cop car's bumper. A few blocks farther up another white St. Louis police car cut in ahead of the first, and one by one more cars joined them, continuing to clear the way until there was a caravan of St. Louis patrol cars leading the agents out of the city.

Tate had their GPS linked to the blip on his phone, and when they cleared the city and the cop cars peeled off and they were once again on their own, Wade knew where to go.

"What's happening?" Wade asked.

Tate's gaze was fixed on the blip. "It's moving slower. I think she must be on foot."

"God, oh, God, don't do this to me again," Wade whispered, picturing Inman dragging her into the woods to kill her—unless he already had and was just dragging her body away to hide it. He pressed his foot harder on the gas, and the SUV fishtailed before grabbing traction and speeding ahead.

Jo had no idea where she was, but she just kept running. Inman was obviously behind her, because she could hear him cursing. Her legs were getting stronger, even though she could feel her muscles jerking from time to time as she continued to run. The trees were thick, the underbrush thicker. She'd long since blocked out the pain on the bottoms of her bare feet. The rain was cold and blinding, frequently forcing her to stagger as she ducked to keep from running headlong into a branch. The rain was in Hershel's favor, making tracking her footprints easy. She needed to run faster, so that the rain had time to wash them away.

One moment she was running, and then the next her foot hit something slick and she was flat on her back, staring up into the falling rain, unable to breathe because she'd knocked the wind out of her lungs.

Help me, Jesus.

She grabbed at her belly and felt the scar.

I lost my baby, and I almost lost Wade. I'm not losing him again.

She made herself roll from her back to her stomach, then pushed herself up onto her hands and knees. The effort made her cough, and then she took a deep hungry breath as her lungs inflated. It was all the impetus she needed to get up, but she staggered and had to grab on to a limb until the world stopped spinning. A few moments later, with her chest still burning, she took off at a lope, but as soon as she got her strength back she stretched out into a hard, mindless run.

Hershel was manic. She'd gotten away from him again. It was women, always women, who brought him bad luck. He had to put an end to this once and for all, but that meant catching her first.

He ran with his eye on her tracks, carrying his rifle loosely in his hands. All he needed was one good look at her and she would be down. Twice he caught a glimpse of her bare back and arms, but both times the trees were so thick that she was immediately out of sight.

A tree limb caught in his wig and pulled it off his head. He kept running.

The places where he'd taken out the stitches were stinging.

He tried to duck under the overhanging limbs, but some of them slapped his face, making it burn.

His clothes were so wet now that they actually weighted him down, and his shoes were full of water. The Luckett woman was barefoot and nearly naked; no wonder he couldn't catch her.

The rain! It was all this damned rain!

When he looked down again to check for her prints, his heart nearly stopped. The rain was washing them away. Since he was moving slower and she was moving faster, her tracks would soon be gone.

He tried to speed up, but he didn't have the stamina. When he finally realized he couldn't find a single footprint, he was so enraged he emptied the rifle into the air.

Jo's heart nearly stopped when she heard the shots. She quickly changed direction and lengthened her stride, ignoring the burning in her muscles and the pain in her side.

Thunder suddenly rolled above her head, and when she heard the loud crack of lightning, she knew it had struck somewhere nearby. She couldn't keep running forever, and her body, weakened by the Taser hit, was already giving out. She had to get out of the weather. She needed a place to hide.

Within seconds she went down again, this time

tripping over a root. She fell forward, hitting knees-first and catching herself with her hands. Every muscle in her body was trembling from exhaustion. The rain was hammering on the back of her head and running down her face, blinding her to everything but what was right before her. She moaned in frustration, then, as she slowly lifted her head, realized she was looking straight into the brush-obscured mouth of a small dark cave.

She crawled forward, shoved aside the bushes in front of the opening and looked in. She couldn't see how far back it went, and she didn't hear any warning growls, so she took a chance and went inside.

Almost immediately, the downpour was muffled. It felt good to be out of the rain, but she needed to make sure Inman couldn't find her.

She pulled at the bushes until there was no sign that anyone had shoved through them and then watched until the rain washed away the last traces of where she'd been. Her heart was pounding, her muscles quivering. She felt like throwing up. Instead, she curled up on her side, laid her head on her arm and closed her eyes. The last thought she had was that Wade would find her. He had to.

Hershel was done. He'd reached the limit of his endurance, and now he needed to find his way out.

He did a one-eighty and began heading back as quickly as he could manage, following his own footprints until they'd all washed away. Then he kept on going, telling himself that he would eventually find the van. All he had to do was keep moving forward.

The rain was beginning to let up a little, which meant the front was passing through. When he was too winded even to jog, he would walk while constantly looking for any sign that would tell him he was on the right path. When he finally came out on a road and saw his van less than a hundred yards up, he was so elated that he ran all the way there. He got inside, and without hesitation started the engine and took off. He had no option but to get as far away from there as possible, and as fast as he could. Once Jolene Luckett was found, they would know what he was driving, and it wouldn't take them long to find out where he'd bought it, and then they would know about Lee Parsons. He had to call the banks where Taliaferro had transferred his money, consolidate the amounts into the nearest of them, withdraw it all and, as the cowboys always said, "Get the hell out of Dodge" before the feds found it—and him.

He didn't know where the road he was on would lead if he kept going, but he knew if he headed back the way he'd come, he could get out. He began looking for a place to turn around.

"How much farther?" Wade asked as he negotiated a particularly sharp curve, then accelerated up a steep hill.

Tate was calculating distance.

"Right now, as the crow flies, she's at least two miles away. By road, at least eight, maybe... Oh, no!"

"What?" Wade said.

Tate's voice was shaking. "The blip is stationary."

"You mean she's not moving?"

Tate nodded grimly.

"Oh, God, do not do this to me again," Wade muttered and kept driving, following the directions from the GPS. At one point, when they realized they'd missed a turnoff and had to backtrack, he was ready to hit something. When they left the blacktop for a muddy, unpaved road, he put the SUV into four-wheel drive and kept going. Almost thirty minutes passed and the rain was beginning to let up when all of a sudden Tate yelled, "Stop!"

Wade hit the brakes. The SUV slid sideways in the mud and then came to a halt at the edge of the road. "What the hell?" he yelled.

Tate pointed. "She's that way. We go on foot from here."

Wade killed the engine, grabbed his phone and jumped out. "Just because she's not moving, it doesn't mean anything," Wade said as he checked his weapon and pocketed an extra ammo clip.

"You're right," Tate said. "She could just be hiding."

Tate's phone signaled a text. He left the app to read it.

"Who was that?" Wade asked.

"The state police are on the way."

"Are they sending a chopper?" Cameron asked.

"Trees are too dense. They can't see anything from the air."

Wade glanced at his phone one last time to make sure he was heading in the right direction and took off into the trees at a dead run, quickly outdistancing his partners and disappearing from sight in the thick forest.

Hershel had to drive almost a half mile farther before he found a place to turn around, then he began retracing his route. When he came over a small hill and saw the dark SUV parked on the side of the road below, he nearly lost it.

It was the feds! How the fuck had they gotten here? How would they know where she was if—

And then it hit him. They'd tracked her. It must have been something in her clothes. He hit the brakes, crawled into the back of the van and gathered up every stitch of her clothing and her shoes, and threw it all out into the bushes. He didn't see them anywhere and hoped to God they were somewhere in the woods, looking for her.

He drove down the hill with his heart in his throat, and when he got to their vehicle, he saw their tracks leading off into the trees. He tapped the brakes and stopped, staring for a few moments at their car, then all of a sudden he was out of the van and running. He took out his pocketknife and dropped down, then scooted beneath the SUV, made a small cut in the brake lines and then crawled out so fast he bumped his head.

He jumped back into his van and started to speed away, and then a thought occurred to him. Instead of leaving, he drove a bit farther up the hill, then parked behind a thick stand of bushes and settled down to wait. He knew it was a risk, but it was his choice. It also wasn't how he'd planned to end the Stormchaser's quest, but it was as good a time as any. He was about to turn himself into bait.

* * *

Wade had been running for more than twenty minutes, stopping more than once to vector her location and adjust his own, grateful that the CIA bug was powerful enough to be picked up in such a remote location.

After a while all he could hear was the repetitive thud of his feet on the ground and rain dripping from the leaves.

Dozens of memories ran through his mind. He remembered their first Christmas together in that cold apartment in D.C. No matter how high they set the heat, the rooms never got warm. Remembered her first big commendation and how proud he'd been—and that the love they'd made afterward had made Sammy.

He glanced down again at his phone, checking to make sure he was still going in the right direction, and couldn't see the screen. He wiped his eyes with the heels of his hands. No crying. Not now. Not yet. Not unless he had a reason.

When his chest began to hurt, it took him a moment to identify it as an emotional pain, rather than a physical one. He was so damned scared that by the time he found her she would be laid out like all the Stormchaser's other victims. If she was, he would die.

He'd been on foot for almost an hour, and when he looked down and saw how close he was to the blip, he realized that if she was alive she would be able to hear him. He stopped to catch his breath and then started calling her name.

"Jo! Jo! Where are you?"

The first conscious thought Jolene had before she opened her eyes was that she smelled dirt. Then she looked around, and for a brief moment the low ceiling and enclosed walls convinced her she'd been buried alive. Her heart nearly stopped as she struggled to get up, and as she did, her vision cleared enough for her to realize she could see daylight in front of her. That was when she remembered. She was in a cave.

She tried to sit up, but the ceiling was too low, so she stayed on her side, watching the narrow view of the world from her hiding place. It had quit raining. She could hear the faint drip of water falling from the leaves onto the forest floor. Her body ached, and what didn't ache was stinging instead. She shivered. Her bra and panties were muddy but drying, and she hoped to God Wade found her before dark. What if some animal used this for a lair? She didn't want to be here when that happened. When she began hearing voices, her first thought was of Inman, still looking for her and still talking to Louise.

Filled with horror at the possibility that she'd run all this way for nothing and was still going to die, she scooted farther away from the front of the cave and held her breath, her heart hammering, listening to the approach. Then she heard Wade calling her name.

Her relief was so great she began to shake. "Here! I'm here!" she shouted, and began to crawl out.

Before she could move, Wade was on his hands and knees coming in, a dark silhouette against the thin gray. But she knew his shape, and she knew his voice, and when he reached toward her, she grabbed his hand, holding on for dear life as he pulled her out into the light.

"You found me!" she said, and collapsed.

Wade caught her in his arms.

Tate raced up then and threw his rain poncho on the ground, and they eased her down on it.

Wade shed his jacket and pulled off his shirt. He began dressing her as if she was a child, helping her with one sleeve, then the other, as her body began to shake.

"Shock," Tate said, then looked down at her

feet in disbelief. "Sweet Lord, Jolene. Your feet are in shreds."

"I got away," she said, and began rocking where she sat. "He came up behind me, shot me in the back with that effing Taser again, and threw me in the back of the van. He stripped off my clothes, duct-taped my hands behind my back, duct-taped my ankles and took off like a bat out of hell."

"You are amazing," Tate said as he briefly touched the top of her head. "One tough lady for sure."

She sat silently, watching the play of emotions on Wade's face as he wiped the dirt from her cheek, and when he stopped they locked gazes. His eyes were filled with tears and her chin was trembling. One wrong word from someone and they would both have been bawling. He touched her face, then her lips, leaned forward and kissed her.

"How the hell did you get free?" Tate asked.

She almost smiled. "Pulled a Houdini on him while he was having an argument with his dead wife, and the rest was pure luck."

Wade stood up and took off his shoes so he could remove his socks. "Guys, I need your socks, too."

They didn't question why as they shed their shoes and handed over their socks.

Wade put the socks on her feet, one pair at a time, until she had three layers of knit fabric between her and the ground.

"It's the best we can do for now. I'd give you my shoes, but they wouldn't stay on your feet," he said.

"I can walk," she said as she started to stand up.

"No. We'll carry you piggyback, trading off until we get down to the car. You're not setting a foot on the ground."

"I'm too heavy," she protested.

"We can all bench-press more than you weigh, and we'll take turns, so that argument won't hold water. I go first because I don't want to let go of you."

Tate touched her shoulder. "Then me."

"You don't look so heavy to me," Cameron said.

Jo was in tears as Wade helped her stand up. He slipped his poncho over her head, then put his jacket back on and squatted just enough for her to climb on his back. She did, wrapping her arms around his neck and then locking her hands just below his collarbone.

"Lead the way, guys," Wade said. "We're bringing up the rear."

"For which you should all be grateful, so I will not moon you as we go," she muttered.

They laughed, and it was the perfect moment

that broke the horror of what she'd gone through and Wade's fear that they would be too late.

"Are you okay back there, honey?"

"Yes." When the others were moving away, she leaned forward and whispered in his ear, "I love you, Wade Luckett."

"I love you, too."

She kissed the back of his ear, laid her head against his and closed her eyes. She was tired—so tired. All she wanted was to go home.

Eighteen

Going downhill was faster than going up. Even though they were carrying her, they made it back to their car in less than an hour. All three of the men had carried her twice, and she was on Wade's back for the third time when they came out of the woods.

"There's the car," Tate said, pointing up the road.

Jo saw it and held on that much tighter to Wade.

He could feel the tension in her arms. She had to be in pain, both from the injuries on her feet and from the second Taser attack, and yet she hadn't said a word.

"Just a little bit more, honey, and we're safe," he said.

She heard him, but there was no need to comment. She was already safe, and had been since the moment she'd seen his face.

They were almost at the SUV when they heard the sound of tires on gravel. Tate was the first to turn around. When he saw the van coming out of the trees, his reaction was shock. "Is that Inman's van?"

Wade turned around.

"It *is* him! Let me down, Wade!" Jo cried, and then slid out of his grasp.

"Wade! Give me the car keys!" Cameron yelled.

Wade hit the button to unlock the doors and then tossed Cameron the keys.

Within moments they were tossing all their gear in the back and getting in.

Wade got into the backseat with Jo. Cameron took the driver's seat and Tate rode passenger. He was already trying to get through to the state police when Cameron began turning the car around.

It was about an hour into his wait when Hershel chickened out. He'd planned to lure them into chasing him at high speed and then witnessing the fiery crash when their brakes went out. But with an FBI agent missing, the woods would surely be crawling with cops before long. It was going to be dark soon and he couldn't wait any longer. He started the van and drove out of hiding onto the main road a couple of hundred yards up from their SUV just as they came walking out of the woods.

He braked. "There you are," he said, watching as they turned toward the sound of his tires sliding on mud and gravel. He saw their reactions to his presence and smiled. They would chase him. Perfect. If he got them going fast enough, he might get lucky enough to watch them die.

The race was on.

He took off, making sure not to lose them until they got themselves turned around to follow, and then, once he saw them come over a hill in his rearview mirror, he floored it.

Tate was on the phone with the state police, who were finally nearing the entrance to the park after being held up by a multi-car accident on the interstate. Once he apprised them of the situation, they sent several cars in and began setting up a roadblock at the exit, leaving Tate and his team to flush Hershel straight into their trap.

"This is crazy," Jo insisted. "He should have been long gone. What was he doing up there? Why did he wait?"

"Who knows?" Wade said. "Buckle up. This is going to be a wild ride."

Cameron had left the SUV in four-wheel drive. His jaw was set, his focus on keeping the van in sight while staying safe on the muddy, rut-filled road. He was finally beginning to gain on the van when it hit blacktop. Seconds later it disappeared.

"Son of a bitch," Wade muttered, and reached for Jolene's hand. "Don't lose him, Cameron. Don't lose him."

The moment Cameron drove off the dirt and onto the blacktop he shifted out of four-wheel drive and stomped on the accelerator. They came over a hill just as the van was disappearing over the next one.

"It's okay," Tate said. "This vehicle maneuvers better than a van in a high-speed chase. Either he'll go off the road, or the state police will stop him. Just keep pushing him."

But Jo felt anxious, and it had nothing to do with their speed.

"I'm telling you. This doesn't feel right. He had hours to get away from us. Why didn't he? Why on earth would he hang around?"

Tate looked over his shoulder at Jolene. "What do you know that we don't?"

"Nothing. It just doesn't fit. He's been so damn careful to stay ahead of everything we do, and now this?"

"She has a point," Wade said. "Why would—"

"Oh, shit!"

Cameron's outburst ended the conversation.

"What's wrong?" Tate asked.

Cameron gripped the wheel as they flew around a downhill curve.

"We don't have any brakes."

Wade groaned. "Now we know why he waited."

"He wants to watch us die," Tate said.

Jo leaned back and tightened her seat belt, then reached for Wade's hand again.

Wade was furious. "Then let's make damn sure the bastard is rudely disappointed," he said. Unbuckling his seat belt, he scooted next to Jo and took her into his arms.

"Buckle your seat belt," she begged.

"I'm not going to sit there when you're here," he said. "Look! I'm buckling up again." He reached for the center belt, matching his actions to his words.

Tate was talking to the state police again when Cameron saw the sharp curve ahead. He looked at the speedometer, and then took a deep breath. "Hang on, everybody. We're not going to make this curve. Take a fast vote. Do we go off the mountain, or do we hit it?"

"Well, shit," Wade said, and wrapped his arms tighter around Jolene.

* * *

Hershel kept watching the rearview mirror as he drove. He had a gut feeling there would be cops waiting for him at the park entrance, and an even stronger feeling that the brakes on the agents' SUV had to be gone by now. He needed to take the upcoming turn or lose his only chance to get away.

If you hadn't stayed to watch more people die, you would already be safe...safe...safe...

"Thank you for the update, Louise. I can always count on you to state the obvious."

Regretting the fact that he was going to miss the fireworks, he took the turn off the blacktop onto a well-graveled road and floored it. According to the map he'd been studying while he waited, he could take this road south out of the park and eventually angle back east until he hit I-55. His plan was to stay on it straight to the Cape Girardeau exit, catch a plane and disappear.

He had just topped a small hill when he heard a loud explosion and braked. He looked back across the trees to his right as a thick black column of smoke began rising into the air.

"See you in hell, you sorry bastards," he muttered and then looked at himself in the mirror.

He was a soldier who'd been at war with the people who hurt him. He had the scars and the

PTSD to show for it, but he'd taken them down. He'd dodged the law and all the storms God could throw at him, and he'd proven he was the smarter man. But without the team to challenge him, he didn't have the heart for this anymore, and he'd made his point. They were dead. Louise was dead. It was time to move on.

Everyone braced for impact as Cameron turned the wheel sharply to the right and headed into the side of the mountain, the lesser of two evils.

The car began to skid. The scent of burning rubber seared their nostrils, and then everything seemed to happen in slow motion. The car was turning and sliding and turning and sliding. The hood was aimed straight at the mountain, but the wheels were turned as far to the right as Cameron could hold them. They were only twenty-five feet from impact when the car suddenly spun. Instead of going headfirst into the mountain, the driver's side hit the unyielding rock. A thousand-plus pounds of metal ran into an immovable object at almost a hundred miles an hour.

Dazed by the impact, Cameron was still hanging on to the steering wheel when smoke began pouring out from under the hood.

Tate's head was bleeding as he tried to unbuckle his seat belt.

Wade was already scrambling to get Jo out. "Tate! Are you all right?" he shouted, and shook his partner's shoulder to make him focus.

"Yes, I think…"

"I smell gas. We have to get out. Get Cameron!"

Like Cameron, Jo was barely conscious as Wade unbuckled her seat belt and dragged her out of the car.

"Hurry! It's going to blow!" Wade yelled as he carried Jo to the far side of the road. "Get down and stay down!" he said, and ran back to help Tate and Cameron.

Tate was still trying not to pass out, but he had Cameron's seat belt undone when Wade appeared.

"I've got him, Tate. Run!"

Tate staggered backward as Wade dragged Cameron out of the car, threw him over his shoulder in a fireman's carry and started running away, with Tate at his heels.

They had just reached Jolene and set Cameron down when the car exploded. Tate grabbed Cameron, who was trying to sit up, and dragged him farther away. Wade had thrown himself onto Jo's body only seconds before the car exploded.

Fire and debris flew in all directions, but they were safe.

Once the fire stopped falling out of the sky, Tate sat up to take a head count. Cameron was shaky but coming to, and Wade had Jolene held tightly in his arms.

"Thanks, Wade," Tate said. "We wouldn't have gotten out in time if you hadn't come back."

Wade wasn't worrying about kudos. "Jo has a knot on her head. Check Cameron. They both hit the windows pretty hard. We might be looking at concussions."

Cameron felt his head, just above his ear. "There's a knot, but I'm not too dizzy," he said.

Jo moaned as she began coming to. "Did we die?"

Wade pulled her closer. "No, baby. We're all still here."

She tried to sit up and pushed the hair from her eyes. "Where's Inman?"

"That is probably going to become the epitaph on my tombstone," Tate said.

Jo groaned. "He got away?"

Tate began looking for his phone, then looked back at the flames still shooting in the air.

"I think my phone was in the car."

"Here's mine," Wade said.

Tate called the state police one more time.

"This is Agent Benton. Do you have Inman in custody?"

"He never exited the park, and the men I sent in haven't driven up on him yet. You should be seeing them anytime now."

"He cut our brake lines. We crashed the car and need an ambulance or three."

The officer was all business. "I'll notify the park service, as well as the state highway patrol. We had already issued a BOLO for the van and driver when we left Springfield, and we have an ambulance on-site. It's on the way."

"Thank you," Tate said, then hung up and handed Wade the phone. "Inman never made it to the main gate. He's either hiding out in the park or he knew a different way out and is long gone."

Wade pocketed the phone in disgust. "This makes me sick to my stomach."

"It's difficult to catch a serial killer with an evolving agenda," Tate said. "Just when you think you know what you're looking for, he changes the game and the rules."

"Will you have to stay here?" Jo asked.

Tate frowned. "I doubt it. We'll go back to work, and when the next natural disaster occurs, we'll wait and see if he's still on the move."

"I hear sirens," Cameron said.

"The state police," Wade said, then groaned as he pushed himself to his feet. "There has to be something to salvage from this mess."

"We know one of his aliases now," Tate reminded him.

Jo was pulling down the hem of Wade's shirt and poncho, trying to hide as much of her long legs as possible.

He saw her and frowned. "They'll have a blanket for you to wrap up in."

She sighed. "Good. I wasn't crazy about mooning the state police, too."

"Just stay put. You're not walking on those feet, and it will take the ambulance a while to get here."

Hours later, the team was finally leaving the E.R.

Jo was in a wheelchair, with both feet in bandages, wearing a pair of donated scrubs from the surgery unit. The knot on her head had turned into a bruise, as had the one above Cameron's ear. Everyone but Wade had a slight concussion, which left him in charge.

They rode back to the hotel in a taxi, grateful that it was night. They made it through the lobby and up to their rooms without drawing anything but a few curious glances.

Tate went straight into the suite with Wade's phone to talk to the Director.

Cameron began writing a report, while Wade took Jo across the hall to her room.

She crawled out of the wheelchair onto the bed and rolled over onto her back with a sigh.

"I got up with every intention of seeing St. Louis from the Arch today and, as my daddy used to say, nearly 'bought the farm' instead. There were a couple of times when I didn't think we were going to make it."

Wade sat down on the side of the bed. He kept looking at the floor instead of at her, and she could tell he was bothered about something.

"What's wrong?"

"We went to all that trouble to bug you, and then I nearly let him kill you anyway."

She frowned. "No way! I'm the one who got hit by a Taser twice by the same perp and didn't see it coming either time. I'll never hear the end of this at headquarters."

He reached for her hand. "I'm sorry. You weren't returning texts or calls, so I checked on your location, and both times it showed you were still in the city. I should have known something was wrong."

"Why? Because you're suddenly psychic?"

"No, but—"

She tugged on his hand and pulled him down beside her.

"No buts, Wade. I'm just so glad we're alive that I could weep."

"Whatever you do, don't cry," he muttered.

She smiled as she pulled his head down onto her shoulder. "You know what?"

"What?" he asked.

"I'm starving."

He was still for a moment, and then he raised his head and grinned.

"I'll order food, and while we're eating, we can decide who's moving. Are you moving in with me, or am I moving in with you?"

"Are you still in our house in Virginia?" she asked.

"Yes. I couldn't bring myself to leave. I know it was where we were the saddest, but it was also where some of the happiest times of my life happened."

Her eyes welled. "My apartment is a sad place. Nothing good ever happened there. I choose going back to you."

"You're not going back. You're coming home, and we're sealing it with a kiss."

When he centered his mouth on her lips, it released the last of his guilt and fears.

Because of Jo's, Tate's and Cameron's concussions, flying was put on hold. By the time they got back to D.C. a couple of days had passed and the Bureau was abuzz with the latest on Inman. It was getting the Lee Parsons alias that had turned the tide. They'd tracked the missing money from the New Orleans bank to banks in Dallas, Seattle and Chicago, with all three accounts under different names.

But by the time they identified the accounts, they were already empty. With unlimited money, Inman could buy any identity, use any disguise and disappear. If he never killed again, the Stormchaser was about to get away with murder.

Reston, Virginia

Wade pulled up in the driveway of his house and then looked over at Jo and saw a muscle jerking at the corner of her mouth. She was trying not to cry. His heart skipped a beat. Maybe this hadn't been such a good idea after all.

"You okay?"

She smiled through the welling tears.

"I'm more than okay. What I am is grateful, grateful you didn't quit on me, and grateful for this second chance."

Wade leaned across the seat and kissed her.

"Ditto that, my love. Let's grab our bags and get inside. It looks like rain."

And he was right. Within seconds of walking into the house, the heavens opened. Jo stopped just inside the doorway, set down her suitcase and let the vibe of the house settle within her.

Wade hadn't changed a thing about the décor or the way the furniture was arranged. In a way, it almost felt like she'd only been away for a long trip and was just now coming home. Thunder rumbled overhead as she reached for Wade's hand.

"I'm taking this as a good sign that we're starting over here. Rain washes everything clean," she said.

He took her in his arms. He was still having nightmares about how close he'd come to losing her to the Stormchaser.

"Everything is good here," he said softly.

She leaned back far enough so that she could see his face.

"Yes, everything is good," she echoed.

He could see his own reflection in her eyes,

and only after it began to blur did he realize she was crying.

"Don't cry, sweetheart. I can't take it," he whispered.

"If we make another baby, I promise I will shelter it with my life."

"Trust me when I tell you that we will make love and babies and loads of happiness here, Jolene."

She sighed, then leaned her forehead against his chest.

"I'm tired. Can we look at the house together later? Right now all I want to do is crawl in bed and sleep for a week."

"You've seen the house before anyway," Wade said. "I vote for bed."

Jo laughed. God, but she did love this man.

Tijuana, Mexico

Hershel rolled into Tijuana in a Volkswagen Beetle under the name Paul Leibowitz, with a suitcase full of clothes and what he called his bag of tricks hidden in the lining. He was there for his first appointment with the plastic surgeon to remove the damaged skin from the burns that scarred his face.

He shaved what little hair he had left, dyed his eyebrows and the small thin mustache he'd grown to a nice matte black, and was on the way to losing the gut he'd carried for the past thirty years. In the few weeks since St. Louis, he'd lost nearly twenty pounds and was working toward at least twenty more before he quit. The weight loss had completely changed the shape of his face, and once he lost the rest he was considering a neck lift as well, to get rid of the flabby skin.

He went into the doctor's office dressed in white slacks and a black shirt with tiny white pinstripes, black sandals and a gold pinky ring with an emerald the size of a pat of butter. He was as far removed from Hershel Inman, Bill Carter and Lee Parsons as a man could be. The last gift Conrad Taliaferro had given him was this identity, with a warning never to call him again. He considered it a good deal.

The doctor came into the examining room well aware that he had an American client, and quickly shifted his language from Spanish to English.

"Good morning, Mr. Leibowitz. I understand you are here about your burn scars."

"Yes," Hershel said. "I am retiring in your beautiful country and would like to be able to enjoy the sun and the beach."

"How did you acquire your scars, if I may ask?" the doctor asked.

"At a family barbecue. The wind blew some of the liquid fire starter onto my face just as someone lit the fire."

"And you have had no plastic surgery on these scars before?"

"No. No money, but now I'm using some of my retirement package to have it done."

The doctor nodded.

Within the hour they'd agreed on an appointment for the surgery in a week to the day. That just gave Hershel time to find a little place to recuperate in afterward. And then, when he was well, he was moving to Lake Chapala, to an area he and Louise had picked out where aging Americans came to retire. It was the last plan they had made, and he didn't have a better idea.

The fact that she'd been completely silent since he'd left Missouri had been worrisome, but she'd warned him that she was going to leave him, so he assumed it had finally happened. In a way, he surprised himself by feeling glad she'd finally given up staying earthbound and gone on to her glory. It was easier on his conscience and his ears.

A week later he was in recovery and coming out from under anesthesia. The doctor was standing nearby, and there was a nurse on either side of the bed. When the doctor saw his patient's eyes opening, he smiled.

"Hello, Mr. Leibowitz! Your surgery is over, and I am pleased with how everything went. Once the bandages come off and the swelling subsides, I think you will be very happy with the results."

Hershel nodded and drifted back to sleep. As long as the scars were gone, or at least minimized, and his face looked different, the rest of his life should be a piece of cake.

Two months later a crazy weather pattern spawned tornadoes across the Upper Midwest. When it did, the team back in D.C. held their breaths, waiting for a text that never came. And while there were deaths from some of the storms, none were attributed to anything but Mother Nature.

A month later, an unusual amount of rainfall in Georgia caused flooding all along the Chattahoochee River. People were stranded in their houses, and some of those living along the river drowned when their houses fell into the flood as the banks washed out from under them.

Again they waited, but the text didn't come and none of the deaths turned out to be murder. They began to believe the ordeal was finally over.

"Do you think he's dead?" Jo asked one night at dinner.

Wade shrugged. "No way to know, but we can hope. In the meantime, would you please pass the scalloped potatoes? They're so good I could eat the whole thing."

She smiled as she watched him dig in and thought about how close she'd come to losing all this.

Reston, Virginia

A few weeks later Jo and Wade were watching television when the Stormchaser case came up on an unsolved-mysteries show.

Wade promptly flipped the channel.

Jo eyed the look on his face. "What's wrong?" she asked.

"It's a sore subject," he said. "I'd like to think the bastard died and is rotting in a cemetery under one of his damn aliases."

"But you don't think so?"

"Until I know for sure, I won't feel settled about this."

She threw a pillow at him, then laughed when he growled and pulled her down onto the floor, where they promptly made love.

The one positive about all of Jo's narrow escapes was that she took nothing for granted. Every day with Wade was a gift, and finding the way through a new relationship was easy, once you knew the route.

It was simple actually, all about trust, an abiding love, and always giving Wade the last cookie.

Epilogue

Lake Chapala, Mexico

Hershel had settled in quite nicely at Lake Chapala, and once he'd finished his weight-loss project and had the extra skin removed from his cheeks and neck, he was a completely different man. In fact, he'd gotten so immersed in his new identity that there were days when the bad parts of his past seemed as if they had happened to another man.

But there was an anniversary coming up that meant a brief return to the States. Louise had died on August 31, 2005, and he hadn't missed a year since of putting flowers on her grave. Despite his reluctance to set foot back on United States soil, he felt it would be bad luck to miss what had become a tradition.

So, two days before the date, he packed up his

carry-on with a change of clothes and a couple of his favorite hats, loaded it into his little Volkswagen and drove into nearby Guadalajara. He caught a flight north to New Orleans, which was just a direct hop across the Gulf of Mexico, and got a room for the night in one of the local hotels.

Within hours of his arrival the familiar sounds of the city, the scent of pralines cooking in the French Quarter and the aromas of Cajun cuisine wafting out of the nearby restaurants made him homesick. He tasted the food, drank the wine and ate a solitary dinner.

When he saw a couple he recognized, his heart skipped a beat, but they only looked at him as if he was a stranger and kept walking. That was when he knew he was safe.

The next morning was the day. August 31. He dressed in a pair of pale blue slacks and a blue and white floral shirt, and walked to a nearby florist to get the flowers before hailing a cab to take him to the cemetery.

As they drove through the gates, Hershel pointed to a road leading off to the left.

"Take that road, and then take the third right. After that, I'll tell you where to stop."

"Yes, sir," the driver said, and drove slowly past the tombstones and mausoleums.

A few minutes later Hershel leaned forward. "Stop at this corner. I'll walk from here."

The driver stopped. "I'll be waiting right here for you, sir, when you're ready to leave."

Hershel nodded, got out with the flowers and started walking.

I almost didn't recognize you.

He stumbled, then looked around nervously as he lowered his voice.

"Louise?"

Who else did you think it would be? Of course it's me.

"What are you doing here? I thought you were gone," he said.

I was thinking the same exact thing of you. You shouldn't be here. You need to go back to Lake Chapala.

"I will as soon as I put these flowers on your grave." He reached the gravesite and then quickly put them down in front of the aboveground tomb.

I remember flowers. I wish I could smell stuff down here again.

Hershel frowned. "You can't smell?"

It doesn't matter. Go home, Hershel. Go home... home...home...

He turned around and headed back to the cab, and the closer he got, the faster he went. By the time he got inside, he was breathless. "Take me back to the Marriott."

"Yes, sir. Right away, sir," the driver said.

Once back at the hotel, Hershel began to pack. He had an early morning flight tomorrow and didn't want to be late. When he eventually went down to dinner, instead of choosing one of the hot spots he knew so well, he ate in the hotel, picked up a half-dozen newspapers from different parts of the country and headed back to his room. It would be a treat to read a larger variety of American papers for a change.

He skimmed through a local paper and then the *New York Times* before he picked up the *Washington Journal*. He was already yawning and about ready to call it a night when he turned a page and realized it was the society section. The photo of the little blonde looked familiar, and he stopped to read the story below it.

He quickly realized it was Laura Doyle, the Red Cross woman he'd worked for during the floods. It appeared she was going to be married, and he kicked back to read further. When he read the name of her fiancé, he gasped.

"What the fuck?"

Cameron Winger? The third fed. The one he'd cracked on the head when he'd kidnapped Nola Landry. He wasn't dead? Why wasn't he dead?

Hershel sat up to keep reading. The notice mentioned a wedding shower being given by Jolene Luckett and Nola Landry. That damn female agent hadn't died, either?

"Son of a bitch," Hershel muttered, and then grabbed his iPad out of his luggage and began running a search of death certificates for Tate Benton and Wade Luckett. He couldn't find either one. "They're alive. They're all alive. Why didn't they die? I thought it was over. I thought I'd won."

He was sick to his stomach as he crawled into bed, and then, when he finally fell asleep, his dreams were filled with long-buried memories of times he'd tried to forget.

When he woke up the next morning he dressed without thought for how he looked, wanting only to get home. He caught a cab to the airport and arrived in plenty of time, but as he was walking to the gate he began seeing Louise. Everywhere he looked she was just walking past his line of sight, or disappearing into the women's bathroom or down a ramp to get on a plane.

"What's going on?" he muttered, but she didn't answer. "What does this mean? If I'm seeing you, does this mean I'm going to die?"

He sat down near his gate, his hands shaking and his heart hammering in a jerky rhythm against his rib cage. Everything had been fine until he'd come back to the States.

Go home. I told you to go home.

"Then why am I seeing you?" he whispered.

If you don't go home, then you will *die. This is the last warning you are going to get.*

"But they aren't dead. They were supposed to be dead."

She didn't answer, and all of a sudden they were calling his flight.

He stood up, grabbed his carry-on and started walking…past the gate, then through the airport until he got to ground transportation and rented himself a car. By the time his plane was in the air, he was in a car driving north.

He knew it was a bad idea, but the worm in his brain was already at work, telling him what to do and how to do it.

Before he left this earth, he needed at least one of those men to know the pain of his loss. Since Nola Landry and Jolene Luckett had already blown past his fruitless attempts to end their lives, it now appeared there was one more lady who'd moved to center stage.

Laura Doyle was set to become a bride, but not if he could help it.

* * * * *

ELIZABETH HEITER

FBI rising star and criminal profiler Evelyn Baine knows how to think like a serial killer. But she's never chased anyone like the Bakersville Burier, who hunts young women and displays them, half-buried, deep in the woods. As the body count climbs, Evelyn's relentless pursuit of the killer puts her career—and her life—at risk.

But the Bakersville Burier has planned a special punishment for Evelyn. She may have tracked other killers, but he vows to make this her last chase. This time it's her turn to be hunted!

Hunted

Available wherever books are sold.

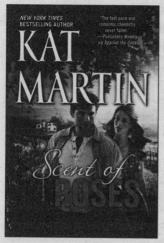

REQUEST YOUR FREE BOOKS!

2 FREE NOVELS
FROM THE SUSPENSE COLLECTION
PLUS 2 FREE GIFTS!

YES! Please send me 2 FREE novels from the Suspense Collection and my 2 FREE gifts (gifts are worth about $10). After receiving them, if I don't wish to receive any more books, I can return the shipping statement marked "cancel." If I don't cancel, I will receive 4 brand-new novels every month and be billed just $6.24 per book in the U.S. or $6.74 per book in Canada. That's a savings of at least 22% off the cover price. It's quite a bargain! Shipping and handling is just 50¢ per book in the U.S. and 75¢ per book in Canada.* I understand that accepting the 2 free books and gifts places me under no obligation to buy anything. I can always return a shipment and cancel at any time. Even if I never buy another book, the two free books and gifts are mine to keep forever.

191/391 MDN F4XN

Name   (PLEASE PRINT)

Address   Apt. #

City   State/Prov.   Zip/Postal Code

Signature (if under 18, a parent or guardian must sign)

Mail to the Harlequin® Reader Service:
IN U.S.A.: P.O. Box 1867, Buffalo, NY 14240-1867
IN CANADA: P.O. Box 609, Fort Erie, Ontario L2A 5X3

Want to try two free books from another line?
Call 1-800-873-8635 or visit www.ReaderService.com.

* Terms and prices subject to change without notice. Prices do not include applicable taxes. Sales tax applicable in N.Y. Canadian residents will be charged applicable taxes. Offer not valid in Quebec. This offer is limited to one order per household. Not valid for current subscribers to the Suspense Collection or the Romance/Suspense Collection. All orders subject to credit approval. Credit or debit balances in a customer's account(s) may be offset by any other outstanding balance owed by or to the customer. Please allow 4 to 6 weeks for delivery. Offer available while quantities last.

Your Privacy—The Harlequin® Reader Service is committed to protecting your privacy. Our Privacy Policy is available online at www.ReaderService.com or upon request from the Harlequin Reader Service.

We make a portion of our mailing list available to reputable third parties that offer products we believe may interest you. If you prefer that we not exchange your name with third parties, or if you wish to clarify or modify your communication preferences, please visit us at www.ReaderService.com/consumerschoice or write to us at Harlequin Reader Service Preference Service, P.O. Box 9062, Buffalo, NY 14269. Include your complete name and address.

SUS13R

SHARON SALA

32941	BLOOD STAINS	___ $7.99 U.S.	___ $9.99 CAN.
32792	TORN APART	___ $7.99 U.S.	___ $9.99 CAN.
32785	BLOWN AWAY	___ $7.99 U.S.	___ $9.99 CAN.
32677	THE RETURN	___ $7.99 U.S.	___ $8.99 CAN.
32633	THE WARRIOR	___ $7.99 U.S.	___ $7.99 CAN.
31548	GOING ONCE	___ $7.99 U.S.	___ $8.99 CAN.
31427	'TIL DEATH	___ $7.99 U.S.	___ $9.99 CAN.
31342	DON'T CRY FOR ME	___ $7.99 U.S.	___ $9.99 CAN.
31312	NEXT OF KIN	___ $7.99 U.S.	___ $9.99 CAN.
31264	BLOOD TIES	___ $7.99 U.S.	___ $9.99 CAN.
31241	BLOOD TRAILS	___ $7.99 U.S.	___ $9.99 CAN.

(limited quantities available)

TOTAL AMOUNT $ _____
POSTAGE & HANDLING $ _____
($1.00 for 1 book, 50¢ for each additional)
APPLICABLE TAXES* $ _____
TOTAL PAYABLE $ _____

(check or money order—please do not send cash)

To order, complete this form and send it, along with a check or money order for the total above, payable to Harlequin MIRA, to: **In the U.S.:** 3010 Walden Avenue, P.O. Box 9077, Buffalo, NY 14269-9077; **In Canada:** P.O. Box 636, Fort Erie, Ontario, L2A 5X3.

Name: _____
Address: _____ City: _____
State/Prov.: _____ Zip/Postal Code: _____
Account Number (if applicable): _____

075 CSAS

*New York residents remit applicable sales taxes.
*Canadian residents remit applicable GST and provincial taxes.

HARLEQUIN® MIRA®
™ www.Harlequin.com

MSS0214BL